BI

FLOWERS

# D.K. HOOD

# BRING ME FLOWERS

bookouture

Published by Bookouture in 2018

An imprint of StoryFire Ltd.
Carmelite House, 50 Victoria Embankment,
London EC4Y 0DZ
www.bookouture.com

ISBN: 978-1-78681-357-2
eBook ISBN: 978-1-78681-356-5

This book is a work of fiction. Names, characters, businesses,
organizations, places and events other than those clearly in the
public domain, are either the product of the author's imagination
or are used fictitiously. Any resemblance to actual persons, living or
dead, events or locales is entirely coincidental.

To Daniel Brown who encouraged me to write this story.

# PROLOGUE

He imagined how she would look dead.

The fixed brown eyes, gaping mouth, and the cool feel of her young, bloodless skin against his flesh.

His would be the last face Felicity Parker would see.

The idea thrilled him; having the power over life or death was something he craved. Felicity would beg and scream but in the end, she would respect him before he cut her throat. He stared at the images lined up on his desk of the girls he had chosen, but for now, he had one girl on his mind.

He traced the trembling tip of his index finger down the image of Felicity. A pretty girl with a full figure and glossy raven hair, long enough to twirl around his fingers. He loved to stroke his girls' hair and let the silken strands slide across his palm. Even in death, their hair remained untainted and he could add a small piece to his collection as a reminder of their time together.

Excitement curled in his belly. Meticulous planning and three long months of watching led to his choice. He had secretly gained intimate details of their lives. She would be his first in Black Rock Falls County.

No one could hide from him.

Inside the confines of their bedrooms, he observed his girls parade in their skimpy underwear, chatting about boys or discussing how they wished the local cowboys would screw them. He had seen the way they enticed with their short skirts and brief tops. The way they used their well-practiced moves and sultry looks to lure men. At the free Wi-Fi benches at the local computer store that sold everything from games to candy, or at Aunt Betty's Café, he would make an excuse to speak to them, but his girls often ignored him. Engrossed in the latest game app, they hardly lifted their heads from their smartphones to take nourishment.

Teeming with anticipation he picked up his bag and got in his car After a short drive, he parked deep in the forest. His last image of Felicity was her tossing her hair over one shoulder and smiling as if she knew he watched her every move. *Girls like her drive men insane with lust.* So many wicked girls to choose from, so many eager to join in the fun. He called them "his" girls because they would all come to him… eventually.

Soon Felicity would come to him.

He let out a long breath. *Time to get into position.* He took the bag from the seat, slid from the car, and headed deep into Stanton Forest. He had planned the route with care, taking a remote hiker's trail rather than the direct pathway to the river, then making his way along the riverbank, walking along the water's edge to disguise his footprints. Forty minutes later, he reached a clearing beside the river. The out-of-the-way nook was a popular place for the local teenagers to make out during summer break. The large, flat boulders running from the riverbank to a secluded clearing in the pine forest offered a place to sit.

Surrounded by dense trees, the area was too far from the road for anyone to hear her screams, and the wall of black mountains opposite offered him complete privacy. He wanted his girls to fight and beg for forgiveness—it made the experience oh so deliciously memorable.

Felicity would approach from the opposite side of the clearing, take Stanton Road, and walk adjacent to Black Rock Falls High School then follow the well-worn path through the forest. She would be relaxed and excited entering the woods. The clearing posed no threat—until now. Oh, how he loved to leave his mark on a town; he would change the idyllic place forever.

As he checked his watch, his belly quivered with anticipation. She would be hot and fragrant from the long walk. He remembered how sweet she smelled the day he accidentally bumped into her at Aunt Betty's Café. His palm still tingled at the memory of brushing her bare arm. He gave himself a mental shake. He needed to concentrate.

He glanced around but the place, as usual, was empty. The preparation would only take a few moments and he had plenty of time to savor the rush of adrenaline. He removed his clothes and pulled on a pair of shorts. After observing the area for a week, he discovered the only visitors in the mornings appeared to be two kids who ventured to the river to fish, and always at the same time. It would be over an hour before they arrived and the teenagers never arrived until the afternoon, no doubt most of them slept until noon.

He selected a flat boulder close to the river but within sight of the clearing to display his offering and another small rock close by but well hidden from view to act as a table. Satisfied he had found the perfect place, he pulled on a pair of surgical gloves and laid out his impedimenta in a row, meticulous to have each item within easy reach. He attached a hunting knife to the belt on his shorts and slipped a sock filled with coins inside a pocket.

The flat boulder would be a perfect canvas, and he would create a work of art for all to see, for all to remember. As he checked each detail, excitement surged into tremors. He strolled back along the path and searched through the bag to retrieve a wrapped packet of cord. His shaking fingers hampered an attempt to untie the skein. He sucked in a deep breath to calm himself then played out the string. After selecting a suitable spot toward the riverbank, he tied the rope between two trees at neck height. If Felicity tried to run, the cord would stop her and she would be his.

His groin ached and he checked one more time for the strip of condoms inside his pocket. A shimmer ran down his spine as he melted into the cover of the trees to wait for his prize. He could creep up on her and she would not hear him. Girls deafened by loud music thumping through their earbuds made such easy prey.

# CHAPTER ONE

Felicity Parker sat at the table and picked at the bowl of cereal her mother had insisted she eat before heading to her friend's house. Dying to read her messages on her phone, she huffed out a long sigh. Her parents hated cellphones at the table, and if she broke their stupid rule, it would mean no phone or social media for an entire long boring week.

Summer vacation meant one thing: the rodeo at the local fairgrounds and the arrival of cowboy stars Lucky Briggs and Storm Crawley. Sure, she had asked her parents—no, begged them—to let her go to the rodeo dance with her friends, and in fact she had made a point of doing extra chores to show her appreciation. Of course, the idea of them being at the dance to watch every move she made would be embarrassing. She had to persuade them that at sixteen she was old enough to attend a dance with her friends alone.

She glanced at her father, who was engrossed in reading a pile of documents. "Dad, have you thought over letting me to go to the dance with Aimee and Kate?"

"Are you planning to go with Derick?" Her father's gaze remained fixed on the papers spread out before him.

Felicity stood and took her bowl to the sink. "No, we had an argument last night and he isn't speaking to me right now."

"I'm not sure why you want to go." Her father lifted his annoyed gaze and looked at her. "It will be a rowdy crowd of cowboys and who knows how many criminals with the number of drifters in town.

I'm not sure I'm happy for you to go. Why are you so set on having no adult supervision?"

Felicity gave him her best tragic stare. "Please, I'm sixteen and Aimee is nearly seventeen. If I don't go, the other girls will make fun of me. It is only one night, from seven until ten. What could happen in three hours? Please, Daddy, let me go."

"She has been doing her chores." Her mother leaned against the counter and sipped a cup of coffee. "Maybe if we drop her at the dance and pick her up it would be okay. I know quite a number of people going who could watch out for her."

"We'll discuss it when I get home." Her father stood and gathered his papers then glared at her. "Don't bother your mom about this again today—understand?"

"Okay. Can I go now, Mom?"

"Yes." Her mother smiled.

Felicity dashed upstairs to her room and dressed quickly. The moment she turned on her cellphone it rang, and to her surprise the caller ID told her it was Derick. "Calling to apologize?"

*"Nope. I don't want you mixing with Lucky Briggs. Don't you know that young girls like you are just another notch on his belt? He'll forget you the moment you walk away."*

Felicity wound a strand of hair around one finger and giggled. "You jealous?"

*"Maybe. Look, can we talk some more about this? I'm going to be close by in ten minutes or so. I have to drop off a car for a customer and pick up the loaner."*

She picked up her bag and slung it over her shoulder. "I don't have time. I'm meeting Aimee and we're going into town." She huffed out a sigh. "You're acting too serious, like we're married or something. I'm going to the dance without you, and if Lucky Briggs asks me to dance, I will so get over it."

*"I don't want us to break up but it's him or me. Make up your mind."*

She smiled. No matter what she did, Derick would come back to her. He was like a little puppy dog that needed a home. "Have it your own way. I've gotta go." She disconnected and headed out the bedroom door.

In the hallway, she called out to her mother, "I'm going over to Aimee's house then we're going into town to hang out."

"Okay, will you be back for lunch?"

Felicity opened the front door, inserted the earbuds into her ears and turned up the music. "No, but I'll be home for dinner."

# CHAPTER TWO

Sheriff Jenna Alton tipped back her chair and yawned. Stepping out of life as undercover DEA Special Agent Avril Parker and into the "safe" role of Sheriff Jenna Alton had not been easy. Since David "Dave" Kane arrived in Black Rock Falls six months previously, life had been interesting to say the least. They had solved four gruesome murders together and she had appreciated his expertise. She had picked him as ex-special forces from the get-go, but whatever his reason to be off the grid in Black Rock Falls she did not care. Having him around as backup was a bonus in spades.

Her new deputy had changed considerably since his arrival. He now sported collar-length hair to cover the scar left from the metal plate in his head courtesy of a gunshot wound received in the line of duty. She had not heard him complain once of the headaches that obviously plagued him, and she hoped the pain had eased with the warmer weather. She liked Dave Kane, and his considerable skills added another asset to the team she needed to do her job. She had learned from the best that in a crisis, a good leader delegated the work to keep sane.

After dealing with psychopaths last winter, and losing Pete Daniels, the rookie her team, her job and that of her deputies had deteriorated into negotiating neighborhood squabbles and finding lost cattle. Life had slowed to a relaxed hum. Cowboy hats and open-neck shirts had replaced the thick winter gear, and women in town wore splashes of color. Summer had arrived with warnings of a crime wave from the impending visit of the rodeo circuit cowboys.

*Anything would be a relief from the current boredom.*

Voices at the front desk drew her attention. The new deputy was due to arrive: Shane Wolfe, a family man with three daughters, and from his résumé, a qualified medical examiner waiting for his license to be issued for Black Rock Falls. She welcomed the idea of dealing with problems in-house rather than relying on a mortician to conduct autopsies and the state forensics team, who took on anything they could not handle. With her experience in the underworld of firearms, vice, and narcotics—and with Kane's profiling abilities, which had already saved her life— the chance of adding another highly qualified deputy to the team was a dream come true. *There will be nothing we can't handle.*

She pushed to her feet and strolled out of her office then waved at Deputies David Kane and Jake Rowley to join her at the front desk. Rowley had shaped up well over the last six months and was as solid as a rock, but having Shane Wolfe on the team would make life easier. Before Kane had arrived, her previous outlet for some serious crime investigation conversation came in the form of old Duke Walters, and she might as well talk to the mop bucket.

"Is that the new deputy?" Rowley pushed his thumbs through the loops on his regulation pants and grinned. "He looks like a Viking marauder."

"Military police background, I believe." Kane strolled toward the front desk. "Professional all the way."

"Are you all settled in?" The office secretary, Magnolia Brewster, or Maggie as she preferred to be called, tossed her black curls and smiled broadly at the tall blond man standing at the counter. "Ah, there is Sheriff Alton."

"Good morning." Jenna held out her hand. "Jenna Alton, nice to meet you, and this is David Kane and Jake Rowley."

Wolfe's handshake was firm and outweighed his weary expression. "Thanks, this place is a little further off the beaten track than

I envisaged." He glanced around the room. "How many deputies do you have on staff, ma'am?"

"Not enough." Jenna frowned. "Right now it's just four. You, Kane, Rowley, and Duke Walters—he is over there taking a statement." She waved toward the gray-haired Deputy Walters. "Come into my office." Her attention moved to Rowley. "Handle the desk with Magnolia. I'm sure you can all get better acquainted later."

"Yes, ma'am." Rowley turned on his heel and went behind the front desk.

Jenna moved behind her desk and waved Kane and Wolfe into the seats in front. She sat down in her squeaky office chair. "Did you find the house okay?"

"Yes, and it is very comfortable, thank you." Wolfe smiled. "It's better than I expected and walking distance from the elementary school and here, which is good. Since my wife died, caring for the girls alone has been difficult." He sighed. "Emily is watching Julie and Anna at the moment but I can't expect her to do it full-time—she is in her senior year at school. Losing her mother and moving here will make it difficult enough for her."

"I can imagine." She towered her fingers. "I'll get Rowley to bring us some coffee." She lifted the phone and spoke to the deputy then disconnected. "I have a list of the available housekeeper nannies and had them checked out. Take whatever time you need to interview them. You can use my office if necessary." She handed him a list. "We don't have many open cases at the moment, and Kane will be able to bring you up to speed." She drummed her fingernails on the desk. "I read from your résumé that in addition to your impressive qualifications in forensic science, you have a degree in computer science. Does that mean you can take a look at our systems? They're pretty old and need a bit of updating."

"Yeah, I can 'tweak' systems." Wolfe leaned back in his seat and the corner of his mouth quirked up in a smile. "What do you need?"

"What we need—" she leaned forward, gripping the arms of her chair "—is a better system for logging case files. Every three months, this system archives all the files, open or closed. We can't compare cases. We have no secure uplink to local systems. It's run on the Boolean system, but if someone gets one letter wrong in a name, all the information goes missing." She grimaced. "We don't have the luxury of computers in the cruisers to check a license plate or a person's criminal record. No on-board camera. Out at night, we are sitting ducks." She sighed. "Unfortunately, my electronics expertise falls into a different area. Luckily, our new mayor, Mayor Petersham, gave us funding for earbuds and power packs. They should be arriving soon."

"Do you have access to the case files using your cellphone? Can you write tickets via a handheld?"

"No, none of the above." Alton waved Rowley into the room and took the tray of steaming coffee mugs from his hand with a smile. "Thanks."

"It all comes down to budget." Wolfe ran a hand over his blond buzz cut and shrugged. "I can write you a new program to run the nitty-gritty, but the other stuff you want costs money." He pulled out his cellphone and checked the bars. "Here in town the reception is good but not so on the way here, so you have blackspots. If you all have smartphones, I can create an app so you can access all areas of the mainframe direct."

"That would be wonderful." Alton sipped her coffee and eyed him over the rim. "Perhaps we have a good reason to ask Petersham to up our budget this year. After all, he has allowed me to employ another two deputies." She looked at Kane. "Although, we haven't had one application for the positions I've posted."

"I guess we could keep looking or manage for another year and use the funding to update the office?" Kane leaned his wide shoulders into the chair.

"Thank you, Kane, I'll give that idea some thought."

Wolfe looked as if he was carrying the world on his shoulders.

Jenna met his gray gaze. "I guess you'd like to get some lunch after your long journey? I'll let you go and leave Kane to explain how I do things around here."

"Yes, ma'am." Kane rubbed his chin and turned to Wolfe. "I'll introduce you around then we'll head down to Aunt Betty's Café; I'm due for a break and I can bring you up to speed. As you need to get your kids settled and hire a housekeeper, I'm happy to cover for you for a couple of days."

"You don't need to." Wolfe emptied his cup and stood. "I'm used to coping under pressure, and my daughter Emily is seventeen and old enough to care for her sisters in my absence until school starts again."

"Maybe so, but I want my deputies to have their minds on the job, not worrying if their kids are okay." Jenna stared at him, allowing no retort, and leaned back in her seat. "The cowboys are drifting into town for the start of the rodeo season and I'll need all hands on deck by the weekend. At the moment, my biggest concern is a domestic disturbance over a cat peeing on a neighbor's car." She waved them toward the door. "Go… I'll contact you if a riot breaks out."

"Okay." Wolfe smiled. "I do appreciate your concern. I'll work on the program at home to make up the time." He strolled out the door.

Kane stared after him then swung around to look at Jenna and raised one dark eyebrow. "Hmm."

"Oh, man." She grinned at him. "I could cut the testosterone in this room with a knife. I think you've met your match with him."

"*Moi?*" Kane wiggled his eyebrows and flashed a white grin. "Never."

*

An hour later, Jenna had finished updating her daybook when the phone rang and Maggie asked her to hold for a call. A woman came on the line.

*"Sheriff Alton, this is Prue Ridley."*

"Yes, Mrs. Ridley, what can I do for you?"

*"I think there's been a bear attack. My son and his friend found a girl in Stanton Forest. I checked her. She is dead and cut up real bad."*

Horrified, Jenna swallowed the bile creeping up her throat and reached for a pen. "Can you give me the exact location?"

*"The northern end of Stanton Forest, near the river. We are waiting by the road."*

"Are you in a safe location?"

*"Yes, I could see no signs of the bear in the area, but if we see one we'll get in the car."*

"Okay, good. Wait there, we are on our way." She hung up the phone and massaged her temples.

Bear attacks were scarce this close to town. *It could be another homicide.* Indecision plagued her of late, but she refused to allow the flashbacks of her kidnapping six months earlier to affect her work. She considered calling Kane then dismissed the idea. Rowley could give him the details. She lifted the phone and called the mortician to attend the scene then explained why her new deputy would be attending the autopsy. Standing, she strode out of her office. "Rowley and Walters, with me."

"Yes ma'am?" Rowley jogged to her side with Walters close behind.

"We have a possible bear attack. Someone found a body with multiple injuries at the northern end of Stanton Forest." She looked at Deputy Rowley. "I want you to take charge until Kane gets back, but first, run down to Aunt Betty's Café and inform him. Tell him to wait for my call, and grab something for lunch while you're there. I'm not sure how long this will take. I'll need to examine the scene and speak to the kids who found the body." She glanced at Deputy Walters. "You're with me. Let's go." She headed for the door.

# CHAPTER THREE

Walking in the sunshine, Kane found it hard to believe the ice-packed snow of winter had vanished. Spring had been a relief, but the first week of June arrived with a rush of color across the landscape and filled the gardens with flowers. A carnival atmosphere replaced the usual lazy-first-day-of-the-week attitude of the townsfolk. Bunting decorated shopfronts on the main road, and a series of signs hung between the streetlights, celebrating the first rodeo in Black Rock Falls on the circuit the coming weekend.

Wolfe strolled beside him, blond head erect, his attention moving from one group of people to another. He said little, obviously taking in the ambience of the town.

Kane glanced at Wolfe, trying to rid himself of a strange feeling he had met him before. Something about him was very familiar and he just could not put his finger on it. He cleared his throat. "I haven't seen this many people on the streets since the last Larks game. This will be my first experience of the Black Rock Falls County rodeo crowd. Sheriff Alton tells me the crime rate goes up by ninety percent over the rodeo circuit weekends."

"Looking at the number of deputies you have, I'm not surprised." Wolfe stood to one side to allow two women pushing strollers to pass. "Why is everyone looking at me as if I have two heads?"

"You're new in town." Kane grinned at his dour expression. "They'll have your picture up on the wall of Aunt Betty's Café before you know it. It's a friendly town."

"Really?" Wolfe curled his lips. "I can deal with friendly." A glistening black SUV screeched to a halt at the curb and he rolled his shoulders. "Now there is another thing I detest." He indicated with his chin toward the vehicle. "Dangerous drivers. Men like him need to have their vehicles impounded and crushed. It's the only way to teach them a lesson."

Kane rubbed his chin and grinned. "It certainly would slow them down, but right now we need a new law passed." He strolled toward Aunt Betty's Café. "This is the best place to eat unless you want to go fancy, then it's the restaurant at the Cattleman's Hotel."

"Who is the guy in the black SUV?"

"Dan Beal, the new captain of the Larks, the local hockey team." Kane snorted. "Don't worry, he doesn't receive any special privileges."

"Nice to know."

Before Kane had time to pull open the door, it opened and Reverend Jones stepped out, giving him a beaming smile.

"Good morning." He turned his attention to Wolfe. "I see we have a new deputy in town."

Kane nodded. "Yeah, Reverend Jones, this is Shane Wolfe." He noticed Wolfe's expression harden but he gave the man a curt nod.

"Nice to meet you." Jones's lips quivered and he dropped his offered hand, but he lifted his chin and met Wolfe's unfriendly gaze with a sunny smile. "I hope I'll see you and your family at Sunday services. You too, Deputy Kane. All are welcome."

"Thanks for the invitation." Wolfe's lips formed a thin line. "Maybe after we get settled."

Wanting to get Wolfe away from any personal questions, Kane tipped his hat. "We have to be going." He moved past the reverend and led the way into the café.

"Damn preachers." Wolfe shook his head. "I saw him watching me with my girls earlier. I pushed them inside the house and shut the door. I am so over preachers right now." Agitation rolled off him. "You should have seen them come out of the woodwork when Angie died. They were like flies—every time I turned around, another was telling me it was God's will. Cancer killed my wife and God had nothing to do with her suffering."

"He means well." Kane frowned. "I'm sure he didn't mean to offend you." He moved through the busy café to his usual table set in the alcove bedside the bay window. He liked the more secluded spot with no one close by to overhear his conversations. "I doubt he'll bother you again unless you seek him out. People need someone to talk to and he fills that spot along with some of the other clergy around here." He sat down and peered at the menu, needing something to do. Noticing the waitress heading in their direction, he cleared his throat. "One thing about being a deputy in this town is we get served ahead of the rest."

"Great." Wolfe grasped the menu and ducked his head. "What's good?"

"Everything. The chili is the best I've ever tasted and I'm pretty sure the cakes are becoming an addiction." Kane grinned and lifted his head as Susie Hartwig sashayed toward him, coffee pot in hand.

"What will you have today, Deputy Kane?"

"I'll have the usual, thank you."

"I don't believe we've met." Susie stared at Wolfe and raised one penciled eyebrow. "I'm Susie Hartwig, and you are?" She filled the two cups on the table and set down the pot of coffee.

"Deputy Wolfe." Wolfe's icy gaze flicked over her then returned to his menu.

"And what can I get you, Deputy Wolfe?"

"I'll have the chili, side order of fries, and apple pie with ice cream."

"Sure, right away." Susie took a notepad from her pocket and jotted down the order, picked up the coffee pot, and wiggled back toward the kitchen.

Wolfe lifted his gray gaze and lowered his voice to just above a whisper. "Now let's cut the chit-chat and tell me why the hell I'm here."

Mind reeling, Kane adopted a nonchalant pose and piled sugar into his coffee. "What do you mean?"

"Don't act like you don't know, ninety-eight H." Wolfe glanced casually around the room then brought his cold gaze back to Kane. "You must recognize my voice. I've been your handler at HQ for the last three years."

Only three people on Earth knew Kane's identity and location. Sure, his handler at HQ was one of them, but why the hell would HQ risk his cover by sending Wolfe to Black Rock Falls? Not easily drawn into a trap, Kane shrugged. "You are talking a load of crap, man. You on some crazy meds or something?"

"Nope." Wolfe rubbed both large hands over his face. "I worked as a round-the-clock handler for you and three other agents during the time I cared for my wife until she died. The moment the funeral was over, three black SUVs rolled up and insisted I accompany them. Two agents drove off with my kids and another escorted me at gunpoint to a chopper. They secreted me in a military base. I underwent intensive training on police procedure, including Montana criminal and misdemeanor law. I have a degree in forensic science but I had to do a refresher course and apply for a license to practice here." He rubbed his temples in slow circles. "I thought I'd kept fit until they put me through intensive physical and arms training. I had an idea they wanted to send me back into service but not to this flea on a dog's back." His attention shifted over Kane's shoulder, and he cleared his throat. "The food is coming."

Kane glanced behind him. Susie Hartwig was heading toward them, carrying a laden tray. Heart thumping against his ribs, he smiled at Wolfe in an attempt to keep the atmosphere casual. "I see, but what has all this got to do with me?"

"I'll be straight back with a pot of coffee." Suzie unloaded the tray and strolled back to the kitchen.

"I have no idea why I'm being forced to take a job as a deputy in a backwoods town, unless you put in a request to HQ for backup and I'm it. Although, I don't know why the hell they picked me. I'm *not* an agent and I've been behind a desk for years. I don't have your training." Wolfe's glare spoke volumes.

Not willing to give an inch, Kane let the man's words percolate through his mind and waited for Susie to deliver the coffee pot. He ate a spoonful of chili and sighed in contentment then lifted his attention to Wolfe. "As a deputy, you will watch my back. It's normal procedure."

"Cut the crap, Dave." Wolfe spit out the words. "I can give you information on the last three calls you made to me. The name of the man you suspected set the bomb that killed your wife. I won't go into details. I know you sent a request to attend your own funeral. The next call was a background check on Sheriff Alton. Don't worry, your cover isn't compromised."

"Really?"

Wolfe sipped his coffee, and his ice-gray eyes observed Kane over the rim of his cup. "You know damn well the line is secure. How else would I know?"

"Maybe you tortured some poor bastard to death for information." Kane snorted. "There's been a lot of that going around here lately."

"That's not my style." Wolfe attacked his meal. "And before you ask, intel on Alton was way above even your security clearance.

What I can tell you is the Department of Homeland Security has her file locked up like Fort Knox. I could hack it but the information wouldn't be worth spending the rest of my life in federal prison."

Not willing to trust anyone claiming to *know* him, Kane placed a plate over his bowl of chili to keep it warm and stood. "I'll be back in five." He walked out of Aunt Betty's and strolled two doors down to the cellphone store.

After purchasing a burner phone, he punched in the number of his contact. When a stranger's voice greeted him, he gave his code name and asked to speak to the chief of operations, code name Purple Sky. A familiar voice came down the line. He sighed in relief. "I'll keep it short. Did you send a man by the name of Shane Wolfe to my location?"

*"Affirmative."*

"Why?"

*"I was informed Alton was recruiting more skilled deputies and we couldn't risk an unknown quantity working alongside you. Wolfe is solid. You can trust him."*

Relief flooded over him and he relaxed. "I don't trust too easy."

*"Does the name 'Terabyte' ring a bell?"*

Oh yeah, he recognized the code name of his handler. The mysterious man at the end of the phone who had saved his life many times. "Yeah."

*"Same person. He is the only one in the loop we could trust. The rest of the world believes he is a desk jockey and retired to care for his wife. He has been unofficially retired for years. It's not as if you are in witness protection or working undercover. Being off the grid makes you vulnerable and without the resources you used to rely on if compromised. We don't intend for that to happen. Sheriff Alton needed boots on the ground and he'll slide in under his own name without question."*

"Before I arrived here, you should have given me the heads-up on Alton. I recognized her as an agent the moment I dragged her out of a car wreck. Up until now, I wasn't sure whose side she was on but had an idea she was in witness protection. I guess you don't have plans to bring me up to speed?"

"*Not exactly. I can tell you she has clearance and you can trust her. We didn't give her a handler because it's not necessary. Some years back, she brought down a major player, and she has enough information in her head to bring down a country. We need her safely tucked away where no one can find her. She was perfect for the job—no family ties.*"

"Why send us all to the same location?"

"*Black Rock Falls isn't the most popular of towns. It's hardly noticeable on the map but big enough to swallow you. Only two people know where you are now: the president and me.*"

"Off the grid, huh? Really? HQ acted like I was finished, retired, and sent out to pasture. Does this mean I will be called back to active duty?"

"*Yeah. You'll be involved with catching the men who killed your wife. I'm sure you and Alton would make a good team when the time comes but for now, nothing has changed and we have zero intel on who was involved. The moment I have more, you'll be informed.*"

"Then I want out now. You know damn well, I'll be able to find the assholes."

"*Not yet. You are far too valuable to risk, and Black Rock Falls is the closest to secure we could find. Play the role, that's an order, and allow us to do our job. Do what you do best and work with Alton. Don't contact me again unless you are compromised—understand? Every call you make puts you both in danger of exposure.*"

Kane scratched his stubble and groaned. "Sure, I'll be a good boy and spend my time filing complaints about cats peeing on cars. Have a nice day." He shut the phone, removed the SIM, snapped it in half, then dropped the phone and SIM down a drain.

Irritated, he walked back to Aunt Betty's and slid into his seat. As he removed the plate covering his lunch, Wolfe cleared his throat and Kane lifted his hand to stop any questions. "I checked you out and we're cool."

"What can you tell me about Sheriff Alton?" Wolfe narrowed his gaze and eyed him critically. "She sure doesn't look like she needs any help." He leaned back in his seat.

"Trust me, Sheriff Alton is as tough as anyone I've worked with but she does have a vulnerability, which in my opinion makes her human." Kane sighed and rubbed the back of his neck. "My orders are to stand down, so it looks like I'm here for the duration too. We might as well make the most of it while it lasts." He shrugged. "Think of it as an early retirement in a sleepy, not-so-little town."

"I'm bored already." Wolfe gave an irritated snort and refilled his coffee cup. "On the upside, I guess it *is* a decent place to raise my kids."

The door to the café opened, bringing a summer breeze and lifting the paper napkins on the tables, and Deputy Rowley strode purposely toward them, grim-faced. Kane swore under his breath then lifted his attention to him. "What's up?"

"Someone found a body in Stanton Forest." Deputy Rowley whispered so low Kane had to lean closer to hear him.

"Did anyone check to see if the victim is actually dead? It could be someone sleeping off a hangover."

"No, the victim is female, and from the woman who examined the body it might be a bear attack. The victim is cut up real bad." Deputy Rowley swallowed and his Adam's apple bobbed in his long neck. "Sheriff Alton is heading to the scene with Deputy Walters. Her orders are to wait for her call. She will examine the scene and speak to the kids who found the body."

"A bear attack?" Kane frowned at him. "Why didn't you call me rather than leaving the office unmanned?"

"Maggie's on the desk and I'm following orders. The sheriff sent me to tell you in person and told me to buy lunch to take back to the office. No one is available to relieve me." Rowley's cheeks pinked. "I'll grab some sandwiches and head back."

*Why didn't Jenna call me?* "Okay." Kane stared after him, confused. "Thanks for letting me know." He flicked a glance at Wolfe. "Did you have to tempt fate by complaining you were bored?"

# CHAPTER FOUR

At the sight of two women fussing over a couple of ashen-faced young boys gripping fishing rods, Jenna pulled her cruiser to the curb on Stanton Road. Two bicycles sat chained to a nearby fir tree. She turned to Walters. "We'll need to split the kids up, take down details, then compare our notes later. Make sure you ask the parents for permission to question their kids. I have their names and addresses. I'll check out the body and when I get back, you take Mrs. Sanders and I'll speak to Mrs. Ridley."

"Right you are." Walters opened the cruiser door and stepped outside.

Jenna slid from the car and took her notepad and pen from the inside pocket of her jacket. Moving toward the group, she smiled at the kids then addressed the adults. "Which one of you called me? Are you the parents of these children?"

"Yes." A young woman pushed a lock of brown hair from her face and patted one of the kids on the head. "I'm Georgina Sanders and this is my son Ian."

"I'm Prue Ridley, the one who called, and this is my son James, Jimmy." The other woman stepped forward and pushed her glasses up the bridge of her nose. "We came as soon as Jimmy called me, and Georgina waited with the boys while I checked the body. I'm a nurse at Black Rock Falls General but the girl was beyond help so I called you. As I said, a bear could have mauled the poor girl, although my boys haven't seen any signs of a bear in the area. We thought it would be best to wait here."

"Yes, the fewer people disturbing evidence the better." She cleared her throat. "Do you mind waiting while I take a look?"

"I really need to get Jimmy home. He's very upset and if it's not a bear, whoever did this might be hanging around."

Jenna sucked in a deep breath. "I doubt that very much but I'll leave Deputy Walters to watch over you. I won't be long." She waved a hand toward the forest. "Where did you find the body?"

Before Mrs. Ridley could reply, Jimmy lifted a trembling finger and pointed to a path winding into the forest. "Down there. It leads to the river. We go fishing there all the time during summer vacation unless the big kids are swimming. We get there early because they don't like us hanging around."

"Okay, thanks." Jenna patted the boy on the shoulder and slipped the pen and notepad back in her pocket. "Wait here with Deputy Walters." She jogged down the pathway and, rounding the first bend, slipped her Glock from the holster. Bear or man, she would be prepared.

The trail ran beneath a canopy of trees, through an idyllic pine forest with points of sunlight highlighting the wildflowers and variegated vegetation. The area had a magical feel and she understood why the kids flocked to this place during the summer. The path wound through rough tree trunks, each wide enough to hide a man with ease, and she slowed her pace, tensing at every sound.

The whine of wind through the trees sounded like a pitiful moan. As she moved forward, the crack of a twig under her boot echoed in the quiet like a gunshot. Aware of her vulnerability to both bear and killer, she fought the panic hovering under the surface and held her weapon before her in both hands. As she moved deeper into the forest, a breeze carrying the unmistakable smell of raw meat hit her full in the face. She slowed to a walk and moved with caution along the winding trail, her gaze shifting from side to side, taking in any signs of a threat.

The thick covering of last fall's leaves masked sound, and anyone or thing could creep up on her, or be hiding behind the packed pines. The forest closed around her in suffocating density and a shiver sent a warning down her spine. She waved the pistol in a sweep, checking every shadow before proceeding.

At last, the path opened onto a large clearing with the river glistening beyond. Heart thudding in her chest, she glanced around, checking in all directions for any sign of movement, then took a cautious step forward. As she turned to face the river, she gagged at the sight before her and staggered backward. With her back to a massive pine tree, and her weapon held at shoulder level, she inched forward, staring in horrified disbelief at the abomination laid out for all to see on a large, flat boulder. No bear had attacked this woman. The atrocity before her was the work of pure evil. "Oh my God."

She pushed down the instinct to run and took a few moments to allow her training to drop into place. The voice of her commander slipped into her mind like a calming balm. *The dead can't hurt you. Swallow your fear and find justice.* Straightening, she pushed away from the tree. To avoid the smell of congealed blood, she breathed through her mouth, scanning the area for any movement and listening. Apart from running into the killer, the smell alone could attract black bears or bobcats roaming the area. The sound of rushing water and the odd bird call broke the eerie silence but no shadows moved within her periphery.

Pushing away the horror before her, she dropped into professional mode. Her heart slowed and the murder scene came into perfect focus. She moved from tree to tree, keeping her back covered and checking the ground for any clues before each careful step. Missing crucial details at this stage of the investigation could hamper the case. She needed to access the scene and get men here as soon as possible.

Moving as close to the victim as possible without contaminating the scene, she caught the low hum of a thousand flies and swallowed the bile rushing up the back of her throat. Adrenaline coursed through her, insisting she get the hell out of Dodge. A wave of panic hit her, sending her mind tumbling back into the past. Men had her tied and helpless. Rope tightened around her neck, restricting each breath. She had to escape. The flashback ebbed slightly and she gripped her Glock, comforted by the smooth handle against her palm. "Get a grip, Jenna." Drawing up her last ounce of willpower, she cast her gaze over the body of the murdered girl.

The victim was young, maybe sixteen. An open gash across her throat gaped in stark contrast to her sheet-white skin, yet no significant amount of blood spatter covered the rock. It was as if the killer had drained her body of blood before laying her out. Naked, with arms out at her sides and legs spread, the killer had arranged her long black hair in a fan around her. The maniac had eviscerated her, and flies covered the spread intestines. Bright red lipstick smeared her mouth and garish red spots highlighted the stark bloodless flesh of each cheek. At her feet lay a posy of blue Michaelmas daisies and wild bergamot picked from the mass of wildflowers in the clearing.

Sick to her stomach, she did a visual sweep of the area and discovered no clothes, nothing at all. The hairs on the back of her neck stood at attention, triggering her flee response. She pushed it down, reluctant to holster her weapon to use her cellphone. *I need backup. He might still be here watching me.* Leaning against the trunk of a Douglas fir, she pulled out her phone and called Kane. "Kane, I need you on scene now. We have a homicide."

*"I'm with Wolfe, do you want me to bring him along? We could use his forensic experience."*

"Yeah, bring him." She swallowed the bile in her throat. "Hurry, okay?"

*"I'm on my way now."* Kane cleared his throat. *"How bad?"*

Jenna swept her gaze over the body and the sight sickened her. "Nasty. The victim is a girl and some bastard has mutilated her. I have the traumatized kids who found her waiting with Walters on Stanton Road but have no one to secure the scene. We need to get boots on the ground to protect the victim before the wildlife destroys the evidence, and I'm all alone here."

*"I'm getting into my vehicle now. Stanton Road is at the river end of the forest, right?"*

"Roger that. Lights no siren. I don't want a crowd of ghouls gathering here. I'm heading back to Walters now to interview the kids." The day was warm but she shivered and goosebumps rose on her arms. "Stay on the line. I'm not sure if I'm alone here."

*"Roger that. ETA fifteen minutes. I'll hand you to Wolfe."*

Jenna pushed the earbud to the cellphone in her ear. With the device stashed in her shirt pocket, she pulled out her Glock and carefully retraced her steps. A breeze rustled the branches setting her nerves on edge. Every small sound sounded like a footstep. Her heartbeat thundered in her ears as she waved her weapon from side to side and moved quickly back to the road. The forest appeared to become darker with each step, and since her close encounter with a couple of psychopaths a few months previously, dark wooded areas freaked her out more than she would ever admit.

Panic shook her legs but she kept moving, and relief flooded over her as the last bend in the trail came into sight. With the Glock back in its holster, she spoke into the cellphone mic. "I'm safe and disconnecting." She pushed the device back inside her pocket.

Jenna beckoned Walters to her side and wandered some distance from the witnesses. "It's a young girl, maybe sixteen or so, and a brutal homicide." She looked up into his shocked expression. "Kane and Wolfe are on their way. I'll talk to the kids." She sighed. "I want your eyes on anything that moves in the forest."

"Yes, ma'am."

Giving herself a mental shake to dispel the horrific images replaying in her mind, she attempted to adopt a natural expression and approached the witnesses. "May I ask your son a few questions? Deputy Walters will speak to Ian, if that's okay?" She glanced at Mrs. Ridley and raised a brow. At her nod of consent, Jenna squatted in front of the young boy. "How old are you, Jimmy?"

"Ten last March." The boy with tousled hair rubbed the end of his nose with shaking fingers and peered at her through lashes still wet with tears. "I'd like to go home now."

*I'll need to arrange counseling for these kids.* "Sure, your mom can take you home real soon but first I need to help the person you found. Can you tell me what time you found her?"

"'Bout ten, we ran away and I called my mom." He dug the cellphone out of his pocket and held it up. "See, I called her at ten fifteen."

Jenna smiled at him. "That is very helpful. So, you arrived about ten. Do you come here to fish often?"

"Yes, we came yesterday, 'bout ten thirty. We bring sandwiches and sit on the big rock and have lunch." Jimmy shuddered. "I'm never going back there again."

She straightened and pulled out her notepad to make a note of the time. "Did you see anyone this morning or any vehicles parked along the road?"

"Yeah, two of the cowboys from the rodeo came out of the forest and took off fast in a red SUV." Jimmy sniffed, pulled a tissue from his pants pocket, and blew his nose.

"Where did you see them?" Jenna stood and waved a hand toward the perimeter of trees. "Here near this path or somewhere else?"

"We rode right past them. They came out of the trail that goes to the rock pool. They'd been swimming because they had wet hair and only wore their jeans and boots." He rubbed his nose. "I know they're from the rodeo, I've seen Lucky ride many times."

Jenna lifted her attention to Jimmy's mother, Mrs. Ridley. "Do you know Lucky's last name?"

"That would be Lucky Briggs, and no doubt the other man would be his friend Storm Crawley. Everyone in Black Rock Falls knows Lucky, his family lives here."

*I've never heard of him.* "I see." Jenna wished she had time to attend a rodeo. Usually the chaos surrounding the contestants clashing with locals kept her busy. "Where is the rock pool located?"

"About fifty yards away in that direction." Mrs. Ridley pointed in the direction of town and gave her a strange look as if she was remiss in not knowing. "There *is* a sign. We don't let the children go there to fish. It's not safe. It's said to be a bottomless pool."

"Okay, that's all I need for now." Jenna took a card out of her pocket and smiled at Jimmy. "If you remember anything at all, even if you think it's silly, ask your mom to call me. I don't want you to talk about this to anyone. I need to make sure her family knows what has happened before the story gets out." She gave Mrs. Ridley a meaningful look and handed her the card. "This wasn't a bear attack, and I suggest you keep the boys close to home for a while. I can arrange counseling for them, if you like?"

"No need, we have someone we can speak to, and don't worry, we won't say a word, not while a maniac is on the loose. He might take it personal like if he finds out my son is a witness." Mrs. Ridley took the card and patted Jimmy on the back. "You'll ride home with me. Get your bike and I'll put it in the trunk."

Jenna nodded. "Thank you for your help. I'll be in touch if I need any further information."

Glad to be in the sunshine and away from the murder scene, Jenna shook her head, trying to dispel the images of horror and the disbelief that anyone was capable of committing such an atrocity against a young woman. It did not take a profiler like Kane to see this murder was different from the cases she had worked in the past, but thank God she had his expertise to figure out the mind of a psychopath. The person or persons who had mutilated the young woman enjoyed the shock value of displaying their victims, which meant they would be close by, absorbing the fear they caused like a sponge. Goosebumps prickled over her skin as if a freezing breeze had brushed her bare flesh, and she glanced around. *Are you watching me, asshole?*

# CHAPTER FIVE

The roar of an engine caught Jenna's attention. She sighed with relief at the sight of Kane's black SUV heading toward her at speed. When Walters moved to her side, she turned to him. "What do you know about Lucky Briggs and Storm Crawley? Right now, they are our prime suspects."

"They are both regular hell-raisers during the rodeo season but seem to keep out of our way most of the time." Walters scratched his cheek and stared at his notes. "I spoke to the kids while you were away. Seems like Jimmy led the way into the clearing, and when he saw the body he pushed Ian back along the track, so Ian didn't see the body at all. He said he just ran for his life. I think both of them are so distraught they can't recall many details."

"I'm not surprised." Jenna tapped her bottom lip with the end of her pen. "I don't remember any complaints against anyone by the name of Lucky or Storm. I think I would remember." She caught Walters' eye-roll and wondered how many good old boys got off with a warning. "How come nobody put in a complaint if these men are as bad as you say?"

"They're not that bad. It's just the young bucks get a bit loud when they're strutting their stuff." Walters barked out a laugh. "They stick to the bar at the fairgrounds and butt heads. Over the years it's been better to leave them be."

*Really?* "No complaints from the local women? I gather they flock to them for attention."

"For some reason women around these parts like a cowboy." Walters tipped back his hat and grinned. "Those lucky enough to spend some time with one don't usually complain."

Jenna shuddered. "Count me out. Men stinking of horse shit and sweat don't attract me one bit."

"But you're a city girl." He grinned at her. "Most here would think it's part of the charm."

She gave him her best frozen expression and waved to Kane as he parked behind her cruiser. "Let's hope their charm doesn't include murder. Where do they usually stay?"

"They'll be at the Black Rock Falls Motel, and with the stakes as high as they are this year, they won't be going anywhere until after the rodeo."

Jenna pushed a strand of hair from her face. "If they murdered the girl they could be hightailing it out of town by now."

"They would know the kids saw them here so they wouldn't get too far. They are known statewide and would stick out like sore thumbs in any town." Walters tipped back his cowboy hat. "More likely they would stay around and compete as usual rather than leave all of a sudden like and appear guilty. This time of day, cowboys competing at the rodeo are likely to be at the fairgrounds preparing for the weekend and checking out the competition."

Jenna considered what he said and it made sense. She glanced up at Walters and frowned. "You sure?"

"I am, ma'am. I know those boys and they won't be going anywhere." He frowned. "I can't see them doing this to a girl. You want me to go check them out, ma'am?"

"No. If they are still there, I'll wait for backup to arrive then talk to them myself." She pulled out her cellphone and called the fairgrounds.

The event manager informed her, he had seen both men not five minutes ago and both were heading for the main arena. After receiving his assurance, he would call her if he noticed them leaving, she disconnected and turned back to Walters. "They are at the fairgrounds and being watched, so we have time to process the scene then I'll take Kane and speak with them." She sucked in a deep breath. She had to secure the area. "Go get the tape out of my car and rope off the trail for me."

She turned to see Wolfe marching toward her carrying a large bag and walked to meet him.

"What have we got, ma'am?"

Jenna grimaced. "I've never seen anything like this before, it's brutal. The killer posed her and laid flowers at her feet."

"No murder is pretty, ma'am." Wolfe dropped the bag on the ground, removed his hat, and scratched his sweaty head before pushing the Stetson back onto his head. "Did the kids or their mothers identify the victim?"

Jenna sighed. "No, I'm afraid not. I'm sure she'll be missed soon enough."

"Do you think it would be better to keep a tight lid on the murder until we identify the victim, ma'am?"

Jenna bristled. "I know the protocol, Wolfe. The last thing I need is reporters contaminating the scene. I've already asked the witnesses not to say anything."

Kane strolled to her side, his face grim. "Do you have any suspects?"

She turned her attention to him. "Two. The kids who found the victim saw two local rodeo cowboys they recognized as Lucky Briggs and Storm Crawley coming out the forest. I want to speak to them the moment we've secured the crime scene." She glanced at Wolfe. "I wish you had your license already. Relying on a mortician to act as M.E. is not in our best interest. I'll give you the keys to my car; follow the mortician back to the funeral home and get me an autopsy completed ASAP. I explained who you are when I called him." She pulled out her car keys and handed them to Wolfe.

"Yes, ma'am." Wolfe pushed the keys into his pants pocket.

She glanced at Kane. "We'll interview the cowboys first, and when we get back to the office, I'll go through the high school yearbooks and see if I can come up with the name of our victim. I doubt anyone has missed her yet; from what I could see, the body appears pretty fresh." She frowned. "I'm sure Wolfe will be able to give me an interim report."

"Do you know if anyone has disturbed the scene?" Kane dropped the crime scene bag he was holding onto the ground.

"The two boys, their mother, and me as far as I know." She chewed on her bottom lip. "Do you have everything you need with you?"

"I never leave home without my kit, and as luck would have it, Wolfe had his box of tricks in his vehicle and we picked it up on the way." Kane gave her a concerned look. "Do you want us to go ahead and secure the scene and do a sweep of the area for clues?"

"No." Jenna swallowed the lump in her throat. During her career, she had seen things she would never forget, and this was one of them. "I'm finished here. Walters can wait for the M.E., and we'll cover the area quicker and get some dignity for the victim if we work together."

"Okay." Kane bent, unzipped the bag, and pulled out bright blue coveralls, booties, and gloves. He handed them around then added face masks.

Jenna grabbed the coveralls. "Suit up and we'll get this done. Make sure you have full access to your weapons."

"Sure thing." Wolfe dressed and turned his attention to her. "Ah, do you want to lead the way, ma'am?"

Jenna lifted her chin. "Yeah." She glanced at Wolfe, who was waiting as if he wanted to ask her a question. "Is there a problem?"

"Would it be possible to have a chat later, ma'am? It might make our working relationship a bit easier." Wolfe shrugged into his suit and raised a blond eyebrow. "The three of us when you have time, ma'am."

A wave of apprehension stopped Jenna in her tracks. She shot a look at Kane but he shrugged. "Right now, we have a mutilated girl requiring our attention. Get your minds back on the job. I'll discuss this with you later."

Her pockets crammed with evidence bags and spare gloves, Jenna led the way down the path to the clearing. She heard weapons slide from holsters and the familiar click as rounds loaded into the chambers. The eeriness of the forest lessened a little with two competent deputies watching her back, but the moment she stepped into the clearing, an inner feeling of dread clutched her stomach.

Throughout her career, she had not been able to view victims of horrific crimes as objects. She never forgot one of them. Her way to deal with carnage came by way of finding justice for the victims. Somehow, in all the horror, she became a different person, as if disconnected from her true self. She had no choice but to put aside her humanity for a short space of time and search for clues to find the animals who committed atrocities.

# CHAPTER SIX

Kane had not missed the color drain from Sheriff Alton's face when Wolfe had tried to speak to her, and he felt like a jerk after promising not to pry into her background. He scanned the forest, noting the way the birds objected to their presence. If someone was close by watching them, they were remaining motionless. He doubted the killer would risk staying behind to observe their reaction to discovering the body, but he had read about psychopaths who liked to display their kills for shock value. Some often joined the crowd of onlookers to enjoy the reaction.

No inquisitive crowd had gathered. Not one word of their discovery had slipped out to the public, and the parents of this poor girl would not suffer the distress of hearing the details of their daughter's murder splashed all over the news. Old Mr. Weems was prone to letting the odd detail slip. As the local mortician, he probably had little in his life to gossip about, and the discovery of a body would make him a celebrity if only for a short time.

The smell of death wafted through the trees, and Kane holstered his weapon and pushed on a face mask. He followed Alton into the clearing and Wolfe moved to his side, cursing under his breath.

"Jesus, she looks about the same age as my daughter Emily." Wolfe gave him a look of disgust, slipped his sidearm back into the holster, then snapped on a face mask. "You told me Black Rock Falls was a nice quiet place to live."

"I thought we'd had our share of crazies for a while." Kane raised both eyebrows. "We had four murders in town six months ago."

"Wonderful."

Examining the layout of the murder scene, Kane winced at the sight of crows pecking at the corpse. He heard Alton's intake of breath at the graphic sight and touched her arm. "Orders, ma'am?"

"Wolfe, go and examine the body. I'd like an interim report." Alton frowned then picked up a small pebble and threw it at the birds. It landed with a crack on the rock. The crows screeched into the air, swirling the dead girl's hair around her face. "We'll leave Deputy Wolfe to do his job and concentrate on finding where the murder took place and work back from there."

Kane noticed a shudder vibrate through her and blocked her line of view to the body. He glanced around the immediate area. "Where are her clothes?"

"Look at the scene, Kane." Alton rubbed her temples then straightened as if gathering herself. She met his gaze head-on with a cool, composed stare. "From the small amount of blood spatter on the rock, I would imagine the killer washed the body or killed her close to the river. Grab a handful of flags and mark any evidence you find. Head toward the river from the left of the rock and I'll take the right; we'll circle around and move in." She glanced at Wolfe. "Do you need any help?"

"No, ma'am." Wolfe surveyed the area and moved closer to the body. "I agree from the lack of blood, the murder happened elsewhere. The victim has defensive wounds on her hands and legs consistent with fighting off a knife attack. She fought for her life, and from the downward angle of the lacerations, we are looking for a man at least five ten. Look for signs of a struggle in the area; if you find any blood spatter, I'd like to see it before it deteriorates."

"Roger that." Alton looked at Kane and tipped her dark head toward the riverbank. "Move out."

"Wait!" Wolfe turned slowly to look at them then pointed to the ground on the opposite side of the flat rock. His mouth turned down and he shook his head. "Drag marks there and it looks like he dropped her. I can see something glistening in the leaves, maybe a gold chain. I would advise you to cover this area first, ma'am. The soil is moist and I can see one set of footprints. Looking at the depth, I would say the killer is maybe 350 pounds. No, make that 220 because I think he carried her to the rock and that would account for the weight variation. I'll need to take a cast." He bent to dig into his open bag. "I have a kit."

"I'll do it." Alton took the containers and a bottle of water from him. "I hope this is enough plaster of Paris. Do you prefer adding sticks to the cast for strength?"

"There are plastic rods in the second container. Mix one-third of the powder with water in the large container and you should have enough for two footprints."

Kane pulled out his cellphone, thankful for the high-resolution camera. "I'll take the shots." He stepped carefully around the rock and bent to take close-up images of the immediate disturbed area then went back and, following Wolfe's competent instructions, clicked away at the victim.

Making a conscious effort to be clinical, he could not prevent rage from bubbling to the surface at seeing such a young woman brutalized. He had not hardened to such sights and doubted he ever would. No, the shock registering on the pretty face would stay with him forever. Her soft brown eyes resembled those of a dead stag and her painted lips hung open in a grotesque smile. He lowered the camera and turned to see Wolfe juggling a recorder. "Do you need any help?"

"Yeah, thanks." Wolfe passed a small recording device to him. "If I record my findings as we go, I won't miss anything for the initial report." He peered at him over the top of his mask. "If you could hold it about a couple of feet away, it will pick up my commentary."

"Sure." Kane glanced on the ground to make sure he would not destroy evidence then stepped closer and turned on the recorder, holding it out for Wolfe to make his report.

"Initial examination. The victim is a female, Caucasian, approximately sixteen to eighteen years old, sixty-five inches tall with dark hair and eyes. Rigor is minimal. Body temperature is ninety-two degrees, which would put the time of death between five and six hours ago. Little blood evidence at the scene. I estimate death occurred between nine and nine thirty as the body was discovered at ten." Wolfe gently lifted the girl's head and examined the skull. His brow creased into a frown. "There is a contusion on the back of the head consistent with blunt force trauma." He ran a hand down her arm, taking in the defense wounds, lifted her hand and then peered at the other. "I will bag the hands for further analysis." He placed plastic bags over both hands. "There is evidence of a burn under her chin and across one cheek consistent with a cord or rope. The killer eviscerated the torso. The neck has a laceration measuring approximately six inches traversing the jugular. The angle of the wound indicates a right-handed person held the knife. The lack of blood in the immediate area suggests death occurred in a different location. Sexual activity to be determined. A large amount of lipstick covers the mouth and cheeks, applied post-mortem. A bunch of flowers was left at the feet." He nodded at Kane and his voice sounded somber. "That's all I need for now, you can turn off the recorder. I'll cover her and give her some dignity while we wait for the mortician." He bent and took a folded plastic sheet from his bag, shook it out, and placed it with great care over the body. When he turned to look at Kane, his eyes held an ice-cold expression. "I so want to get this animal."

Pushing back a wave of anger, Kane handed him the recorder. "We'll get him." He slapped him on the back.

"Right now, the best thing we can do is look for clues." Alton grimaced. "Killers like this believe they are invincible but sooner or later they make a mistake."

"I agree." Wolfe's pale gaze narrowed. "Ready to search the area, ma'am."

"Go ahead but keep each side of the footprints." Alton's gaze narrowed as she moved around Wolfe and bent over the prints.

Kane followed Wolfe, taking the opposite side, and examined the glint of gold Wolfe had spotted. He moved the leaves with care and found a cross then a chain. The links had snapped as if dragged from the victim's neck. "I have a necklace here with a cross. Looks like the killer tore it from her neck." He photographed then bagged the items and slipped them inside a large evidence bag.

"Signs of a struggle here and blood spatter, not enough for the injuries sustained, look here." Wolfe pointed one long finger at the sandy edge of the river. "Deep marks in the river mud. I'd say he killed her in the water."

Trying to push the image of the murdered girl from his mind, Kane took more shots and followed Wolfe around the area for another twenty minutes. "Whoever did this covered his tracks pretty well. We had a murder before Christmas with little to no evidence, much like this. I blame TV shows: They're informing killers how to avoid leaving DNA or other trace evidence." He led the way back to where Alton was finishing the plaster casts of the shoeprints.

"We have a significant problem with this murder." Wolfe plucked at his face mask, his gaze fixed on the shrouded figure lying on the flat rock. "This isn't his first kill. The way he disrespected her by smearing on the lipstick and posing her to make her look like a prostitute, then as if in a sudden pang of conscience, he left her a posy of flowers. This is an advanced escalation of psychopathic behavior, and the way he laid her out—he is proud of what he has done."

"I agree." Alton placed the plaster of Paris kit containers into the forensic bag. "This is why we need a database link with other towns. From the look of this victim, the killer has probably been committing murders all over the state, and this time it's Black Rock Falls' turn." She straightened and stood, hands on hips. "I believe he wanted to deliver the ultimate shock value and is close by waiting for the fallout."

"I'll bet he'll be one of the mourners at her funeral." Kane rubbed the back of his neck. "He will be in his element, feeding on people's grief."

"Then we'll need to haul ass and catch him before he strikes again." Alton straightened. "Thoughts?"

"This is a man out of control." Wolfe shook his head slowly and stared at Kane. "You are one of the best profilers I know. Do you agree he enjoyed killing her and will want a bigger thrill next time?"

A cold chill ran down Kane's spine as he nodded. "I do. Prepare yourselves for worst-case scenario because it's going to get nasty." He sighed. "Right now, we don't know his cycle. They all have a limit to how long they can go before their next fix. If he is passing through Black Rock Falls, we need to be on alert. He could strike again in days or even hours."

"Wolfe, I want a positive ID of the victim like yesterday, and tell the M.E. I don't want this leaking to the press. The last thing we want is the media contacting the parents before we've had the chance to notify them."

"I'll make it crystal clear, ma'am."

Alton's expression hardened as she glanced up at Kane. "The kids identified a couple of cowboys coming out of the forest, and we need to get over to the fairgrounds and interview them straight away." She brushed a lock of black hair from her eyes. "Ah, there's the acting M.E. to collect the body. I'll leave the victim in your capable hands, Wolfe and send Walters back to the office to bring Rowley up to speed. Email me the findings of the autopsy ASAP." She glanced at Kane. "Let's go."

# CHAPTER SEVEN

Trailers and pickups packed the parking lot at the fairgrounds and people moved around setting up tents and food-vending caravans. Brightly colored signage pointed to different arenas. A massive poster hung over the front gate proclaiming cowboys and cowgirls would perform death-defying feats of athleticism on the wildest beasts in the west.

As Jenna made her way from the parking lot, murder was not foremost in her mind. Deputy Wolfe's words at the crime scene filtered into her brain at a relentless rate. *You are one of the best profilers I know.* A trickle of worry ran down her spine. Kane had not mentioned knowing the new deputy, and in fact, the body language between them on meeting had been more like two stags during mating season rather than acquaintances. Yet after their visit to Aunt Betty's Café, they acted like old friends, and then Wolfe had practically ordered her to a meeting. She trusted Kane and could find no reason why he would withhold information about Wolfe from her. *What is going on?*

She turned to Kane and could not temper the harsh tone of her voice. "Have you met Shane Wolfe before? You seem to get on like old friends."

"This morning was the first time I laid eyes on him but I like him. He has experience in all the areas we need—especially today."

His gaze had been direct, his manner convincing; either he was the best liar she had ever met or he had told her the truth. She nodded. "I agree. I wish we had another six like him."

"I'm not sure if you can twist the mayor's arm for another six—maybe one and a rookie." Kane indicated with his chin toward a poster stuck to a board beside the ticket office. "I'll speak to the guy in the ticket office but I would say, looking at the events, Lucky Briggs is a bull rider and roper; no doubt he is taking part in quite a few events."

She stared at the pixelated image of a dark-haired man, his face shadowed by a black Stetson. "That photograph isn't much to go on but he is obviously well known. I had no idea there would be so many events, including a Rodeo Queen competition. I've always preferred to remain in town during the celebrations to handle the complaints."

"There is a dance on Friday night as well. I'll buy tickets."

Jenna gaped at him. "Don't be ridiculous. Apart from it being inappropriate after what has happened, we'll be on duty not boot-scooting, even if I knew how to boot-scoot."

"I should be crushed but I wasn't *exactly* asking you out on a date. Don't you agree, blending in is sometimes the best way to find out information? Liquor loosens people's tongues." His mouth quirked up at the corner. "I'm sure you can manage a Texas two-step after living here for over three years."

"Not really but I guess we could use it as an excuse to keep an eye on the locals and see if anyone is acting suspicious." She shrugged. "I don't have time to shop for an outfit. We're running a murder investigation, in case it slipped your mind."

"An undercover assignment works for me." He grinned. "These dances are not formal. I'm sure you have a pair of blue jeans, boots, and a shirt with a fringe. You're wearing a cowboy hat." His smile flashed white. "Well?"

After informing her he had suffered a painful breakup, they had become close friends and spent a lot of downtime together. She placed both hands on her hips and blew out a long sigh. "I'm sure you are used to having women fall at your feet but we are trying to do a job here."

"Exactly."

Jenna threw her hands up in the air and turned away. "Fine, I'll go to the dance with you but only to back up the deputies on duty—understand? Go and buy the tickets. I'll check the stables and ask around if anyone has seen our suspects." She headed toward the row of horse trailers lined up alongside a building. From the smell blowing in her direction from the freshly painted barn, it had to be the stables.

Sidestepping the piles of steaming manure and streams of urine, she moved inside the humid building. The scent of horse, straw, and leather wafted toward her from the dark abyss. Coming out of the bright summer's day, she paused in the entrance, allowing her eyes to adjust to the dim interior. Streams of sunlight dancing with dust motes spiked down from skylights in the roof and illuminated rows of horses' heads peering over the stall gates.

She strolled along a center aisle, past a rack of saddles, and approached a man filling a wheelbarrow with horse dung. She waited for him to lower the pitchfork then cleared her throat.

"Have you seen Lucky today?"

"Maybe I have and maybe I've not." The attractive man in his late twenties moved his dark gaze from her face slowly down her body then back up again. "They sure don't make deputies like you in my neck of the woods. Ah, Lucky don't get on with cops but if you want a date for the dance, come see me. I love a woman in uniform."

Jenna wanted to cringe at his sexist remarks. As handsome as he was, he made her feel dirty, but she could play his game. "What's your name?"

"Storm Crawley but you can call me Storm."

A chill walked its way up Jenna's spine and she forced her hand away from the handle of her Glock. *He could be the killer and armed with a pitchfork.* Absently, she waved a hand toward the horses and took a step closer to the nearest stall, feigning interest. "Do you ride?"

"Oh, yeah." A smile slashed across his tanned face. "Maybe I'll show you how good I am after the dance?"

Ignoring his not so subtle innuendo, she pushed her lips into a semblance of a smile and turned her attention to the back of the barn. "That sounds like fun but right now, I have to speak to Lucky. Do you know where I can find him?"

"See the door right down the end there?" He jabbed the handle of the pitchfork in the direction. "He'll be in there cleaning his saddles. I'm all finished here and need to wash up, so I'll see you at the dance." He sauntered away in a chink, chink, chink of spurs.

The arrogant asshole had not even asked *her* name. No doubt the notches on his belt did not require names. Then again, his total disregard for her as a person could reflect a psychopathic killer. She had learned more intricacies on profiling since Kane arrived. Turning, she stared toward the entrance, hoping Kane would be close behind her. Walking into an enclosed space with a potential killer was a fool's errand.

The sound of a tap running caught her attention and she turned. Standing shirtless on the other side of the building, Storm was splashing water from a tap over his face and chest. Confident that bathing would occupy him for some time, she waited four beats of her heart and strode to the room at the back of the stable. Seeing the door ajar, she pushed it open and peered through the entrance.

A tall man, muscles bulging as he hoisted a saddle onto a rack, lifted a sinfully handsome face in her direction. As he raked her with his eyes, a frown wrinkled his brow.

Immediately accosted by the smell of saddle soap, leather, and stale sweat, she moved inside the room. Her gaze moved down his frame looking for weapons, and she absently wondered if he had his jeans sprayed on. *He would be more lethal as a lover than a killer.* Wanting to slap herself for ogling a potential psychopathic killer, she swallowed the lump in her throat. "Are you Lucky Briggs?"

"Yeah." He turned his back on her and strolled deeper into the room. "I didn't touch her."

A wave of fear clutched her chest. No one had released any information about the murder. She moved into the room, kicking the door wide open until it clicked onto a stop. "Didn't touch who?" She followed him past the rows of saddles.

"I didn't ask her name." He collected rags and a tin of saddle soap then dropped them into a box. "I met her at the Cattleman's Hotel at the bar. She followed me back to the motel but I'd been drinking and wasn't interested… if you know what I mean? I'd been driving all darn day and I just wanted to sleep. Man, I even told her Storm would be willin' if she was needy."

Jenna watched him closely. "Then what happened?"

"She went ballistic, tore her shirt, and came at me with her nails. Said she would call the cops and say I raped her." He turned to face her and displayed a line of scratches down his neck. "I pushed her out the door and went to bed—alone."

The chink, chink, chink of spurs and the sound of footsteps came from behind her. She glanced around the room seeking an alternative means of escape but found nothing. The hair on the back of her neck stood at attention and every muscle went on alert. *Storm is behind me. If they jump me, I'm trapped.*

# CHAPTER EIGHT

Assessing the threat, Jenna took three steps closer to Lucky and turned casually to place her back to the wall. From her position, she had the men in clear view. Both carried hunting knives attached to their belts in leather sheaths, and the image of the gutted young woman flashed into her mind. She had seen cowboys in action, the way they jumped from their horses to rope a steer. The agile, strong men on each side of her could move like lightning, and although Kane had taught her some new moves, they could restrain her without breaking a sweat. She had her weapon, but without reasonable cause, she could not draw on them.

When Lucky gave Storm a knowing grin and moved in close, she could smell him. Fear gripped her in a rush. The choking feeling heralding another flashback rushed to the fore and she dragged in deep breaths to push it back into the dark recesses of her mind. She needed to take control of the situation. "Take a step back, Mr. Briggs."

"Have a problem with men movin' into your comfort zone, Sheriff?"

*Where are you, Kane?* She met Lucky's overconfident gaze head-on, refusing to show fear. "Just stay where you are and answer my questions then we can all be on our way."

"Sure, ask away."

"Did anyone see you at the motel?"

"Yeah, Storm was making out with some girl in the parking lot outside my motel room." Lucky nodded at his friend. "You saw that woman attack me, didn't you?"

"Sure did. The crazy bitch had been chasing after Lucky all night." Storm moved inside the room and leaned against the saddle rack. "I tried to calm her down and told her I'd be happy to have both of them, but she spat at me and took off." He grinned. "I mean, look at me, who wouldn't love a night in Storm's arms?"

*Not me.* "Can you describe her? How old was she? What color hair?"

"Older than you, maybe forty or so, hard to tell with all the makeup." Lucky shrugged. "Blonde, the kind out of a bottle, black stilettos, nice tits. I'm guessing she was a hooker. She sure looked like one but I don't need to pay for company and maybe that's why she got pissed." He smiled. "Shame you're a cop. You look real nice. I'm afraid it seems to be the young ones or the hookers who chase after me. They want a cowboy to show them some lovin'. I'm starting to check their IDs."

"But I'm *not* chasing after you, Mr. Briggs."

"Really? I sure thought by the way you looked at me before you had a hankering for some prime cowboy— and call me Lucky."

Giving him a dismissive snort, she narrowed her gaze. "I don't think so, Mr. Briggs."

"Sassy too." Lucky's gaze rested on her breasts then very slowly moved back to her face. He grinned at Storm. "Now I know why you like women in uniform."

She ignored the inappropriate remarks and glared at him. "Do you want to make a formal complaint against this woman?"

"Nope." Lucky rubbed the back of his neck. "I don't need any trouble."

Storm ruffled his damp hair and moved a few steps closer. Jenna's heart went into overdrive. Muscles tensed and ready to fight, she planned her moves. One kick to the knee would smash his patella, tear the tendons, and ruin Storm's career, but it would startle Lucky, giving her the split second required to pivot and crack her heel into his jaw.

She took a step away from the wall to give herself room and rested her hand on her pistol. Storm had noticed the subtle movement and raised one fair eyebrow then moved between her and the door. Lifting her chin, she used her authoritative voice. "Okay, but before I go, can you tell me your whereabouts this morning between eight and ten?"

"Yeah, earlier I was helping old Joey move Lightning and the stupid animal threw a fit and slammed me into the side of the truck. I bruised my hip and we went to the rock pool in the forest over yonder so I could soak in the cold water. We go there a lot, as in all the guys on the circuit go there for a cold soak. It's good for injuries." Lucky unzipped his pants and pulled them down to exhibit a massive black bruise over one slim hip. "I have to compete with this injury this weekend. I had to get the swelling down. I'll be back there again tomorrow and maybe later this afternoon."

Before she could comment, Kane's voice boomed out in a clipped tone from behind Storm.

"Cover up before I book you for indecent exposure." Kane flashed her a look to stop time and his mouth flattened into a thin line. "Did you see or hear anyone else in the area while you were soaking your injury?"

Biting back a sigh of relief, Jenna took the opportunity to stroll to Kane's side and waited for Lucky to reply.

"Yeah, a couple of kids on bikes waved to us on the way back to the car." Lucky zipped up his pants and shrugged. "Didn't hear anything unusual but the waterfall covers a lot of noise."

"Why swim there and not further up in the clearing? There's a beach there and it must have been difficult climbing out of the rock pool with an injury." Kane glared at him.

"You kidding me?" Lucky snorted. "We went skinny-dipping and the rock pool is secluded. Kids hang out at the clearing. Adults usually go to the rock pool at the weekends and never that early. The water is damn near freezing." His gaze narrowed. "Why the third degree?"

"Just routine questions following a complaint." Kane slid his cold gaze over her. "Anything else you need to ask them, ma'am?"

Jenna understood Kane's concerns for her welfare. She wet her lips and took out her notepad and pen. "I need your cellphone numbers and shoe size, and are you willing to submit to a DNA test?"

The men rattled off the information and she made notes. "I have DNA test kits at the sheriff's office. It's painless."

"You already have our DNA on file." Lucky shrugged. "The other sheriff took samples from most of the guys in town when a girl from Blackwater was raped four years back."

"Yeah, we couldn't leave town for weeks. The sheriff had to send the samples to Helena to be processed." Storm shook his head slowly. "We lost a lot of money and our ratings that year. Everyone thought we were guilty. It turned out to be her boyfriend, and the girl didn't want to rat him out."

"Where can I find old Joey?" Kane turned an ice-cold stare on the two cowboys.

"Most likely in the cattle shed. The building by the main arena." Lucky ignored Kane and smiled at her. "He'll tell you what happened."

"Okay, that's all I need for now." Jenna closed her notepad. "Thank you for your cooperation."

"I'll see you at the dance." Storm gave her a meaningful smile. "Or maybe afterward?"

"That is so *not* going to happen." Kane's voice boomed out and he glared at him with such intensity, Jenna's mouth went dry.

She headed for the door without a backward glance. When Kane fell into step beside her, she sucked in a deep breath and let it out slowly. "Thanks."

"*Thanks?* Have you lost your ever-loving mind walking into a situation alone with two murder suspects again? Have you forgotten how close you came to being raped and tortured by a pair of psychopaths not three months ago?"

She gaped at him. *He is becoming overprotective again.* "Chill out, Kane. I'm hardly going to forget killing a man who used to be my friend, am I?"

"What is it with you and trusting cowboys?" Kane's voice had dropped to a whisper. "Did you overdose on Roy Rogers when you were a kid or something?"

"Don't use that tone with me, Deputy." She ignored him and kept walking.

"Jenna, stop. *Please.* What use am I as your deputy if I'm not supposed to care about your safety?" He glared down at her, but despair etched his handsome features. "They had you surrounded with your back to the wall."

"I was armed and could have taken them down before they made a move, and you know it."

"Maybe it would have been nice if you'd told me where you were going. I turned my head for a few seconds and you'd vanished. You scared the crap out of me, Jenna. There are ten stable blocks on these fairgrounds. It was only by sheer luck I walked into the right one and heard your voice. If those cowboys were the killers, they would work together. One would get you turned around and the other would sneak up behind you. You know I'm right." He stormed off toward the cattle shed.

*I guess it's nice to know he has my back.* Jenna stared after him. With two ex-military deputies on staff, she had no excuse to investigate alone. *He is right. I need to stop acting like I'm infallible and use him for backup.*

# CHAPTER NINE

Joanne Blunt strolled along Stanton Road enjoying the sun on her face and the smell of the pine forest laced with the fragrance of an abundance of wildflowers. Summer break had to be the best time of the year, and spending time with her cousins in Black Rock Falls during rodeo week would be heaven. No parents to report to, and during the day when her cousins were at work, she could roam around without a worry in the world.

The trails through the forest were familiar, having visited on numerous occasions, and she had all day to visit the rock pool. With luck, she might run into some of the cowboys, who frequented the place in the summer. They always had free tickets and she might find one to take her to the dance. She tucked a rolled-up towel under one arm and strolled into the dense forest. Along the way, she collected wildflowers and tied them with a strand of grass.

At the falls, she noticed a man strolling back and forth as if contemplating something important. Although she did not want to disturb him, she didn't want to leave either. She had walked some distance to enjoy the falls. Sweat trickled down her spine, and although the water would be freezing, a quick dip to cool off would be wonderful. When he turned and stared at her, she gave him a wave then placed her bunch of flowers in a puddle.

After spreading out her towel on a boulder, she kicked off her shoes, pulled her shirt over her head, and wiggled out of her denim shorts. Underneath she wore a skimpy yellow bikini. Proud of her suntanned body, she liked to show it off; she glanced across the pool but in the short space of time, the man had vanished. She shrugged and sat on the edge of the rock pool, dipping her toes into the cool water.

It was so quiet; apart from the rush of the falls it felt like she was the only person alive on Earth. A strong smell of sweat reached her and she turned to see the man walking out of the trees. He had an amused expression and waved as if he knew her. She waved back. "Nice day for a swim."

"Yes, it is a nice day, a very fortunate day." He moved closer and his gaze slid over her body. "Did you come here alone?"

Suddenly uncomfortable, she pushed to her feet and went to grab for her towel. In her periphery, she noticed something in his hand sparkling in the sunlight and a wave of breath-stealing panic raged through her. *He has a knife.*

Trying to act nonchalant, she shrugged. "My friends are on their way."

"I doubt it. You're here to go skinny-dipping with the cowboys." He chuckled. "You missed them, they were here earlier."

The way he moved the knife, tossing it from one hand to the other, sent shivers cascading down her spine. She wanted to run but with him blocking the path and the water at her back, he had her trapped. Deciding to bluff her way out of the situation, she gathered up her clothes and lifted the flowers out of the puddle. "If you'll excuse me, I have to be getting back."

He ignored her and stared at the posy in her hand, almost mesmerized by the sight of it, then his attention moved back to her.

"You brought me flowers. How nice." He moved closer, blocking her path. "Put down your clothes, you're not going anywhere today."

Terror made her legs like lead but her mind was working fine. She threw her clothes and the flowers at him and dashed into the dense forest, running hard. Tree branches whipped her cheeks and bracken tangled around her legs. She could find another path if she could just run another twenty feet. Lungs bursting, she pushed through the trees searching in every direction for the elusive path and safety. Heavy footsteps thundered behind her and moments later heavy breathing. Pulled to a stop by her hair, she screamed at the pain tearing through her scalp. "Let go of me!"

Blinding agony and white flashing lights shattered her vision. She had not seen the punch. Her legs gave way and she staggered, falling against him. The smell of him made her gag but she used the chance to knee him. Like a professional street fighter, he sidestepped and she caught him on the outer thigh. She went for his face but he spun her around and punched her hard in the belly. Retching, she doubled over, but the moment she tried to stand he hit her again. She looked through tears at his ginning face. "Oh God."

"God won't help you now." He pulled her hard against his stinking body then licked her cheek. "I'm going to have so much fun with you."

# CHAPTER TEN

Desperate to identify the victim, Jenna leaned on her desk and stared at the photographs of the crime scene, trying to concentrate on the clues. Old Joey had corroborated Lucky's story about the injury but the weather-beaten old man had informed her he was sure the two men had left the fairgrounds before eight, which gave them plenty of time to commit murder, wash, and return to their vehicle.

Kane's anger toward her at the fairgrounds and his stony silence on the ride back to the sheriff's office disturbed her concentration. Of course, he had a point and was only watching her back. She would try to smooth things over with him later after he returned from attending the autopsy. *Good luck with that.*

Dragging her mind back to the case, she stared at the girl's face. Deputy Wolfe had taken the image after removing the makeup at the post-mortem. No permission was required for an autopsy in the case of an evident homicide, and Mr. Weems, the mortician and acting M.E., had agreed to perform the official examination immediately. The victim looked so young and innocent without the smeared red lipstick, yet it was after five and no one had reported her missing. After instructing Deputy Rowley to contact the local hospital and ask them to call her if anyone called looking for their daughter, she had hit a brick wall.

She turned to her computer, accessed the local high school's yearbook photographs, and scrolled through the sophomore images. Not three pages into the file, she found the cheerleader squad, and there in the front row was her victim. She zoomed in on the image and compared the smiling face staring back at her to the blank staring eyes of the victim. With trembling fingers, she scrolled to the bottom of the photograph and read the list of names. Not trusting the accuracy of the printer or photographer to have the correct names corresponding to the people, she copied the identities into her notebook. She would start with the three girls on the front row, but Felicity Parker, wearing her hair tied up in a ponytail and a cheerleader uniform, was most likely her victim.

The last name rang a bell and she called out to Rowley. When the young deputy stepped inside her office, she lifted her gaze. "The librarian, isn't her name Parker?"

"Might be, I haven't been to the library since Google." Rowley grinned. "I'll ask Maggie, she reads all the time." He strolled from the office and returned a few moments later with Maggie close behind.

"Why are you asking about Jill Parker? She isn't in trouble, is she?" Maggie's eyes rounded. "Oh Lord, the body isn't her, is it?"

Jenna cleared her throat and gestured for Rowley to close the door. "No, I'm looking for Felicity Parker—is she related, do you know?"

"That would be her daughter." Maggie's brown gaze slid to the images spread out on Jenna's desk and one hand went to her mouth. "Oh no, not Felicity." She dropped into the chair and covered her face with both hands.

Selecting one image and turning over the pile to hide the contents, Jenna cleared her throat. "If you know this girl, I'll need you to take a closer look. Is this Felicity?" She stood, poured a glass of water from the cooler, and handed it to her. "Maggie, can you look at the photograph?"

Maggie lifted her tear-streaked face and took a deep breath then glanced at the image. She turned her head away and sobbed. "It's Felicity. I've known her since she was a baby."

"I'm so sorry. Can you tell me where Mrs. Parker lives?"

"Number six, Elm Street. Down near Stanton Forest." Maggie took a tissue from her sleeve and mopped her eyes.

"Is her husband at home?" Jenna wanted to hug her but had to ask questions. "She'll need someone with her when we inform her. Does she have any family or friends nearby?"

"Yes, Sean gets home about five thirty and her sister lives in town. I know her number, I'll write it down for you." Maggie blew her nose then took Jenna's pen and wrote down a name and number.

"Thank you." Jenna sighed. "Go home, I can handle things here."

"I'm sorry for your loss." Rowley helped her to her feet. "I'll give you a ride home. Don't worry about anything. I'll come back and help Sheriff Alton lock up."

Jenna nodded. "Yes, thank you. Can you send in Kane and Wolfe before you leave?"

"Yes, ma'am." Rowley slid one muscular arm around Maggie's shoulder and led her away.

A waft of aftershave preceded Kane and Wolfe's entrance. Both men had attended the autopsy then showered and changed before returning to the office. She glanced at them. "Do you have anything we can use?"

"I have a copy of the recording I made at the scene and will have an initial report for you first thing in the morning. The M.E.'s official report will take longer—I insisted on a full blood screen and DNA samples."

"Was she raped?"

"Yeah." Wolfe's forehead crinkled into a deep frown and he cleared his throat. "I'm afraid so. No evidence of semen. Right now, we have zip to find this guy."

She tried in vain to push the dead girl's face from her mind and tucked a lock of hair behind one ear. "Maggie identified our victim as Felicity Parker and is really upset, poor woman. I would like you to go and break the news to her parents. They should be home by five thirty." She handed Kane the address. "I would come with you but I'll need to remain here until Rowley returns. He has taken Maggie home." She turned her attention to Wolfe. "I know you wish to speak to me about a confidential matter but I understand if you need to get home to your girls."

"I've arranged to interview the housekeepers this evening. I have three coming over from seven thirty. All can start straight away and one is prepared to live in, which will be the best option, especially since the house has a separate apartment over the garage." Wolfe smiled but it did not reach his eyes. "I really appreciate the trouble you took finding these women for me and making sure they are suitable candidates."

Perturbed by his complete lack of emotion, she wondered if working with dead bodies gave him the skill to turn off his feelings. She cleared her throat. "I don't take chances where kids are concerned. The references checked out and Mrs. Mills I know personally. She is a very kind lady and took care of Duke's grandkids for two years. He gave her a glowing reference and will give you any information you need to know about her. She is a widow in her fifties and I think you'll like her."

"Thanks. I have a nanny cam as well. I don't trust anyone with my kids." Wolfe straightened to his full impressive height. "I'll head home after we've spoken to the Parkers. You'll want one of them to do an official identification?"

"I'll handle that part of the business. You go home to your kids." Kane nodded at him then turned his deep blue gaze on her. "I know you have a lot on your plate right now, ma'am, but we would appreciate twenty minutes of your time to speak to you in private. My house would probably be best. If the housekeeper works out, we could go to my house when convenient. It's safe from prying eyes and ears." He rubbed the back of his neck, clearly uncomfortable. "I know you're upset with me right now but it's important."

*Here they go again.* Jenna's heart picked up the pace and she lifted her chin. "I'm not annoyed with you at all. Okay, if it is as urgent as you say, I'll speak with you tomorrow morning at seven at your cottage. Rowley can open up in the morning." She flicked a stare at Wolfe. "Kane will give you directions."

"I'll drop the Felicity Parker case paperwork in here before I go home." Kane gave her a long, considering stare. "You look tired. Will you meet me for dinner at Aunt Betty's café? After delivering the bad news, I'd rather not eat alone tonight."

She shook her head. "Thanks, but not tonight. It's been a long day and I'm going to spend the evening going over what evidence we have so far, then I need to get some rest to get my head straight. I'll speak with you in the morning."

"You have to eat and I'll be back within the hour if you change your mind." Kane let out a long, exasperated sigh. "I would *really* value your company."

After staring at the paperwork on her desk for some moments, she lifted her head slowly and met his gaze. "I'll think about it." She returned to her paperwork, glad at the sound of the door shutting behind him.

The one thing Jenna hated above all else was untrustworthy people. She believed her friendship with Kane was rock solid, but the comfortable feeling she experienced with him was evaporating fast. Sure, she knew he'd come straight from a branch of the special forces, more likely special ops or marines, but they had come to a sort of truce, agreeing not to pry into each other's past, then the moment a new deputy walks into town, Kane acts as if he wants everything out in the open.

Right now, she had so many bells and whistles going off in her head she could not think straight. After three years of perceived safety off the grid, hidden in Black Rock Falls in wonderful obscurity, the rug had been well and truly pulled out from under her feet. There was no way Shane Wolfe recognized her as Special Agent Avril Parker. After intensive facial reconstruction, the agents she had worked with would not know her. Yet it was obvious Wolfe had discussed something of great importance with Kane.

A secret bond had grown between them in milliseconds; in fact, about the same time as her intolerable unease had returned. If Kane and Wolfe were both ex government agents, had something she said triggered Wolfe's memory about her case? If he had discovered her new identity, would he discuss the matter with Kane? Almost four years ago, after the government had recruited her for a special undercover mission due to her lack of family ties, she had testified against international underworld kingpin Viktor Carlos. The trial received extensive media coverage, with her face plastered all over world news. The moment the verdict came down as per her agreement with the Department of Homeland Security, she had vanished. No doubt, after Carlos threatened her in court, he would have offered considerable bribes for information of her whereabouts.

She chewed on her bottom lip. God help her if Wolfe being here had compromised her security after over two years of obscurity. Dammit, she had just started to feel safe again. She had one option: to divide and conquer. Wolfe seemed a hard nut to crack but Kane had at least offered her dinner. As three years of hiding unraveled in seconds, she pulled out her Glock and placed it on the desk then reached in the drawer for her backup Sig. Cleaning the weapons helped her to think, and if Kane had joined forces with Wolfe, she would need to up her game—and fast.

# CHAPTER ELEVEN

Exhilarated, the man pushed through the row of pines and across a clearing to where he'd parked his car. The isolated area was perfect, hidden away but close enough to the road for convenience, and his vehicle could negotiate the narrow trail with ease. He pulled on a baseball cap then slipped behind the wheel. No one would ever discover his secret; he could clean the plastic-covered seats in his car with bleach and incinerate his clothes.

He shook with the thrill of killing and took a few precious moments to tie a band around the lock of hair he had taken from the girl in the woods. He ran his fingers over the silken strands and rubbed it over his lips. Pressing the hair to his nose and inhaling, he caught the scent of apple shampoo, and a quiver went through him. He could still taste her, and the ecstatic sensation of holding her as her life drained away shuddered though him again like a climax. She had been special, an unexpected gift.

The time with her had been far too short but someone might have arrived and caught him with her. He regretted hurrying to finish his work. Never mind. He had enjoyed every second of the rush and his next girl would receive his undivided attention. His plans for her would give him as long as possible with her. Ideas seeped into his mind, arousing him again.

He smiled. The stranger had even picked her own flowers.

The bouquet had been the sign. The girl was his for the taking.

The sight of her smiling and waving at him flashed through his mind. He had not met her before, which somehow made the anticipation of having her more thrilling. Jerking himself back to the now, he started his car and headed home, but the memories of the stranger flashed through his mind in an endless parade of desire.

He preferred to plan his kills and made sure he gained the ultimate pleasure by savoring each one. His pretty stranger had surprised him. In fact, the stimulation of catching her mid-flight had been incredible, powerful. His muscles twitched, reliving the feel of her squirming beneath him. He loved the way she fought like a wild animal. Who would believe someone so small and pretty like her could fight like a cat?

He had killed his cat.

He had enjoyed killing her more.

# CHAPTER TWELVE

Breaking the news to a family of a murdered child had to be the worst job Kane had ever encountered. His training had been nonexistent but he had suffered the pain of loss and understood the need to keep the facts clear and concise. He stared at the inquisitive faces of Mr. and Mrs. Parker. "I'm sorry to inform you, we found a body in Stanton Forest we believe to be Felicity. Your friend Magnolia Brewster identified her photograph."

"Oh my God. I've been calling her for an hour." Mrs. Parker fell against her husband. "This can't be happening."

"What happened to Felicity, was it an accident?" Mr. Parker hugged his sobbing wife.

Kane took out his notepad and pen. "The cause of death is undetermined until the results of the autopsy but we believe it was a homicide."

"Murder! Who would kill our little girl?" Mr. Parker's face paled and his hand shook as he held his wife. "I can't believe anyone would do such a thing. Are you sure it's Felicity?"

"I'm afraid so." Kane watched the couple gaped at him in shocked disbelief. "Would you like to sit down? Is there anyone I could call, a family member perhaps?"

"No!" Mr. Parker's voice trembled. "Why aren't you out looking for her killer?"

"We have every man on the case but we need your help and I really need to ask you some questions."

"Ask your damn questions but I don't know how we can help."

He hated intruding on the family's grief. "When did you last see Felicity?"

"At breakfast." Mr. Parker gazed at him with unseeing eyes as reality set in. "She mentioned she would be meeting up with some of her friends later."

"Did she say what friends? Does she have a boyfriend?"

"Yes, Derick Smith, but they fell out over the upcoming rodeo dance. I'm not sure if they made up or not." He gave him a tragic look. "You don't think he killed her do you? Dear God, I allowed him to date her."

"We don't have him as a suspect but we'll be checking everyone Felicity knows. Do you have his address and cellphone number?" Kane looked at Mr. Parker. The man was trying to keep control of his emotions but now anger had replaced the shock and disbelief. "Anything else you can tell me about Derick?"

"Yes." Mr. Parker took out his cellphone and scrolled through his contacts. "I made sure I had his contact details before I allowed her to go out with him." He rattled off the information. "Derick has a part-time job at Miller's Garage on Saturdays and during summer break."

"Thank you." Kane kept his notes brief and pushed the questions, hoping they would elaborate a little more. "Do you think she might have paid him a visit this morning?"

"No, she wouldn't go and see him without telling me." Mrs. Parker choked back a sob. "To be honest, I'm not sure what she was talking about this morning, I wasn't listening to her. It's my fault."

Kane sucked in a deep breath. "You're not to blame but you can help me catch the person who hurt Felicity. Do you remember anything at all about her movements this morning? Had she spoken on her cellphone or mentioned doing anything specific?"

"I heard her talking to Aimee before breakfast." Mr. Parker absently rubbed his sobbing wife's back. "She mentioned walking to her house.

Aimee has a car and they go into town and hang out there or at Aunt Betty's Café. I'm sure Aimee will tell you everything they planned to do."

Kane could feel the emotion flowing from the couple. "Do you know who else Felicity could have been meeting?"

"Dear Lord, how many more questions? Can't you see my wife is close to collapse?"

Kane pushed on, aware the couple were crumbling before him but he needed the information. "Anything you can tell me might help, Mr. Parker."

"You know girls, they have cliques and I've lost count of who is in and out these days." Mr. Parker frowned then lifted tear-filled eyes to Kane. "Although, Felicity wouldn't need to cut through Stanton Forest, Aimee lives on School Road."

Kane made notes. "Do you know Aimee's last name?"

"Aimee F-fox." Mr. Parker stumbled over his words. "The family are close friends."

"Thank you." Kane scribbled in his notebook. "What time did she leave this morning?"

"Early, before eight." Mr. Parker blinked away tears.

"Can you remember anything else at all?" Kane leaned forward in his chair. "What kind of mood was she in—happy?"

"She was excited at breakfast. I remember her asking us if she could go to the dance at the fairgrounds on Friday night with her friends." Mr. Parker sighed. "I said I would discuss it with her mother but if she went, we would drop her there then pick her up at ten."

"She is a good girl, Deputy." Mrs. Parker rubbed her eyes. "She did all her chores and stopped playing games at the dinner table. She deserved to go to the dance this year. Now she's dead—Oh God, this has to be a mistake." She sunk back into her husband's arms.

As their devastation washed over him, Kane ground his teeth, trying to keep a professional persona and get through the interview. "Does she have a computer? I'll need to take it back to the sheriff's office."

"Yes, a laptop. She uses it for schoolwork. I'll get it for you." Mr. Parker turned away and climbed unsteadily up the stairs.

Kane waited for him to return, unfolded a large evidence bag, and pushed the laptop inside then asked Mr. Parker to sign the seal. He hated distressing Felicity's parents any further but had to keep going while details remained fresh in their minds. "Do you remember what she was wearing when she left home and did she have a cellphone with her?"

"Wearing?" Mrs. Parker lifted her tear-stained blotchy face and glared at him. "Don't you know?" She let out a wail, broke away from her husband and fell against the wall. "Oh my God, what did he do to her?" She threw herself at Kane grasping the front of his shirt. "You have to tell me. I must know what happened to her."

The woman's long fingernails pierced his skin but he kept his voice, calm and professional. *How the hell can I tell her what happened?* He gently pushed her away and sucked in a deep breath. "I am asking routine questions, ma'am. I don't have a list of her personal effects." Kane swallowed the lump in his throat at seeing her distress. "I want to make sure nothing is missing, no article of clothing overlooked or any personal possessions."

"He is only doing his job." Mr. Parker, close to collapse, took a shuddering breath in an obvious attempt to remain strong and gripped his wife's shoulder. "She had on a pale blue top with a butterfly on the front and a denim skirt." He rubbed his chin. "Pink cowboy boots. She wears a gold cross around her neck." Mr. Parker raised both dark eyebrows. "She received it as a birthday present when she turned thirteen and never takes it off." He gave his wife a little shake. "Is there anything I've missed?"

"Yes, she has a c-cellphone with her all the time, she never takes her eyes off the screen." Tears cascaded down Mrs. Parker's cheeks. "It is a smartphone and has a p-pink cover."

"May I have the number and would you mind giving my department permission to check her calls and social media, in case she spoke to anyone prior to her death?" Kane wrote down the details.

"I'll sign anything you like." Mr. Parker seemed to crumple into himself. "Just find the person who did this."

"We'll find him." Kane swallowed the lump in his throat. "We would like to give you time to inform your relatives before this is leaked to the press. Keeping it out of the media for twenty-four hours will give us time to investigate. I know you want this person caught but a media frenzy isn't the best course of action." He sighed. "The sheriff has advised everyone concerned not to tell anyone. If the killer doesn't think we have found Felicity, they'll be careless."

"I don't want to give this animal the satisfaction of becoming famous on the damn news." Mr. Parker shook with anger. "We won't say a word."

"I want to see her." Mrs. Parker gripped Kane's arm. "Where is my baby?"

Kane looked into the woman's distressed face. "I can take you to see her now but I only need one of you to positively identify her. Perhaps you might prefer to remain at home?"

"I want to see her." Mrs. Parker swayed to her feet. "It has to be a mistake."

Kane bit back a sigh of regret and nodded. "Yes, of course. Felicity is at the local funeral home. Do you want me to lead the way?"

"Yes, please." Mr. Parker placed one arm around his wife.

Straightening, Kane turned on his heel and left the house.

*

Drained after the emotional viewing and signing of the necessary documents, Kane headed back to the office. He had been relieved to see the mortician had made Felicity appear asleep. The sheet covered her completely and came up to her chin to hide the horrendous injuries.

Not having the energy to tangle with Sheriff Alton again, he bypassed her door and went straight to his desk. After scanning the paperwork into the system, he added his notes from the parents' interview then pushed to his feet and headed for the coffee machine. The pot of freshly brewed coffee filled his nostrils. He should have been famished but had no appetite with the haunting memory of his wife's shocked eyes fixed in his mind, so much like the expression on Felicity's young face. He leaned one shoulder against the wall and rubbed the throbbing scar covering the plate in his head.

"You okay?" Jenna moved to his side and placed her small hand on his arm.

He forced his mouth into a small smile, surprised by her change of attitude toward him. "I'll do. I have entered all the information including my interview notes with the parents into the file. I've informed the parents not to talk about the murder to give us some time to chase up the leads we have, and they agreed."

"Any suspects?"

"Yeah, we will need to follow up on the victim's boyfriend, apparently they argued recently." He sighed. "His name is Derick Smith and I have his details. I called his workplace, Miller's Garage, and spoke to George."

"Did you ask him if Smith was acting any differently?"

"Yeah and George said he was acting normal." He scratched his cheek, aware of the stubble. "I'll need to speak to him but from what George said he is a pretty solid young man. If he argued with Felicity, he would more likely storm off and sulk than kill her."

"Okay, that's good enough for me. It's late and we can interview him in the morning." Jenna met his gaze. "Anything else?"

Exhausted and with a headache from hell, he nodded then immediately regretted moving his head. "Yeah, I obtained a formal ID on the victim and all the permissions we need to check her calls, et cetera, but telling the parents was brutal."

"It's the worst job. It was nice of you to send Wolfe home. I guess he is a little raw after losing his wife?"

"He is not alone." He met her concerned gaze. "I lost someone close to me as well. You never forget seeing someone you care for dying and you can do jack shit about it. Life sucks sometimes." He sighed. "Can we change the subject?"

"Do you like Chinese?" Jenna raised one dark eyebrow in question.

"Yeah, but I haven't tried that new place in town." He rubbed his stomach. "I'm not really hungry."

"You will be once you smell the sweet and sour chicken." Jenna filled two takeout cups with coffee and handed him one. "I'll leave my cruiser here, if you'll drive me home. My order should be arriving soon and we can eat at my place. Rowley will lock up and Walters is on the 911 line until six in the morning."

Suspicious of her sudden change of attitude toward him, he rubbed his chin. Perhaps the idea of having two men confronting her in the morning was a problem, but she was as tough as nails. He relented and smiled. "Okay, I'd like your thoughts on the case."

"Deal." She turned as the front door opened with a delivery guy carrying two carry-out bags. "How's that for timing?"

He pulled out his wallet and offered her some bills, but she ignored him.

"I paid by card over the phone." She headed toward the front desk. "Your treat next time, okay?"

# CHAPTER THIRTEEN

Contented and tingling from his kills, he sat near the window of Aunt Betty's Café and sipped his coffee. From here, he could watch the world go by and sense the mood of the town. Outside, the carnival atmosphere of the upcoming rodeo shrouded the truth, and people went about their everyday business ignorant of the knowledge he had snatched two young girls from under their noses. He smiled a secret smile, an all-knowing smile. *Soon they will all learn about my work and every man in town will be under suspicion.*

The six o'clock news had come and gone without a mention of the young boys' discovery of one of his girls. He had wanted to see their horrified expressions on his TV screen, but never mind, the boys would carry the vision of his work in their minds forever.

It would be a constant reminder to avoid girls like her.

Images flashed through his head as if he hit the fast-forward button in his mind then paused for him to savor each unforgettable moment. He wet his lips and sighed, remembering the feel of warm flesh against his palm, such a contrast to the cold, white skin when he laid them on the rock. The welling of blood as he moved the knife. The way Felicity's mouth moved as if pleading him to stop.

He would never stop.

The sheriff and Deputy Kane drove by in a black SUV. He could see by the way she smiled at Kane that being in law enforcement had not prevented her from using sex to get her own way. Although he preferred to kill girls, the world would fit back into place without

Jenna Alton. A man would make a far better sheriff, and no matter what her occupation, no woman deserved his respect. Perhaps he would show her what happens to women like her.

He stared after the black SUV. Taking her would be difficult. He had no way to make her come to him. *It will take some planning, but if I have time, she will be mine too.*

# CHAPTER FOURTEEN

After finishing their meal at the kitchen table, Jenna encouraged Kane to join her on the sofa in front of the TV. Leaning back, she considered the man beside her. In the months since he had arrived in Black Rock Falls, she had come to rely on his unfailing loyalty and support. She enjoyed his company and tried to keep their relationship between work and home separate, yet since Shane Wolfe had walked into the office, Kane had changed. He usually had a relaxed, laid-back nature around her off-duty, as if he really wanted them to be close friends, but now something had wound him up so tight that any second he might bust a spring.

She turned down the TV and glanced at him. "Head aching again? Do you need to keep a check on the plate in your head, have the occasional brain scan or whatever?"

"My head is aching and no the plate doesn't shift around, it's bolted in place." His dark blue gaze settled on her face. "My mind was on the case. That girl was so young and seeing her like that is playing on my mind. The man who did this is one sick son of a bitch." He cleared his throat. "Sorry, ma'am, it just makes me feel useless."

"It's fine and I happen to agree." She reached for her coffee and eyed him over the rim of the mug. "This is where your expertise comes into play. I can see the killer is trying to make a point by the way he displayed the body but why the flowers? Wolfe mentioned it was as if the killer is apologizing. What do you think?"

"He wants to shock and is proud of what he has done but there is regret there as well. As if he is a child being naughty then bringing his mother flowers to say sorry." His full lips thinned into a line. "This is not why you asked me to dinner. What's on your mind?"

She had to admit, asking him to dinner had confused him but she wanted to make up for her hostility toward him at the fairgrounds. After all, he did spend every morning working with her to hone her defense skills and knew her weaknesses, but his anger at finding her in a potentially dangerous position surprised her. He should have known she would use her weapon if threatened. She allowed her gaze to linger on his handsome features and wet her lips, not that her feminine wiles ever worked on him. Although, she noticed the way he looked at her sometimes and knew he would protect her with his life. *You are a strange man and I like the strong, silent, mysterious type. Ah well, I can dream, I guess.*

"Jenna? If you have something to say to me, spit it out." Kane leaned back in his chair and stretched his long, muscular legs. "I know when you're worried about something. We're friends and you can confide in me, even after you tore me a new one."

"So, what is so important we need a secret meeting tomorrow?" She grinned. "Do I need to erect a cone of silence or something?"

"Have you taken a paranoia drug or something?" Kane gave her a long, considering stare and rubbed the dark stubble on his chin. "It's just a meeting so we can discuss how we can best use Wolfe's talents."

"God, you talk a crock of shit sometimes. Do you think I was born yesterday? You two are up to something." She glared at him. "Spill the beans."

"Nope. I'm not saying a word. It's best if Wolfe is here to explain." Kane reached for his beer. "Talking about suspicions, I've often wondered how you discovered this is my favorite brand of beer."

*Oh, you're good.* "I didn't know. I used my superior intelligence." She giggled at his eye-roll. "I got the most popular brand from your home state. Why ask me now? You've been living in my cottage for over six months. Before you ask, I also worked out the size of your uniform from the details on your driver's license. It's not too difficult when you know the height and weight of a man. It's not as if I needed your bra size, is it?" She sipped her wine. "Stop avoiding the question. You *know* him, don't you?"

"Not *exactly*." Kane narrowed his eyes, making his forehead crinkle. "I spoke to him on the phone after you interviewed him for the position." He sighed. "We have similar backgrounds, we both served in the marines, but anything else, he'll have to tell you."

Happy to have gained ground, she pushed a little more. "Do *you* have anything else you need to tell me about?"

"Not really, but as sure as hell, I think *you* are carrying a trunk-load of secrets. For a sheriff who carries two weapons at all times, you are the jumpiest person I know." He turned in his seat and his eyes bore into her. "Why are you in Black Rock Falls? And don't tell me it's because you absolutely love being sheriff or appreciate the incredibly low salary because you could be earning a hell of a lot more working for the government."

"Maybe I think working for the government is too dangerous." She shrugged. "In any case, then I wouldn't have *you* to watch my back, would I?"

"Trust me, you'll be a whole lot safer with Wolfe and me watching your back." Kane pushed to his feet. "We'll sort this out in the morning if you don't mind, ma'am. Thanks for dinner and don't forget to set the house alarm." He headed for the door without a backward glance.

She gaped after him, stymied for a few moments, then stood to follow him and bolted the front door. After entering the code to activate the alarm, her attention went to the window. The bright automatic floodlighting around her property illuminated Kane's strong figure striding along the pathway to his cottage. Her mind went into freefall trying to digest his words. She had interviewed a few candidates for the deputy position, but after reading the other applications, Shane Wolfe shone out like a bright light.

At the time, Kane obviously had not recognized his name or face but admitted they had spoken by phone. If he had cause for alarm, or Wolfe had confided information to him earlier in the day, it would mean only one thing: Kane was working off the grid for the government and Wolfe was his new contact. Kane fit the profile and he had to be way above her old pay grade.

Collecting a glass of wine and the bottle, she headed into her office. If word had leaked about her new identity and whereabouts, she doubted the Department of Homeland Security would send him to protect her. After working undercover on one case, she hardly rated the expense. More likely, the DHS would swoop in and relocate her again, but so far, hiding in plain sight had worked. She dropped into the chair in front of her computer and refilled her glass then stared at the wall of flat screens. *Why is he here?*

Her mind turned to the murder. She needed to organize her deputies and use the assets of her team. She grabbed her notepad and made some notes. After listening to the brief report from Wolfe at the scene and Kane's conclusions, she had a few of her own. Although Lucky Briggs and Storm Crawley made her skin crawl, the crime scene had told her one man was involved. Yeah, after the antics in the tack room, she believed either of them was capable, but would they work alone?

The staging of the victim and the fact her face was not touched led her to believe the killer was unlikely to be her boyfriend. She had seen enough victims of domestic abuse to know men angry with their wives or lovers went for the face. The murder was gruesomely artistic, which meant the killer had murdered before. One thing Wolfe mentioned had been significant. Killers who mutilate their victims start slow. They start with their pets and move up to murder as the need grows. From the carnage she witnessed in Stanton Forest, whoever had brutally murdered Felicity had plenty of practice. If her murder followed his usual modus operandi, his kills would be easy to trace—and people make mistakes. Without the ability to search the local databases for similar crimes, she drafted a letter then sent it out to all the police and sheriffs' departments in the state.

She leaned back in her seat and made plans for the next day. In the morning, she would ask Rowley to trace Felicity's cellphone and collect a list of calls or texts she had made from the server. Having her parents' written permission gave the sheriff's department instant access to her accounts. Rowley could also check her social media for clues. She needed some idea of Felicity's movements from the time she left home until approximately nine thirty. A list of her friends would be helpful. She would send Kane to interview the boyfriend, Derick Smith, and see if he had an alibi for the time of death. Whoever Felicity had met during the short time between leaving home and reaching the forest had murdered her. The face of Felicity Parker filled her mind. *Why did you go into the forest, Felicity?*

# CHAPTER FIFTEEN

Kane did the usual sweep of his house, checking for any intruders or bugs. Confident his home was secure, he emptied his pockets, removed his holster, and stripped off his uniform. He dropped the garments into the washing machine then headed for the bathroom. He had a lot to think about and the shower was his refuge of choice. The arrival of Shane Wolfe had surprised him but he would be an asset to the team. Wolfe had spent his time wisely by continuing his studies to become top in his field in forensic and computer science. Once his wife died, the government ordered Wolfe back to active service. *Why put the three of us together? It makes no sense.*

He stepped from the shower and dressed. His gaze settled on his notepad and his immediate priorities slammed into place. He had a young woman lying on a slab in the mortuary, and he owed it to her and her family to find her killer.

After dragging on a T-shirt and jeans, he padded barefoot to the bedroom he'd converted into an office. Set up much like Jenna's, he had a full CCTV network of cameras around Jenna's property linked to flat screens. Luckily, Jenna had convinced Mayor Petersham to fund a system for the town and public areas. He sat at his desk, turned on the laptop, and went over the information he had taken from his visit to the Parkers.

His experience in profiling suspects had often meant life or death for him in the past. He studied a person's behavior or reaction, and the flicker of eyes or beads of sweat spoke volumes. The interview with Felicity's parents had told him one thing: Neither of them had anything to do with her murder. He watched their reaction at the viewing of their daughter's body. Both had responded normally; that kind of shock, horror, and anger did not come from a killer.

His experience in dealing with grief was limited, and standing beside the couple during the viewing was disturbing. No one could ever forget seeing a loved one murdered. Disturbing memories remained forever, and no matter how hard he tried, he could not forget the faces of the men he had killed in the line of duty. To him, not one was "the target," the term used by the kill squad to eradicate the human element from the shooter's mind. He remembered the names and faces of them all.

He scanned the files Wolfe recently added to Felicity Parker's case and found his conclusions solid. Although the results of soil samples and bodily fluids would take some time, the forensic examination of the scene was impressive. Wolfe had noted the absence of Felicity's footprints in the immediate area, which would mean the killer, or one of her killers, carried her to the rock. The autopsy proved the killer had viciously raped her but Wolfe had found no evidence of that happening on the rock. *She was raped and killed in a different place—but where?* The killer had eviscerated her post-mortem on the flat rock. He concluded the act was ritual in nature and if two men were involved one would be dominant and calling the shots, while the other looked on. He could not discount the fact one man was responsible, in fact it was uncommon to have two serial killers working together. *They don't like to share.*

Kane rubbed the back of his neck. He had studied murderers and interviewed serial killers and sociopaths from every walk of life. The fact he had used her then "cleansed" her in the river before cutting her throat followed the pattern of one person's very disturbed mind. The lewd positioning of the body and makeup made him believe the killer had suffered prolonged abuse as a child, perhaps from a woman who wore bright red lipstick. The killer would have despised her but craved the love she denied him. The flowers were significant. Violated children often tried to placate their abusers.

Had Felicity gone willingly into the forest with her killer? Was he someone she trusted? He did not recall any signs of a struggle on the footpath and he doubted a girl of her age would leave the trail and risk plowing through dense undergrowth alone in the summer. She was a local and would be fully aware of the wildlife. He scrolled through the photographs of the scene, zooming in on each one. As he moved his mouse over the image of the footprints surrounding the rock, goosebumps ran up his arms.

*Holy shit!* The footprints all led *away* from the river and *toward* the rock where the body lay. He searched the images, zooming in on the far side of the clearing, and his stomach clenched. Practically concealed by bushes, a second path led from the opposite side of the clearing. He cursed under his breath and pulled up every photograph of the area. From a different angle, he could make out a bend in the path turning it toward the river and not deeper into the forest. As none of them had known the area, they had no idea which was the regular path to the riverbank. On arrival, they had been engrossed with the murder scene and the trail of footprints leading from the river; none of them had considered the victim or killer had taken a different route on the way to the riverbank.

He grabbed his cellphone and called Jenna. When she picked up, he explained what he had found. "Do you want me to take Wolfe with me after our meeting and take another look? I hope the scene is secure. Walters put tape across the entrance to the area and posted a sign."

*"How did we miss the other pathway? We should have had Rowley with us. A local would have known it existed."*

"We were all concerned with gathering evidence from the scene. The problem is if we missed any evidence, the killer could have returned by now to sanitize the place. I am surprised he didn't try to cover the footprints."

*"The kids might have disturbed him before he had the chance?"*

He stared at the computer screen and sighed. "Maybe. I would like to know how he knew no one would be there at that time of day. He has to be a local. And how did he lure Felicity to the riverbank? We know she was heading in a different direction. I believe she knew her killer and he planned the murder ahead of time."

*"It's a bit far-fetched to believe an obvious psychopath not only planned for her to be in that location but managed to, as you say, 'lure' her to the riverbank. Why would she change direction and head for the forest when she had planned to meet her friends and head into town?"*

"Do you believe teenage girls never tell lies or keep secrets from their parents?" Kane cleared his throat. "For all we know, she made a date to meet someone, her boyfriend or someone else in the forest. She must have gone there willingly or we would have found signs of a struggle on the trail into the forest from Stanton Road. Don't forget there are cowboys in town and they are attractive to teenage girls. Add the fact she left home wearing pink cowboy boots, and after the act Lucky and Storm put on yesterday, they are on the top of my list."

*"Why not the boyfriend? We can't rule him out yet."*

"I'm not leaning heavily toward the boyfriend. The profile doesn't fit a teenage killer—it says older man to me, probably late twenties or older, Caucasian and has killed before."

*"Her boyfriend is twenty and on the college football team, so he'll be big. At that size, age doesn't come into it, does it? He would be more than capable of killing her and we haven't had time to check him out."*

"For me, he remains a suspect mainly because of motive. I would like to know why they argued —what if she was pregnant?"

*"The laying of flowers too."*

"Yes, and not jealousy or a crime of passion." Kane stretched and yawned. "We need her phone records pronto to see if she made or received a call before or after leaving home."

*"I'll have them by the morning but until we get the lab results we're flying blind. I understand your concern—I want to catch this monster too."* Jenna sighed. *"It's late and I'm exhausted. You must be too and we all need to be on our toes right now. I'm done for the day, I'll see you in the morning."*

The line went dead.

Kane stared at the call-ended message on his cellphone in disbelief. He had so many theories to discuss with her. The meeting they had planned for the morning had ruffled her feathers. With luck, what he planned to reveal about her two deputies should smooth them back down.

# CHAPTER SIXTEEN

The moment Jenna's cruiser, with Deputy Wolfe at the wheel, drove past her house, she opened the front door, set the house alarm and stepped onto the porch. The morning chill refreshed her on the walk to Kane's cottage. The secrecy of the meeting troubled her. What had Wolfe discovered about her? Damn well nothing. The DHS had sealed her file in concrete. She straightened, needing to appear confident and in charge, although weariness dragged at her. After receiving Kane's call, she had not slept and spent long hours going over the images of the crime scene. How many times before Kane arrived in town had she failed to notice important details? No wonder he'd been frustrated with her after the incident at the fairgrounds. Three years ago, she had been at the top of her game. *Am I losing my edge?*

Kane had failed to arrive for their usual workout at six. Perhaps now Shane Wolfe was in town, he had made other plans. She had enjoyed going through a routine of punishing exercise with him, and of late, he had taken her defensive skills to a higher level by showing her different moves. Letting out a long sigh, she stepped onto his stoop and knocked on the door.

"Come in, Dave is pouring the coffee." Wolfe smiled at her. "The live-in nanny is already settled, I moved her in last night. You were right, she is a gift and my kids love her, she reminds them of their grandmother."

She returned his smile and strolled past him through the family room and into the kitchen. The rich smell of Kane's favorite coffee filled the room and she relaxed a little. "That's wonderful and such a weight off your mind."

"Take a seat." Kane handed her a steaming mug.

"I feel as if I've entered the Spanish Inquisition."

"Nothing of the sort." Wolfe sat beside her and reached for his coffee.

"We decided it would be better if we had everything out in the open." Kane turned a chair around and straddled the seat, resting his arms on the hooped back. "We have to work together and it would make life easier if we told you how Shane and I know each other."

*Kane lied to me.* Jenna adopted her best blank expression then looked from one to the other. "Oh, so why tell me you'd never met?" Both men remained silent just staring at her. Annoyed, she pushed to her feet. "Oh, never mind, we don't have time for this. In case you've forgotten, we have a homicide to solve." She headed for the door.

"Jenna." Kane sprang to his feet. "Wait! We know you're in witness protection."

Fear gripped her throat. She stopped mid-stride and turned slowly to face them. "I'm not sure what you're talking about but *do* go on, this story is better than fiction."

"*Please* sit down." Wolfe pulled out the chair beside him. "We believe you should be aware of who we are and why we know about your situation."

Dropping into the seat, she glared at Kane. "You knew about me all this time?"

"Nope." Kane shrugged nonchalantly. "This was a shock for me too. Until Wolfe arrived, I was under the impression I was here to start a new life." He lifted his troubled gaze to her. "He used to be my contact at HQ. I didn't know his real name and yesterday was the first time we met."

Heart pounding like a marching band she eyed them suspiciously. "How much do you know about my situation?"

"Zip." Kane sipped his coffee and eyed her over the steaming rim. "Other than if you're compromised it will open up a can of worms."

"What's *your* story?" She massaged her temples. "Is the head injury a lie too?"

"Unfortunately, it's true and I honestly believed I came to Black Rock Falls to semi-retire." Kane rubbed his chin and dropped his blue gaze to the table. "But if I disappear one day it's because I've been compromised." He gave her a long look and a nerve in one cheek ticked. "That's all I'm prepared to tell you."

"How bad can it be?" She gaped at him and came close to losing her hard-fought composure. "Look, Dave, it's obvious you're special forces. I'm not stupid."

"It's not pretty but I'll give you an abridged version. Just for the record, I'm *not* in witness protection. I spent five years in DC's Special Forces Investigation Command as a sharpshooter. Enemy agents placed a bomb under my car. The blast killed my wife and caved in my skull. To take me off the radar, I went off the grid and became Dave Kane, a retired homicide detective injured in the line of duty."

The jigsaw fell into place. His superior skills, the way he handled trouble. Kane could think and act fast in a crisis. She bit back a moan. No wonder he had avoided her and other women. The poor man was mourning his wife. She reached across the table and squeezed his arm. "I'm so sorry for your loss. Why didn't you tell me you'd lost your wife?"

"In Dave Kane's life, she doesn't exist." Kane covered her hand. "If we intend to stay alive, we have to live the lie."

"The problem is the hackers are getting smarter by the second." He cleared his throat almost apologetically, then shrugged. "It may be years or weeks before or if anything happens but these people rarely give up. We need to watch each other's backs."

"Why are *you* here?" She withdrew her hand from Kane's arm and turned to Wolfe.

"What you see is what you get." Wolfe chuckled, and for the first time, his pale gray eyes sparkled. "I'm clean but I'm the ears and eyes the bad guys won't be expecting. I'll soon have a fail-safe on every device you use and we'll know the moment anyone puts your names in a search engine."

"I think you have quite a team at your disposal." Kane leaned back in his chair and his blue eyes narrowed at her. "Unless working with me is a problem for you now, ma'am?"

She swallowed the lump in her throat. He had gone to hell and back yet been supportive and kind to her from the first day he arrived. He had become her rock and she had to say something, give *him* something in return. "I worked undercover for the DEA."

"Okay, say no more." Kane's worried gaze moved over her face. "Now I know why you stuck a gun in my face the day we met."

"She what?" Wolfe's mouth gaped open.

"Leave it alone, Shane." Kane drained his mug then flashed a white smile at her. "We are BFF's now."

"Right." Jenna laughed.

"You don't know, do you?" Wolfe looked from one to the other in amazement. "Viktor Carlos's right-hand man turned informant and gave up the entire gang. The next day someone murdered Carlos in prison. It happened the day before I left home. I guess it didn't make the news here. You are safe, Jenna. It's over. He can't hurt you."

She gaped at him in disbelief. "So why am I still here?"

"Because you know too much." Wolfe sighed. "It's the way of things, I'm afraid. I guess you could ask to be reassigned?"

Suddenly feeling as if a great weight had lifted from her shoulders, she looked at the men. "I happen to like being the sheriff of Black Rock Falls."

"So are we good?" Kane scratched his chin.

"Yeah and now we have cleared the air, are you ready to catch a killer?"

"Yes, ma'am." Kane's grin had not faded.

She stood and pulled out her notepad. "I'll need my car keys." Flipping open her notes, she looked at Kane. "I sent emails out to the other sheriff departments in the state requesting information on similar cases. I cc'd you in, Kane, so the emails will go straight to your cellphone." She sucked in a breath. "I gather from your talk with Felicity's parents, the boyfriend, Derick Smith, has a part-time job at Miller's Garage on Saturdays and during summer break? I want you to interview him just to see if he is as squeaky clean as George thinks. He lives on Pine Forest Road, a block away from Felicity's house, he could have driven past her on the way to work."

"Yes, ma'am."

"After you're done with Smith, pick up Wolfe and head back out to the crime scene and check out the other trail." She glanced at her notes. "Something you said last night made me think. It wasn't hot yesterday and yet I didn't notice any pools of water at the scene. The victim's hair was damp but the killer had taken the time to brush it. I studied the images as well and didn't notice any muddy footsteps leading away from the rock in any direction as you mentioned. You were correct. All the footprints led *away* from the river. If the killer placed the body on the rock, cut her up, dried her hair and brushed it, then picked flowers before he left, somehow he left no trace of his movements in or around the clearing."

"We'll look closer." Wolfe gave her a determined stare. "I'll break down the area into a grid and we'll search every damn inch. I'll find something we can use." He handed Jenna her car keys.

"Do you mind if I grab Rowley and take him with us?" Kane rubbed his chin. "As he's lived here all his life, he'll know all the tracks throughout the forest."

Jenna nodded in agreement. "Good idea. I'll be out of the office for an hour or so." She headed for the door. "Maggie will have to manage for a short while. I'm going to visit Aimee Fox and see if she can shed some light on Felicity's movements before her death. I'll call first to make sure one of her parents is there before I question her." She stopped walking and gave Kane a long look over one shoulder. "I'll take Deputy Walters as backup."

"Good idea." Kane followed close behind her. "I'll call you if we find anything."

She turned and flicked a gaze over both men. "I'll do the same."

# CHAPTER SEVENTEEN

Kane strolled into Miller's Garage to interview Derick Smith with his military mindset fully loaded. A familiar calmness descended on him, bringing everything around him into perfect clarity. If Derick had killed Felicity, his instincts would scream, "Guilty." He avoided the office and walked past the gas pumps and into the garage.

Two cars sat on the hoists with a man working on each. He had spoken to George Miller, the owner of the place, many times, so the young muscular man in dirty coveralls had to be Derick. He took in the size of him—not only young and as strong as a bull but he could plainly see marks on one forearm resembling scratches. The strong, fit football player could render a full-grown man unconscious with one punch, and overpowering a sixteen-year-old girl would be a piece of cake.

The image of the mutilated body and the surprised look of horror etched into her expression flashed into his mind. Anger welled and he fought hard to swallow his emotion. He approached Mr. Miller. "Hey, George, mind if I have a quick word with Derick?"

"Oh, it's you, Deputy Kane. Would you like my daughter to bring you a nice hot coffee? We have a fresh pot—no trouble." George smiled and wiped his hands on an oily rag.

Kane had avoided Mary-Jo after a date six months previously. As he valued Jenna's friendship and the comfortable ease he enjoyed with her off-duty, he had not asked Mary-Jo out again. Her father regarded him as son-in-law potential and tried to force her onto him at regular intervals. He smiled at the older man. "Thanks, but if I drink any more coffee I won't sleep for a week. It's been one of those days."

"I know what you mean." George went over to Derick and tapped him on the shoulder. "Deputy Kane wants a word with you, son."

"Sure." Derick pulled out his earbuds and gave Kane a worried frown. "My folks okay?"

"As far as I'm aware." Kane led him to a more secluded area of the workshop. "Do you know Felicity Parker?"

"Yeah." Derick looked over Kane's shoulder at the tools lined up against the wall, each in their marked position. "She's my girl."

Kane stood feet apart and rested one hand on the handle of his Glock. He had mentioned her in the present tense, not something a man would do if he knew she had died. He pushed him a little to see if he had the temper he expected. "Bit young for you, isn't she?"

"She turns seventeen in a couple of months." Derick shot him a worried glance. "It's not like that either. I respect her and plan to marry her someday."

"Uh-huh." Kane narrowed his gaze. "I hear you had one hell of an argument over Felicity going to the dance on Friday night."

"Yeah, we did disagree." Derick glanced down at his soiled work boots then lifted his chin. "She wanted to go with Aimee, and that troublemaker is only interested in getting laid by Lucky Briggs. I objected is all." He huffed a deep breath. "Lucky is the guy you need to be talking to about underage girls, not me, and I have her parents' permission to date her."

"When did you last see Felicity?"

"Sunday." Derick shuffled his feet and avoided Kane's gaze. "We went for a walk and talked some but she insisted on going to the dance without me."

Kane waited a few beats hoping he would spill the entire story but the young man appeared to be deep in thought. "And?"

"I told her straight. If she preferred to hang around Lucky Briggs and become another notch in his belt, she wasn't the girl for me." Derick frowned and straightened, looking him in the eye. "Would *you* chase after a woman who trashed your heart as if the time we spent together and the respect I gave her meant squat?" He dragged a filthy hand through his hair, making it stick it up in all directions. "She tempted me beyond reason but I kept my word to her parents and never touched her."

"I see." Kane remained noncommittal and reached inside his pocket for his notepad and pen. He made a few notes. "So, you had no contact with her from what time on Sunday?"

"'Bout four thirty." Derick's expression turned from anger to concern. "Why are you asking me all these questions about Felicity? Her parents haven't put in a complaint against me, have they?"

"No, they haven't." Kane jotted down the details. "I'm speaking to everyone who was in the area of Stanton Forest, Sunday through Monday." He cleared his throat. "So, Sunday afternoon about four thirty was the last time you spoke to Felicity. Is that correct?" After reading Felicity's cellphone records, he would know if Derick was lying.

"Has something happened to her?" Agitation rolled off the young man.

"Just answer the question." Kane lifted his gaze from the notepad.

"Not until you tell me what's going on!" Derick made a step toward him, fists clenched.

Kane straightened and gave him a "back the hell off" glare. "Felicity was involved in an incident on Monday morning and like I said before this is a routine inquiry."

"I called her on Monday morning, early from here. I've called her since but she has turned off her damn phone."

"How early?" Kane raised an eyebrow. "Had you started work?"

"Yeah, so around seven thirty, I guess." Derick stared at his boots. "I was waiting around for George to do the paperwork on a repair. He wanted me to deliver the car and pick up the loaner before I got my clothes all greased up." He wrinkled his nose. "I took the car out to Stanton Road around eight and got back here around nine."

"It took you that long to drive a forty-minute round trip?"

"The customer, Mrs. Bolton, insisted I go over the repairs listed on the bill then made me wait for her to write out a check." Derick pushed both hands into the front pockets of his coveralls. "She held me up, some."

"I'll need her address." He wrote down the details Derick willingly supplied to corroborate his story. "Would you object to giving me a sample of your DNA?"

"My what?" Derick's cheeks reddened. "Here? Why would you need my DNA? What happened to Felicity?"

"I am not at liberty to discuss the case at this time but whatever incident may have involved her, a sample will eliminate you from any list of suspects we might have." Kane narrowed his gaze at the flustered young man. "I just need to swab the inside of your mouth. Quick and painless."

"Oh—sure. I ain't got nothing to hide."

Kane pulled a DNA collection kit from his inside pocket and performed the test, making sure the evidence was sealed and the documentation required for collection signed. "Okay, thank you for your cooperation."

He headed over to George Miller and smiled at him. "Do you remember what time Derick arrived yesterday morning and how long he was away delivering the car?"

"He is a punctual lad, starts seven each mornin', is never late, does his job." George rubbed his chin. "He must have brought the loaner back around nine because I was in the office giving my daughter an order for apple pie. We take a break at nine fifteen like clockwork every day. Mary-Jo goes down to Aunt Betty's to pick up our orders around nine."

Kane made notes and lifted his gaze. "Thanks." He pushed the notepad and pen back inside his pocket.

"The lad ain't in no trouble, is he?"

"No, just routine inquiries." Kane gave him a wave and headed back to his black SUV.

He pulled out his cellphone and called Wolfe. "Grab Rowley and meet me out front of the office, we'll go check the other trail to the crime scene."

*"Roger that. Rowley said there is another trail that runs past the falls."*

Kane spun the car around and accelerated toward the sheriff's department. "Let's hope we find enough evidence to stop this animal."

# CHAPTER EIGHTEEN

After arranging to speak with Aimee Fox and picking up Walters from the office, Jenna made her way to School Road. Confident that two men in the top of their field and one very capable deputy would be scouring Stanton Forest to discover just how clever the killer had been in covering his tracks, she would have time to interview the victim's friends and get a better handle on her timeline. She sucked in a breath as the image of Felicity Parker's lacerated body flashed across her mind. "We have to catch this guy."

"We sure do." Deputy Walters waved a hand toward the windscreen. "Next left. The Foxes live in the house with the stone wall."

She found the house and parked at the curb then noticed a girl about sixteen heading in their direction, head down, looking at her cellphone, and wearing earbuds. She appeared oblivious to her surroundings. The girl ignored the cruiser, turned into the Foxes' driveway, and headed for the house. Jenna stared after her for a few moments. "Have you noticed since cellphones kids never talk to each other anymore? I wonder if they'll manage to communicate out in the real world." She pushed open the door and climbed out.

"My grandchildren are the same." Walters ambled up beside her. "When they come to visit, all I see is the top of their heads."

The girl had entered the house and a woman waited on the doorstep. Jenna smiled to put her at her ease. "Mrs. Fox? I'm Sheriff Alton and this is Deputy Walters. May we come in and have a chat with Aimee?"

"What is this all about? I know you mentioned 'routine inquiries' but why would Aimee be able to help you?"

"I am speaking to friends of Felicity Parker concerning an incident yesterday morning." Jenna took out her notepad. "Aimee is on our list and might have some valuable information."

"Very well, you can catch two birds with one stone." Mrs. Fox stood to one side to allow them to enter. "Kate, Kate Bright, has just arrived. She is a friend of Felicity as well."

"Do you have her parents' number? I will require their permission before I speak to her." Jenna glanced around. The houses on this side of town made a statement of wealth. Rather than ranches, these homes sat in the middle of huge, well-tended gardens. The owners enjoyed being part of the university faculty or medical profession.

"Yes, of course." Mrs. Fox pulled her cellphone from her pocket and gave Jenna the information.

After obtaining the required permission to allow Mrs. Fox to be a proxy, Jenna followed Mrs. Fox into the family room. She gaped at the impressive display of Civil War rifles and other collectables displayed on one wall. "That is an amazing collection."

"Yes, my husband spends a fortune at auctions. He loves weapons of all description." Mrs. Fox sat between the two girls sitting on the edge of the sofa. "Turn off your cellphones. Sheriff Alton wants a word with you." She patted a girl with tawny hair on the knee. "This is my Aimee."

Jenna left Deputy Walters standing beside the door and sat in a comfortable leather chair opposite. She smiled at the girls. Both had dressed the same in short skirts and T-shirts with cowboy boots. The makeup on the girls surprised her and it made them look older than their sixteen years. Lucky's words echoed in her mind. *I seem to attract the young ones.* With Kane's interview notes running through her mind, she decided to ease the information from the girls rather than reveal Felicity had died. "Can you tell me what you usually do with Felicity over a typical week of summer vacation?"

"That depends if the rodeo is coming to town." Aimee grinned. "Sometimes we like to ride around town and hope to get a glimpse of some of the riders. This year we are going to the dance."

"You have a car?" Jenna jotted down notes.

"Yeah, Dad gave it to me for my birthday." Aimee patted her hair and yawned. "I have my license."

The girl, bored by her questions, constantly fiddled with her cellphone.

"What else do you do? Where do you go, who do you usually speak to?"

"We go all over. Sometimes to the library, Aunt Betty's Café, but yesterday we planned to hang out at the computer store in town. It sells games, computers, cellphones, and all types of gadgets. It has free Wi-Fi." Kate Bright grinned. "The guy behind the counter is a real nerd but if we are nice to him he helps us with the games."

The hairs on the back of her neck prickled. "Define 'nice' and why do you need help with a game?"

"Oh, we pick up his lunch and do other stuff." Aimee sighed. "Or he has to kick us out and lock up the store."

"Does he give you games?"

"Nah. Don't be silly." Kate giggled and looked at her as if she was crazy. "We download them onto our smartphones. You are just like my mom. She can't even send a text message. Games are free from the internet. Lionel knows how to cheat at most of the games and shows us how to get up the levels faster is all."

"Do you know Lionel's last name?"

"Provine, I think." Aimee fiddled with the cushion on the chair. "Why are you asking questions about Felicity? Has something happened to her?"

"I'm afraid Felicity was involved in a serious incident yesterday."

"What kind of incident?" Aimee leaned forward in her seat. "Did someone hurt her?"

Jenna sighed. "I'm not able to disclose that information just yet but I must caution you to be very careful and don't go out alone. Keep away from the forest right now it's not safe."

"That's awful." Aimee looked at her friend. "We'll go and see her."

"No, she isn't at home." Jenna glanced at Mrs. Fox. "I'll explain everything to your mother when I'm able." Jenna turned her attention back to the girls. "I need all the information you can give me. When did you last see Felicity?"

"Sunday at church but I spoke to her yesterday morning before breakfast." Aimee met her gaze. "She said she would drop in here before nine. We planned to go into town. Lionel sent all of us a bonus card for one of the new games and I guess she got engrossed in the game because she didn't show. She is totally addicted to games, so I wasn't really surprised. We all are and sometimes I get so involved I'd rather play than go out with my boyfriend." She shrugged. "I did call and leave a message but she didn't get back to me." She sighed. "Then Lionel closed the store for almost two hours and we had to cool our heels in Aunt Betty's."

*This is way over my head.* Jenna blinked and wrote down as much of the girls' ramblings as she could remember. "Okay, so I gather these 'bonus cards' are ways to move up levels in the game faster? I'm afraid I've never had time to be a gamer."

"Yes, and they are like gold. They can be awarded as you complete the tasks or missions and you can share or swap doubles of them too." She let out a long sigh. "I know old people don't understand but these days most teenagers play games or talk online."

Jenna flicked a glance at Mrs. Fox, who gave her a non-judgmental stare, then moved her attention back to the girls. "So, where did you go yesterday around nine?"

"I picked up Kate and we went into town." Aimee chewed on her bottom lip. "We spent most of the day in the computer store with Chad and Lucas but I didn't give them a ride. They always catch the seven-thirty bus into town. Dad doesn't like me having boys in the car."

"May I have their full names please?"

"Yeah, Lucas Summerville and Chadwick Johnson." Kate twirled a strand of blonde hair around her finger.

"Did you speak to anyone other than them and Lionel or see anyone on the way?"

"We spoke to Mr. Rogers at the stoplight. He crossed the road in front of the car and I called out to him." Kate smiled in a flash of straight white teeth. "He is one of the new teachers that started this year."

Jenna flicked over another page of her notebook. "What did you talk about?"

"Not much. We didn't have much time before the light changed to green. He was coming back from looking for his dog. I guess he'd been running. He was all sweaty and had bits of grass and wildflowers stuck to the Velcro on his sneakers." Kate giggled. "He ran off in such a hurry with them trailing out behind him."

The mention of wildflowers prickled the hairs on the back of her neck. The coincidence plus the timeframe was significant. "I take it he lives close by?" She looked at Mrs. Fox.

"Yes, with his wife at the far end of Stanton Road, number 206, I believe." Mrs. Fox patted her auburn hair and frowned. "Is this about Felicity's boyfriend, Derick Smith? He is far too old for her, I don't know how her parents allow her to see a boy over three years her senior."

Jenna straightened and stared at Aimee. "I heard they'd broken up."

"That's because of Lucky Briggs." Kate giggled. "Felicity thinks he is all that and plans to dance with him on Friday night. Derick got real mad and stormed off. He is such a jerk. As if Lucky Briggs would be interested in Felicity. Everyone knows he prefers blondes."

"How do you know Lucky?" Jenna moved her gaze from one girl to the other.

"Who doesn't know Lucky?" Aimee smiled. "He comes from Black Rock Falls and his ranch has been in his family forever. He is a star and everyone loves him."

"We can't wait to watch him ride on Saturday." Kate's eyes sparkled with excitement. "I wish we could follow him on the circuit. I will the moment I turn eighteen."

"Me too." Aimee turned on her cellphone and held it up. "I have his photograph as my wallpaper. He is so hot."

"I see."

"You can put that man right out of your mind, young lady." Mrs. Parker's cheeks reddened with anger. "She is not usually so forward."

"Teenagers are a handful, so I'm told." Jenna took in her horrified expression. "Maybe Aimee will be at college by then and Lucky Briggs will be a distant memory."

"I live in hope." Mrs. Fox cleared her throat. "Is that all?"

Jenna smiled. "If you wouldn't mind, while everything is fresh in their minds, could I get written statements from Aimee and Kate? Then I won't need you to come down to the office. If you could witness them as well, otherwise this information is hearsay."

"Yes of course, I have a couple of notepads they can use." Mrs. Fox stood and left the room, returning with pens and paper. "What do you want them to say?"

"In your own words, what time you saw Mr. Rogers, what he was wearing. Everything you can remember about what you said and how he looked, then sign and print your name on the bottom."

Jenna waited for the girls to write their statements, collected them, and stood. "Thank you for your cooperation." She headed for the door and Mrs. Fox followed her outside.

"Has something bad happened to Felicity?" Mrs. Fox searched her face. "From the questions, I gather the situation is serious."

"I'm afraid I can't go into details but keep a very close eye on your daughter. Don't let her go out alone and inform Kate's mother as well." Jenna raised both brows. "If you see any strangers hanging around or anything that seems out of place, please call me." She took a card from her pocket and handed it to her. "I'll be able to release details to the media in a day or so."

"I will keep her at home today. Thank you." Mrs. Fox turned toward the house.

Jenna followed Walters back to her cruiser, slid behind the wheel, and turned to him. "The moment we get back to the office, start the check into the victim's phone logs. We have her parents' written permission."

"Yes, ma'am."

She took out her notepad and read each page of the interview, adding a few comments to make sure she had everything. The talk with the girls had pointed the finger at two new suspects: Rogers and Provine. The cowboys and boyfriend remained on her list. Their eagerness to give up their information might stem from knowing the killer had left no damning evidence. She tapped her pen on her bottom lip, running through the interview again. Her timeline for Felicity's movements from the time she left home was non-existent.

Somebody must have seen her walking along Stanton Road. She had left home at the time people living in the area would be heading to work. After making a note to find and call a number of local residents, she glanced at her watch and wondered if Kane had discovered anything of interest at the crime scene. Not wanting to disturb him, she huffed out a sigh and headed back to the office. *I'll need to set up my whiteboard again to unravel this mess.*

# CHAPTER NINETEEN

After picking up Wolfe and Rowley from outside the sheriff's department, Kane drove to the outer edge of Stanton Forest. Rowley's local knowledge was invaluable. He described the trails throughout the forest and the most likely one a killer would use to access or leave the crime scene undetected. The day had started out cool with a cloudless blue sky but as the group trudged deeper into the forest, humidity surrounded them. Sweat spilled into Kane's eyes in an annoying, salty stream and insects attacked without mercy. He dodged another patch of poison ivy and kept alert for wildlife. The walk had not depleted his energy and Wolfe met him stride for stride. After so many years in the service of his country, he could survive most of what nature and man threw at him, but Rowley was showing signs of fatigue.

His cellphone rang. It was Alton. "Kane."

*"I've just been notified a girl is missing. She fits the killer's type: sixteen, long hair, pretty. Her name is Joanne Blunt."*

"When was she last seen?"

*"The neighbor saw her walking toward Stanton Forest carrying a towel after lunch yesterday. She got to town yesterday morning and is staying with relatives for the rodeo week. She could have been heading for one of the swimming holes but there are tons in that area. I'll organize a couple of deputies from Blackwater to search the west side. You are on the Stanton Road side, so as far as I know, there are three main ones on your side."*

Kane frowned. "Okay, we're in the area, we'll check them out." He ended the call.

After relaying the information to the other deputies, he followed Rowley along a narrow, winding path deeper into Stanton Forest, with Wolfe close behind. As the sound of running water reached his ears, he tugged on Rowley's shirt to get his attention. "Hey, where is the river? I thought it was in an easterly direction from here?"

"This trail leads to one of the waterfalls. It's not the one Lucky Briggs took to get to the rock pool. I reckon animals made this track but it's on the hiking map. We can get to the first water hole from here then it's an easy walk to the rock pool."

"Lead the way." Kane rubbed his chin. "How come this is the first time I've heard of a hiking map?"

"They are for sale everywhere. Aunt Betty's Café has them on the counter on a display marked, 'Things to do in Black Rock Falls County.'" Rowley wiped sweat from his brow and reached for a water bottle inside his backpack. "Most visitors here during the hunting season use the trails. Little Falls is one of the recommended areas. Hikers like it because it is picturesque but it's a bit small as a swimming hole and one hell of a long walk for the locals. Big Falls is the better option, and only a short walk from the road."

"Hold up." Wolfe dropped his backpack on the ground. "We've been walking for half an hour and I need a break. I've noticed at least three trails leading off this one. Where do they come out?"

"They end up against the mountain range, bear caves mostly." Rowley removed the cap from the water bottle and drank, spilling drops onto his chin, then lowered the bottle with a satisfied sigh. "I doubt anyone would use them at this time of the year. Black bears are hungry and on the move." He waved in the direction of the trail. "It's not much further, maybe five or ten minutes. I can hear the waterfall."

"Okay. Keep moving." Kane glanced at Wolfe. "Someone has used this path and recently." He followed Rowley but indicated with his chin toward the cobwebs dangling between the trees. "I've not seen anything blocking our way, not a cobweb or a branch, but the covering of leaves and pine needles is so darn thick even my boots aren't making an impression."

"I've noticed a few damaged plants, and as you are both sticking to the middle of the path, it's not you. Back there—" Wolfe gestured behind him with his thumb "—I examined a crushed fern. Problem is, with bears and deer in the area, we can't be certain a person used the trail."

"I don't think so." Rowley glanced back at them. "I haven't seen any deer droppings or bear scat and they shit all the time." He shrugged. "No recent claw marks on any of the trees either."

The small trail opened out into a rock formation with a drip-fed pool. The place was deserted and the water so clean they could see the bottom. They split up and searched the surrounding forest but found nothing.

Kane stared at a wide path leading in the direction of the roar of water. "This way, I gather?"

"Yeah." Rowley smiled. "Five minutes max."

As the sound of water became louder, the damp earthy smell of the forest faded into the distinct smell of death. "Oh shit, can you smell that?"

"Oh yeah." Wolfe moved to his side. "Victim number two?"

"I hope not." Kane strode into the picturesque clearing and stopped in his tracks.

On an orange towel lay a young girl, eyes staring into nothing. He bit back a moan of dismay and held back an arm to prevent Rowley from entering the scene. "Same M.O. as before."

"Looks that way." Wolfe dropped his bag on the floor and opened the zipper. "Suit up then I suggest you call it in and ask the boss for orders. We are running out of time to check the other crime scene before any evidence is destroyed."

Kane made the call.

Moments later, he joined Wolfe and Rowley. "The sheriff is on her way, with Walters and Mr. Weems." He sighed. "Orders are to secure the area, take the shots, and complete a preliminary examination of the body then wait for her to arrive. As we have to check the other crime scene, she'll take over here." He pulled out a roll of crime scene tape from his pocket and handed it to Rowley. "You know the drill."

He used his cellphone to capture the images and could hear Wolfe dictating his findings into his recorder. After collecting the girl's clothes and shoes, he moved to Wolfe's side. "Find anything different?"

"Not really but from the scratches all over her, I gather she tried to run away from the killer. The marks are consistent to running through the undergrowth and low tree branches." Wolfe let out a long sigh. "We have her clothes but apart from that, it is a mirror of the first murder, right down to the flowers."

Kane rubbed his chin. "He is escalating faster than I imagined. Time of death?"

"I'd say yesterday, not long after she was last seen. So, he killed twice in one day." Wolfe covered the victim with a plastic sheet. "This is a lot worse than I imagined."

By the time he had packed the evidence into labeled bags, Jenna and Walters arrived on scene with Weems and his assistant pushing a gurney. He drew Jenna to one side. "Same killer."

"Okay, leave the evidence bags with me. I'll take it from here." Jenna glanced at Wolfe. "Come back to the office after you've re-checked the other crime scene. The autopsy can wait until the morning."

"Yes, ma'am." Wolfe moved away and removed his coveralls. "I'll have my initial report on your desk this afternoon."

# CHAPTER TWENTY

After Alton left the forest, Kane stripped off the face mask and his crime scene gear. He glanced at Wolfe and Rowley. "Okay, move out. We still have to check out Felicity Parker's crime scene again."

He led the way down the path and back into the forest. A short while later, they joined the original trail and headed toward the river, keeping up a good pace.

"It would make sense the killer used this trail to the river." Wolfe moved beside Kane. "It's isolated as hell, a great way to get to the location and leave without being seen."

Kane nodded in agreement. "To escape the scene for sure but we have no evidence to suggest the killer knew the victim would be in the forest. Felicity's parents believe she was going to a friend's house and heading in the opposite direction." He rubbed the back of his neck. "I spoke to Jenna last night about this and we agreed the murder was not a random thrill-kill. It looks as if Felicity knew her killer and went with him willingly. I've spoken to the boyfriend but I'm not finished with Lucky Briggs and Storm Crawley either."

"Or someone she knew called her after she left home and she met them here." Wolfe stood, hands on hips. "We won't know shit until we check the phone records."

"The kids didn't see anyone else that morning so if the killer used this path to get away, he must know the area." Rowley grimaced and moved along the trail.

"Makes sense." Kane shrugged. "Assuming he was soaking wet after murdering Felicity in the water, he would likely wade in the river again to clean away any residual blood. By the time he walked back to the road, he would be dry—sweaty but dry."

"And nobody would think a thing about seeing a sweaty hiker coming out of the forest." Rowley slowed his pace. "Whoa, on the right under the leaves—is that a condom wrapper?"

Kane edged his large frame around Rowley and crouched down to look. "Yeah, it certainly is, and there is more than one concealed under leaves. I'll get my gloves." He stood, removed his backpack, and went through the pockets. "Got them, and by the look of them they haven't been here long. Of course, they could belong to any of the kids who make out here." He dropped the foil wrappers into an evidence bag. "I doubt these are his, from what we've seen so far, he is too smart to leave DNA evidence. If they are his what did he do with the used ones?"

Kane did a visual scan of the area but found nothing disturbed. "He would drop them and the wrappers into the river; it flows fast, and apart from washing away any evidence they would be carried miles away. My guess is the wrappers belong to someone else."

He moved ahead and the sound of the river became louder with each step. He slowed his pace as he caught glimpses of sparkling water through the trees. "Okay, if we assume the killer left the clearing using this trail, we need to search for clues to trace his movements in and around the clearing."

"The victim had blunt force trauma to the back of her skull, which would indicate he came up behind her, knocked her senseless, then dragged her onto the riverbank." Wolfe moved into the perimeter of the clearing and turned slowly as his pale eyes scanned the area. "The main track to the river from the clearing splits into two. I suggest we split up. You start there and take a path each. I'll follow this trail and see if I can find any evidence."

Kane ducked down the main path from the clearing. The leaf-strewn pathway gave way to fine rocks and sand, offering no trace of footprints. He meticulously checked the bushes along the way for any hair caught on branches and underneath for evidence. He berated himself on the way for not checking the area at the initial visit, but collecting the evidence in the immediate area around the crime scene had been a priority. He heard Wolfe call his name and retraced his steps, meeting him at the edge of the clearing. "I haven't found a thing."

"I have." Wolfe led the way along the narrow trail.

The path opened out to display a fallen log, and by the indent in the ground, locals had used it as a seat for some time. "What did you find?"

"Here." Wolfe pointed to a piece of torn paper with a green brand mark. "That is from a skein of twine, the plastic type. I used the same brand to tie down the load on my trailer recently." He collected the paper and placed it inside an evidence bag. "It seemed irrelevant until I noticed the marks on the trees on opposite sides of the trail." Walking ahead, he indicated to the small scrapes on the bark of two trees. "I would say the rope was tied between the two trees, and at neck height if we're talking about Felicity. The twine is dark green, and if someone was moving along here at a jog they wouldn't notice it until they ran into it."

Kane examined the evidence and crouched to examine the ground. "The gravel has been disturbed, scuffed-up in places. A struggle took place here." He stood slowly, peering at the bushes thick along each side of the trail. "There, that is hair. Long and brown, we have to assume it belongs to the victim."

"Right." Wolfe snagged the hair and secured it in a bag. "We can assume Felicity jogged down this path, hit the cord, and fell into the bushes. The killer struck her over the head, rendering her dizzy, but she remained conscious—the autopsy revealed the blow wasn't hard enough to knock her out. There are no drag marks, so he must have carried her to the riverbank."

Concerned he might disturb evidence, Kane stepped slowly forward, checking ahead before each step. The river glistened before him. Opposite, a wall of rock kept the small, secluded beach from prying eyes. As he moved onto the small beach, he noticed a spot of blood on a stone and disturbance in the sand. "How the hell did we miss this?"

"That's where he raped her and I bet he had her on her knees with a knife to her throat. He nicked her to pacify her and probably told her once he had finished he would let her go." Wolfe flicked him a look of stone-cold rage then crawled around on hands and knees, checking every inch of the area.

"Over here." Rowley's voice came from further down the small beach.

Circling the area with care, Kane glanced back at Wolfe. "Grab some photographs. I'll go and see what he has found."

"Just a minute." Wolfe indicated ahead with his chin. "Those marks look like two sets of footprints. I'd say she got away from him and ran from here along the water's edge." He pointed to a raw patch on a nearby tree. "After he'd killed her, it looks like he swept the area with a tree branch. He is smart and probably chucked the branch into the river, walked along the water's edge, then went through the forest and back to the trail we used to get here."

"So, we need to find the spot where he killed her."

"It would help." Wolfe gave him a grim half-smile. "But I'd bet he attacked her in the water. He has done this before and knew he needed to minimize blood spill, which means he was concerned someone would see him covered in blood. I bet he lives in town and is known locally."

"Then he travels a lot, because we both know he has killed before and often." Kane headed toward Rowley, keeping away from the disguised footprints. He constantly scanned the area and reached Rowley moments later. "What do you have?"

"Fabric by the look of it, and I think I can see a boot in the water but it's a way from the bank." Rowley's face had paled. "It's unusual for anything to remain that far out in the water for long; the flow is very fast in the middle, and deep. When the kids swim here, they keep to the inlet further down."

"Where the footprints led from?"

"Yeah, that's a shallow area but as you can see it all joins together. It would be easy to drag a body from the river's edge into the inlet and carry it to the flat rock." Rowley swallowed and his Adam's apple bobbed up and down. "Looking at the scrap of cloth, if it is part of Felicity's clothing, the killer must have cut off her clothes—this doesn't look torn."

Unease grabbed Kane's gut as he bent to check out the blue cloth with a sequin attached. It did not take a forensic scientist to tell him someone had used a hunting knife to hack through the material. The sequin could have formed a part of a butterfly and the color was a match. "Photograph it and bag it." He straightened and tossed Rowley a pair of gloves. "Where is the boot?"

"See the black rock sticking out of the water. Look to the left at the bottom." Rowley pointed to the river. "Do you want me to go collect it?"

"Nah. I'll do it." Kane headed to a large boulder upstream, checked around for evidence, and finding nothing of interest stripped to his underpants. He waded in then dived under the fast-flowing river and did a visual scan along the swirling riverbed. His ability to remain underwater for considerable time came in handy and he reached the black rock with only resurfacing once.

Blinding pain from the cold water zipped across his head but, determined, he pushed on. He found the boot, pink with sparkles, and his stomach gave a twist of anguish. He climbed onto the rock and tossed the boot like a quarterback to Rowley, who caught it with ease. After doing a reconnaissance of the riverbed for some distance in the direction of the rushing water he discovered a second boot, but all other traces of Felicity Parker had vanished.

# CHAPTER TWENTY-ONE

After relaying the terrible news to the relatives of Joanne Blunt, Jenna returned to the office feeling emotionally drained. She needed a break; every crime scene brought flashbacks, and the thought of losing control with a serial killer on the loose was distressing her to the max. Without time to visit a shrink, she needed to confide in someone and talk through her worries. Kane came to mind. Dependable, he would have seen post-traumatic stress disorder cases in the marines. She would take his advice without hesitation.

After watching Walters sneak into his cubicle carrying a paper sack filled with homemade goodies from one of the stalls lining the main street, Jenna decided to get away for a few precious moments. She walked past the front counter and gave Maggie a wave. "I need some sugar. I'm going to the store."

Stepping out into the sunshine, she sidestepped a bunch of kids on skateboards and weaved her way through the throngs of people toward the tables lined up outside the community hall. The townsfolk had draped bunting over the front of the building and it continued along the front of each stall. Bright, handwritten signs decorated the wall, giving the prices of what was on offer.

She moved slowly, taking in all the treats and purchasing everything from cookies to fudge. As she strolled across the road at the end of the block, she had the strange feeling someone was watching her. Goosebumps rose on her arms and her scalp prickled. She glanced around, expecting to catch someone following her. The crime scenes had put her on alert and awoken memories of her kidnapping six months earlier, but why would she be suffering flashbacks on the main street?

Dropping into secret-agent mode had saved her many times. She walked head erect and used the shop fronts to keep a close eye on who was behind her. All she could see was the milling crowd and no one in particular stood out. She stopped at an impressive display of pies and, pushing down the rush of nerves, selected four then waited for the woman to place them into a box for her. On the other side of the street, she noticed Aunt Betty's Café had joined in the celebrations, with posters advertising the rodeo and flags.

She waited to cross the road and every hair on her body stood at attention. *What is wrong with me? It's broad daylight and the place is crowded, I'm safe, Carlos is dead..*

Hurrying across the road, she pushed open the door to Aunt Betty's and went straight to the counter. After ordering coffee, she stood with her back to the wall and checked out the customers. The tourists she did not know, but she spotted the computer guy Lionel Provine eating lunch with Aimee, Kate, and a group of kids. He could have been watching her. *Hmm, I wonder if their mothers know they are so friendly with him. At least they are out in a group.*

She started when Reverend Jones touched her arm, and she gazed at the man's concerned expression. "Did you want to speak to me, Reverend?"

"No." Jones gave her a warm smile. "Miss Hartwig has been trying to get your attention. I think your coffee is ready."

She looked into his compassionate gaze and smiled. "Oh, yes, thank you. My mind was on something else."

"Are you okay? You seem a bit jumpy." He squeezed her arm with his large hand. "Would you like me to walk you back to the sheriff's office? I'm going in that direction the moment my order is ready. It would be no trouble, no trouble at all."

She gave him her best bright smile. "I'm fine but thank you so much for your consideration." She picked up her coffee and headed for the door.

As the sensation of someone watching her slid over her again, she hoisted her box of purchases under one arm then turned to look back at Aunt Betty's and straight into the dark eyes of Lionel Provine.

# CHAPTER TWENTY-TWO

After returning to her office, Jenna dropped into her chair, leaned back, and stared at the ceiling trying to absorb all the information gathered on Felicity's murder over the last twenty-four hours and compare it with what she knew about Joanne Blunt. They had nothing in common apart from age. Joanne did not live in town and she had no friends in the area apart from her cousins. All of them had alibis, and as far as they knew, she had not met or conversed with anyone since her arrival. Jenna had absolutely no suspects or leads whatsoever. A knock at the door drew her attention, and she noticed Deputy Wolfe standing in the doorway. "Did you find anything?"

"Yeah, a pair of boots and a scrap of blue cloth likely from the victim's T-shirt." Wolfe moved into the room and pushed the door closed behind him. "I think I have a pretty good idea of the sequence of events at the scene."

Jenna pushed to her feet. "Photos?"

"Yeah, we all took tons. I'll upload them ASAP. Rowley is waiting outside the evidence room. Who has the keys?"

"Kane and myself. Tell Rowley to drop them down the evidence chute and we'll log them later." Jenna headed for the door. "Where is Kane?"

"Ah, he had to go home and pick up some underwear." Wolfe stood to one side. He gave her a lopsided grin. "Rowley noticed a boot in the river and Kane volunteered to go in after it. Searching underwater he found the second boot, then we had the long walk through the forest back to the car. The insects are a bitch."

"Why didn't you leave a cruiser at both ends of the trail, it would have saved you a long walk?" She stared at him in amazement then laughed to herself. *This is going to be a very long day.* She headed for the coffee machine.

"Well, it was like this, ma'am." Wolfe followed her out the office. "Kane had the theory the killer would be wet, as in soaking wet. We both believe the murder took place in the water, as there is no substantial blood evidence on scene. The killer carried her to the flat rock to cut her up after he cut her throat and let her bleed out. It would make sense he would be wet after washing in the river. But after dressing in dry clothes by the time he walked back along the trail, his hair would be dry enough not to draw attention."

Jenna refilled the coffee maker. "And was Kane's hair dry when he reached the road?"

"Nearly, but he was wet all over. He went into the river fully dressed." Wolfe took four mugs down from the shelf. "That's why he headed home." He sighed. "I'll get started on the Joanne Blunt preliminary examination now."

"I'd like to hear all your theories because I need proof both victims weren't killed elsewhere then carried to the forest to be put on show." She turned and leaned her back against the counter. "After interviewing Felicity's friends, my list of suspects is a mile long for her murder but I have absolutely nothing for Joanne Blunt. She literally arrived in town and someone killed her."

"Kane thinks it's a local who moves around, maybe in his job, but there *are* differences in both murders. We know Joanne Blunt was heading to the rock pool for a swim but Felicity Parker had no reason to be in the forest. I think the Blunt murder was opportunistic. The killer came across her, chased her down. From the bruising, she fought back. He pulled her hair and punched her rather than using a weapon. From what I could determine, he used one knife not a variety." Wolfe went to the refrigerator and took out the cream. "But both murders are ritualistic and I have no doubt he has killed before and will again, very soon."

She glanced up to see Kane strolling through the door carrying an Aunt Betty's takeout box. His blue gaze moved around the room and rested on her, and he headed in her direction. "There he is now. If you handle the coffee, I'll go with Kane and place the items you found into the evidence locker."

"I've picked up some food. I'm guessing you haven't had time to eat either." Kane smiled at her and dropped the takeout box onto the counter. "We have a lot to discuss."

"Thanks, but I've collected enough pies and candy for a month." Jenna returned his smile.

"Great!" He grinned. "You hungry?"

"Famished. I've been waiting for you to get back. Once we've taken care of all the evidence you've collected, we can eat." She turned to Wolfe. "I'll send Rowley to give you a hand. Take the coffee and food into my office, we won't be long."

"We found a pair of cowboy boots, pink with sparkles. They fit the description of the pair Felicity was wearing the day she went missing. There is a scrap of blue material with a sequin, which might be a part of her top."

She strolled beside Kane and they met Rowley outside the cage. The young deputy appeared a little frazzled. "Thanks, we'll take it from here. Go and help Wolfe—Kane was kind enough to pick up our lunch so we might as well eat and discus the case."

"Yes, ma'am." Rowley handed the box of evidence to Kane. "Thanks, I could eat a horse right now."

She waited for him to go, and they used their keys to unlock the evidence room. As she entered a description of each article into the book then the computer, she glanced up at Kane. "I had the strangest feeling someone was following me today."

"Did you see anyone?"

"Not following me but I went to pick up coffee from Aunt Betty's and Lionel Provine was there with some kids. When I left, I had the same feeling. I turned around and looked straight into his eyes."

"We have an inbuilt radar. Instinct or whatever." Kane shrugged. "It may be nothing but we'll keep an eye on him. I'm glad you told me."

She sighed. "Okay, back to the job at hand. Any thoughts?"

"You mean apart from knowing this animal is a psychopathic, exhibitionist, murdering son of a bitch?"

"That would be the general consensus but you have a knack for figuring out how a killer's mind works. How long do you think before he strikes again?" She closed the book and stared up at him.

"Right now I don't have a clue." Kane rubbed the back of his neck. "I'm hoping the emails I sent out last night to the sheriff's departments of other counties might be able to shed some light on this monster." He followed her from the cage and pulled the door shut behind them. "There have to be other murders with the same M.O. The murderer is making a distinctive statement and I'm sure will kill again. These crazies usually have a pattern: They start slow, as long as six months between kills, then the hunger gnaws at them and the distance between each murder becomes smaller. Think of killing to them as an addiction: Once they are hooked, they keep needing a bigger fix and crave it more often. So, with two on the same day, we can expect him to act again very soon."

Jenna headed into her office and took her seat behind the desk piled high with takeout cartons of cakes and sandwiches. She lifted her gaze to Kane. "How much do I owe you? After the trek you did through the forest, this meal is on the department."

"I'm good." Kane slid into a chair. "There is nothing to spend my money on around here, is there?" He selected a packet of sandwiches. "I didn't have to pay for the tickets to the dance on Friday night either. The guy gave me a bunch for nothing and said we were all welcome to attend." He glanced at Wolfe. "As you requested, I arranged for four deputies from two other counties to help out Friday night and all this weekend, so we can be undercover at the heart of any trouble if you agree?"

Jenna shrugged. "Sure, but I want uniforms as well. Rowley and Walters can pull the night shift during and after the dance. The three of us will be at the dance, and I'm sure Shane would like to take his daughters out for the evening, or a part of it?" She glanced at Wolfe and smiled. "At least your seventeen-year-old will want to join in the fun."

"Yeah, Emily has been harping about going since we got to town. Not the other two, they can stay at home with the nanny. I can't watch all three at once, and we have a killer in town, in case it slipped your mind?"

"I'm not likely to forget seeing the bodies of Felicity Parker or Joanne Blunt anytime soon." Jenna selected a sandwich and peered inside. "Aside from the articles we logged in the evidence locker, run me through what else you noticed on scene. So that we don't get confused, just Felicity Parker's crime scene for now."

"First and most significant is I'm sure the killer murdered her in the river. The evidence tells me he lay in wait for her to arrive and had everything he needed on hand." Wolfe placed his cup firmly on the desk. "He killed her then carried her to the rock to act out his fantasy."

"First impressions on the evidence so far?" Jenna looked at Kane.

"I agree with Wolfe. The killer planned the murder. He had too much stuff with him for it to be a random thrill-kill. We found evidence of rope, condoms, not to mention the evidence proves he used more than one knife." Kane took a bite from a sandwich, chewed, swallowed, then shrugged. "What I can't get my head around is Felicity told her parents and her friend she was heading in the opposite direction. What happened around the time she left home to make her go into the forest alone?" He reached for his coffee, took a gulp, then cleared his throat. "The timeline we have for her movements makes no sense at all."

"What do you mean?" Rowley leaned forward in his seat and frowned. "We know the time of death was between eight and ten. It has to be. Felicity was seen at eight and found just after ten."

"No, you have me all wrong." Kane placed his sandwich back in the box and looked at him. "We have to assume the killer planned the murder. People don't carry all that equipment around just on the off chance a girl will wander into the forest alone. The killer had the scene set up to trap her if she tried to run. He was there well before she arrived and lay in wait."

"That makes sense." Wolfe scratched his blond buzz cut.

"Yeah, it makes a lot of sense." Kane's blue gaze moved from Wolfe to Jenna. "So how could he possibly know Felicity would be in the forest at that precise time?"

Jenna stared at her deputies across her desk and a cold shiver slid down her spine. "There is only one explanation. Felicity knew her killer. He might have arranged to meet her or maybe he bumped into her on the street and talked her into going to the river with him." She glanced at Kane. "What do you think?"

"I'm sure he didn't meet her accidentally. From the evidence at the crime scene we have to assume he set up the killing area well ahead of time." Kane met her gaze and raised one dark eyebrow. "I would like to know how the killer knew what time she would be leaving the house. You mentioned Aimee usually drops by to give her a ride into town. So, if the killer had been watching Felicity, he wouldn't be expecting her to walk to Aimee's house."

"You said she had an argument with her boyfriend." Wolfe raised his ice-gray gaze to her. "Has anyone checked to see if he called her? Young women can be secretive about their boyfriends. If she planned to meet him at the river to make up after their argument, it would make sense she wouldn't tell her parents and make an excuse to walk to Aimee's house."

Jenna swallowed her sandwich and nodded. "Yeah, that's a possibility, but her mother mentioned she made a habit of telling her if she planned to meet him."

"We don't know what peer pressure she was under from her friends. Maybe going out with an older boy and then breaking up, she couldn't take her friends 'told you so' attitude and kept the meeting to herself. What do we know about this boyfriend?"

"Not much." Jenna picked up her notebook and flicked through the pages. "He is twenty, on the football team at college."

"Would you like me to check the cellphone records and see if he called her at any other times, ma'am?" Wolfe shrugged. "That would be a place to start."

Jenna let out a long sigh. "Walters is downloading them as we speak." She glanced at Kane. "What was your impression of the boyfriend?"

"Derick Smith doesn't fit the profile but I don't think we should discount anyone at the moment. We know he delivered a car and picked up the loaner but we don't know the timeline and George can't give an exact time he returned to work." Kane rubbed the stubble on his chin absently. "We'll need to check out the owner of the car, Mrs. Bolton."

Jenna made a few notes in her daybook. "Okay, I'll keep him on the list."

"Although, I'm sure this wasn't a crime of passion, her face wasn't touched. It is unusual for this type of psychopath to kill women they care for. He did say he planned to marry her." Kane's brow wrinkled in concentration. "And we know the same killer murdered Joanne Blunt."

"Maybe she decided to end the relationship and he lost his temper and killed her accidentally then took it out on a stranger as well." Rowley's young face paled. "It happens."

Wolfe flashed Rowley a look that could kill. "I want you to take a real long look at the crime scene photographs and tell me why you think what that monster did was accidental."

"Ah well... I guess." Rowley's ears went bright red.

Jenna cleared her throat. "Hey, settle down, Wolfe. Rowley has a right to an opinion. This is a discussion and I value everyone's views." She stood and walked to the whiteboard. "Okay, we have a very minimal gap between the last time Felicity's parents saw her alive and when the kids found her body." She wrote Felicity's name on the whiteboard and underneath, "Last persons to see her alive," then added Mr. and Mrs. Parker and the time of approximately eight. She turned to look at Wolfe. "Did Weems confirm stomach contents?"

"Yes, cereal and milk." Wolfe glanced at his notes. "In fact, my observation on that alone would place the time of death before nine; no digestion had taken place at all."

"At that time of the morning, people in the area would be leaving for work. It might be an idea to release it to the media." Kane sipped his coffee. "Someone must have seen something, a car, a person walking their dog, a man strolling along the road. The killer couldn't have been invisible."

Jenna frowned. "I'm not sure I want the media scouring the forest just yet, not with two murder scenes sticking out for all to see, but

I can see your point. I'll put out a media release to say we found the bodies and urge the public to be cautious. I'll ask for anyone who saw the girls in the vicinity of Stanton Forest and see if anyone calls in with information."

"There would be about thirty residences along Stanton Road near both crime scenes." Rowley clasped his hands in front of him on the desk and gave her a determined look. "It would be faster to call everyone in the area tonight around, say, six. Most people will be home from work by then and we could cover the entire neighborhood in a couple of hours."

"Half that time if Walters gives you a hand." Jenna nodded. "Good thinking."

"Main suspects?" Kane lifted his pen expectantly.

"We have one man in the vicinity seen coming out of the forest. Steve Rogers is a teacher, known to the victim. From his driver's license, he weighs 195 pounds, five ten, age thirty-six. When I interviewed Aimee Fox and Kate Bright, Kate said they spoke to him on the morning of the murder around nine. She said he was looking for his dog and she made a comment about him being in a hurry."

"I don't recall you mentioning him before." Kane gave her an inquisitive look. "He ticks all the boxes and we should be shaking him down. Did they say anything else about him? Did they mention him being wet, for instance?"

"No, she said he was in a hurry, sweating and had flowers stuck to his shoes." She checked her notes. "I made a point of asking them about his appearance. They spoke to him close up and would have noticed, so for me that point alone is significant."

"I agree." Kane scribbled notes in his book.

Jenna made a list of suspects on the whiteboard. "Okay, I want boots on the ground today interviewing suspects. As we have already spoken to Lucky Briggs, Storm Crawley, and Derick Smith, that leaves the guy in the computer store, Lionel Provine, and Steve Rogers. Kane, you can speak to Rogers." She glanced at Wolfe. "You will be with me today. The computer store is on the main street." She turned to Rowley. "I want you to check Felicity's social media." She returned to her desk, searched for Derick Smith's cellphone number, wrote it down, and handed it to him. "Then see if Walters has her cellphone records and check this number against incoming and outgoing calls Sunday through to Monday morning and check it against Kane's notes. Make a note of any calls from Saturday through Monday. I want a list. I'll give you her laptop from the evidence room before we leave and you can check her social media accounts."

"Unless Rowley has the necessary hacking skills, I would advise against allowing him near her computer." Wolfe filled his cup with coffee and added cream and sugar. "Leave that part of the investigation to me, ma'am. Problem is these days most kids of her age use their laptops for schoolwork and their cellphones for social media. As we don't have her cellphone, it will be difficult to follow her on social media without the necessary passwords. I'll be able to get into her account."

"That sounds like a plan." She glanced at Rowley. "We had better make our coffee to go."

"I'll get some takeout cups." Rowley headed to the kitchenette.

Jenna looked from Wolfe to Kane. "I want everyone in the loop at every step of this investigation. I want you to add your interviews to the file and pertinent information to the whiteboard. I want to know at a glance where the suspects were at the time of the murder and the witnesses for their alibis."

"Yes, ma'am." Kane pushed his hat onto his dark head then his phone chimed. He pulled the device out of his pocket, and after bending over the screen, he whistled. "You have an email from Deep Lake's sheriff's department. Six months ago, they had two murders, two weeks apart, sixteen-year-old girls, almost the same M.O. They found the bodies of both victims inside their houses and believe the murders took place in the bathtub. They have no leads and all their suspects came up clean. They want to be in the loop if we find any new evidence. This could be the same man. If it is, he is escalating fast."

"If you forward the email to me, I'll send them what we have on file to date." Rowley walked into the office carrying a pile of takeout cups and lids.

"Ask them to send the files and complete autopsy reports on both girls to me." Wolfe frowned. "Two weeks apart." He rubbed his chin thoughtfully and his pale eyes slid to Kane. "If this is the same killer, he had a break for four months before killing Felicity."

"If it is, then I wonder what happened to slow him down." Kane keyed in a reply to the email and lifted his concerned gaze to Jenna.

"Maybe he was in transit from his last killing ground?" She cleared her throat. "He has not murdered anyone here before, so we have to assume he moved here since his last kill."

"Or like Derick and the cowboys, he moves around a lot, like with a football team or in a rodeo and didn't need to get his fix in his hometown. There could also be other victims in nearby towns unaccounted for, or something substantial prevented him from pursuing his activities for a while. Perhaps he was in jail. Psychopaths at this stage of madness don't slow down, they escalate." Kane frowned. "The fact we can determine Joanne Blunt was a thrill or opportunistic kill means he is out of control."

Jenna chewed on her bottom lip, thinking. "Rowley, get me a list of men recently released from jail. We have a list sent monthly, it's in the files."

"Yes, ma'am." Rowley pulled out his notepad and pen. "Right away."

Gripped by the horror of finding another mutilated girl, Jenna pulled hard on the years of training she relied on to keep her sane and kept her tone calm and professional. She looked at Kane. "How long do you estimate we have to catch him before he kills again?"

"It depends how much control he has over the beast." Kane took one of the takeout cups Rowley handed him and reached for the coffee pot. "Maybe a week, maybe a couple of days, or maybe he has killed again already." He gave her a long, steady look. "This animal enjoys killing and wants to show his skill to the world, and from Joanne Blunt's murder, we can tell that although he prefers to plan his kills, if a suitable girl comes along, he'll take advantage. He likes to shock and his next thrill ride could be hours away."

Her stomach cramped with concern for the safety of the local girls. "Then we need to move faster if we plan to catch this guy. I want you out there interviewing our suspects immediately."

"Yes, ma'am." Wolfe nodded in agreement.

"Kane, when you talk to Rogers, I want to know why he was in the forest. He is married. Speak to his wife as well. Find out what you can about him, as in does he often sneak off during the day?" She picked up her car keys and coffee. "Okay, move out."

# CHAPTER TWENTY-THREE

He watched the girls as they chatted. The girl in the forest had been a gift but he'd wanted more time to play with her and now the ache inside was intolerable. He ran his fingers through the pile of carefully tied skeins of hair, enjoying the silky-smooth remembrance of his girls.

His head filled with a colorful screensaver capturing their confused expressions as he gave them what they craved. Their pleas rang in his ears and he gazed down at his hands, imagining hot sticky blood dripping from his fingers. The moment Felicity's flesh whitened, clean in the water, he felt empowered. Vivid images slashed across his brain, exciting him. *I must choose another tonight.*

Aimee and Kate stared at their friends, unaware of his presence. They were so close he could almost reach out and touch them. He wanted to caress their cheeks and trace their lips with his fingers. "Eeny, meeny, miny, moe, which one of you is next to go?"

His finger pointed to Kate.

A rush of euphoria hit him, and in his mind, he traced his thumb across her delicate white throat, seeing the knife in his hand. He would taunt her with the glint of the sharp blade and enjoy her gasp of surprise as he cut deep. The spurt of crimson blood gurgling over his flesh would excite him, but he craved the delightful shudder they all made as life slipped away.

Blissfully unaware of his presence, the girls chatted to their boyfriends as usual on Skype. Kate made plans to sneak out to meet

Chad the following evening at the high-school football ground under the bleachers.

"Someone will see us." Chad ruffled his dark brown curls and grinned at her. "We could go into the gym for a time and maybe after go skinny-dippin' in the pool. I have the combination to the locks."

Kate's cheeks pinked. "I think we all have the combination. The cleaners are so dumb the janitor has to use the numbers one, two, three, and four on every lock."

"So, I'll see you tomorrow at six thirty? I'll meet you outside the gym."

Kate smiled. "Sure but I'll call you later."

"My dad confiscated my cellphone and laptop for twenty-four hours. I'm grounded tonight but I convinced Mom to allow Lucas to come over. He snuck in his laptop so we could talk to our girls." His white grin flashed in a tanned face. "I'll see *you* when I get out of jail."

The boys left and Kate turned to Aimee. "I can't wait to see him." Kate curled her long blonde hair around her finger. "His kisses make me tingle all over."

"All you ever talk about is boys. They are just boys, and Lucas looks good but he is a terrible kisser, all tongue. Now Lucky Briggs, he's a *man*. All muscles and tight jeans. He is sooo hot." Aimee chuckled.

"He'll never put his boots under your bed." Kate ducked a slap from her friend. "I'm his type. My boobs are way bigger than yours and he prefers blondes. I heard him tell my brother last year."

"Oh, pleeeze, like I'd believe he'd turn *me* down. Lucas is always trying to get into my pants."

"I am so over watching you drool over Lucky Briggs." Kate pulled a face. "I think I'll head home, my mom is expecting me for lunch and if I'm five seconds late I'll get a lecture. Since your mom told her about Felicity she won't let me out of her sight. I want to do extra chores so she doesn't bug me when I'm supposedly in my room playing games tomorrow night." She bounced to her feet and tucked a strand of long blonde hair behind one ear. "Why don't you call Felicity again, you might find out what happened to her."

"I've tried and I called the house, no one is answering the phone." Aimee scowled as she watched Kate head for the door. "No one is saying anything."

A tingle of excitement skittered up his spine. Confidence flowed over him; he had chosen well and everything he needed would be at hand. He stared at Kate for a few moments longer. Her name lingered in his mind for a millisecond then faded. Once he had made his choice, their names vanished from his thoughts.

They meant nothing to him.

# CHAPTER TWENTY-FOUR

Kane drove down the main street and noticed Jenna's cruiser parked at the curb. She and Wolfe would be interviewing Lionel Provine. He checked the time then headed to Stanton Road. His next stop would be to interview Mr. Rogers—the teacher Aimee and Kate spoke to on the morning of Felicity's death. The trip would give him an accurate travel time for Derick Smith's car delivery on Monday morning. As the two people lived relatively close to each other, he would drop by to speak to Mrs. Bolton and check the timeline.

Heading downtown, traffic slowed in a procession toward the fairgrounds. The influx of visitors and the number of people crowding the streets surprised him. The line outside Aunt Betty's Café went halfway round the block. He smiled. Being a local deputy had benefits. Earlier, he'd walked past the waiting customers, and Susie Hartwig had filled his order at once, all smiles and blushes. The tempting smell of fresh coffee wafted through the window and the sign advertising apple pie à la mode called to him, but he ground his back teeth together, promising the ever persistent rumbling stomach he'd drop by later.

He arrived at Mrs. Bolton's address and an elderly woman was outside weeding her garden. "Mrs. Bolton?"

"That's me. What can I do for you deputy?"

Kane took out his notepad and smiled at her. "I gather you had your car repaired at George's Garage? Do you recall what time Derick Smith dropped it by and how long he was here?"

"Yes, I do. I was eating breakfast so it was around eight." She wiped her hands on her apron. "He was only here a few minutes. I had a check ready—they had given me a quote—and I gave him the keys to the loaner. He left straight away."

Kane made a few notes. "So, less or more than ten minutes?"

"More like five." She screwed up her eyes at him. "Is there a problem?"

Kane closed his notepad. "No not at all. Thank you for your help." He touched his hat and strolled back to his car. *Next stop Rogers.*

The house at number 206 Stanton Road was an impressive log home with a wide veranda out front, similar in style to most of the homes in this end of town. He pulled his vehicle into the driveway, made a note of the time of arrival, and headed up the steps. A dog barked from inside and he could hear a man's voice and footsteps. Before he had time to knock, the door opened and a man in his thirties stepped onto the porch.

Dressed in uniform, Kane's arrival would usually cause a modicum of concern, but Mr. Rogers' expression gave no clue to his inner thoughts. "Mr. Rogers?"

"I am." The man folded his arms against his chest. "Lovely day, don't you think?"

Taken slightly aback, Kane nodded. "Yeah, it sure is pretty around here in the summer." He reached inside his pocket for his notepad. "I'm Deputy David Kane and I'd like to ask you a few questions."

"I *know* who you are." Rogers let out a long sigh. "Which kid has got themselves into trouble this time?"

"Why would you believe I'm here for that reason?"

"It's summer break." Rogers shuffled his feet, impatiently. "I'm not available to help them maneuver around the cyberbullying rampant online at the moment. I guess a parent complained and you came straight to me to sort out the problem?"

Kane straightened and shook his head. "No, and we have resources to handle a variety of cybercrimes in the department. I came to question you about something entirely different. I need you to account for your movements between the hours of eight and ten on Monday morning."

"Monday morning?" Rogers appeared agitated. "In relation to what? I am entitled to know if I am a suspect in a crime before I answer your questions."

*Why are you being so defensive?* "We received a complaint about an incident that occurred between the hours of eight and ten on Monday morning and I am speaking to people seen in the area." He met his gaze with a hard stare. "Would you mind telling me what you were doing in Stanton Forest before nine?"

"I don't have to tell you anything." Rogers scowled at him. "I have the right to remain silent."

Kane nodded. "I wasn't arresting you but I think we'll take this conversation down town. Do you want to call your lawyer? He can meet us at the sheriff's office."

"This is police harassment." Rogers stepped back inside the house and Kane could see him punching numbers into a landline telephone.

He reached for his cellphone and, eyeballing Rogers, called Jenna. "I need to bring in Mr. Rogers for questioning."

*"The school teacher? Why?"*

"He refuses to answer my questions, is acting real weird, and we have two witnesses who put him in the right place at the right time. We have probable cause. I'm staying here to watch him. Will you send someone out with the arrest warrant? I want to do this straight down the line."

*"Sure. I'm waiting for Lionel Provine to show. He's had an 'out to lunch' sign on his door for over an hour. I'll arrange the documents now and come out to your location."*

Kane huffed a sigh of relief. "Thanks. Will you be able to take him to the office? I haven't finished talking to people in the area."

*"Not a problem. Wolfe is riding shotgun."*

"Okay, I'll be close behind you. I have to check on an alibi. It shouldn't take long."

*"I'll bring coffee."*

The line went dead and Kane leaned back against the porch railing and folded his arms. His gaze fixed on the movements of the man inside the house. Rogers fitted the profile and was as jumpy as a cat on a hot tin roof. Guilty men usually demanded their rights from the get go. Most people are happy to clear their names and answer questions to convince him they are innocent.

The wide windows and open drapes gave him an almost unrestricted view inside the house. A nicely furnished family room with a Chinese rug led to an open-plan kitchen, and a staircase led to the floor above. His attention moved over the man talking fast on the phone and he remembered Jenna mentioning Rogers was married. Yet with all the yelling, he had not seen a woman moving around the house. The hairs on the back of his neck prickled. He wanted to kick down the door and do a complete search of the property but hunches did not constitute probable cause.

His life had been easy before moving to Black Rock Falls. Find the target, one bullet, one kill, or hang around and protect the president. Now, living as deputy, following procedure, and making a solid case to hand on to the prosecutor, he had to do everything by the book. He scowled at the man cowering in the hallway, his telephone fixed to his ear, and he wanted to scream in frustration. *If this maggot is our killer, I hope he tries to run.*

# CHAPTER TWENTY-FIVE

With Mr. Rogers safely locked in a cell, Jenna headed back out with Deputy Wolfe to see if Lionel Provine had returned to his store. Kids ten years old and up packed the computer store, which appeared to be an old feed supply conversion. The vast display of various devices on sale and the flat screens devoted to the latest games filled the front of the store. Toward the back area, groups of kids huddled around samples of the latest devices. Jenna noted the chains connecting each device to the tables and smiled. Mr. Provine was no fool. Along the front window, kids sat along a long bench engrossed in games, no doubt taking advantage of the free Wi-Fi on offer.

She glanced around, searching for the proprietor, and her attention landed on a tall man wearing glasses, bending over a computer, and surrounded by teenage girls. Raising her voice over the noise of battling gameplay, she turned to Wolfe. "That's Mr. Provine. As you know more about computers than me, will you take the lead on this interview?"

"Sure thing, ma'am." Wolfe shot her a smile. "Don't speak the language, huh?"

"Not at this level."

As if Provine heard her, he glanced up and a deep frown crossed his face. Moments later, he straightened, said something to his admirers, and strolled toward her. She offered him a smile. "Lionel Provine?"

"Yes, is there a problem?" Provine pushed his hands into the front pockets of his jeans and peered at her through black-framed glasses.

"Nice place you have here." Wolfe offered his hand. "Deputy Shane Wolfe."

"Thanks, I have worked hard to make this store a going concern." Provine frowned but shook his hand. "How can I help you?"

"Do you supply command-and-control servers and associated hardware?"

"I can order anything you need." Provine raised both eyebrows then lowered his voice. "Are you planning on setting up remote control of multiple targets because hacking of personal information, as I'm sure you are aware, is against the law?" He rubbed his chin. "Oh shit, you don't think I've been supplying a Black Hat, do you?"

"Not at the moment. Not many people would know that term for a superior type of hacker. You surprise me, Mr. Provine." Wolfe towered over the man. "Supply of individual hardware items is not against the law. In my case, the sheriff's department's computers need an upgrade and to be working via a secure department server, so I'll be sending you an itemized list as soon as the funds are approved."

"If you need a technician, I am fully qualified." Provine brightened seeing a potential massive sale.

Jenna blinked at Wolfe; his tech-talk was way over her head but she had to join in the conversation. "Some of the kids mentioned you often send them bonus cards. Why?"

"Ah, Sheriff, I *earn* the cards during gameplay and share them with other players. We all share bonuses—it's part of the online gamer environment." Provine glanced up at Wolfe and hunched his shoulders. "You know your stuff and yeah I've used cheat codes, *but* I didn't write them, I traded them online."

"Uh-huh. Do you recall where you were between the hours of eight and ten yesterday morning?" Wolfe took out his notebook and pen.

"Yesterday?" Looking slightly bemused, Provine rubbed the back of his neck. "Here, I live in the apartment out back of the store—why?"

"Just routine inquiries." Wolfe made a note in his book and his cold gaze moved over the smaller man. "Can anyone verify your whereabouts?"

"Yeah, I open the store at nine and a delivery arrived about the time I opened." Provine shrugged. "The kids started to arrive around that time as well. During school vacation the place is usually packed. It's the free Wi-Fi but they do buy games and their parents stock up on the latest tech for birthdays and holidays."

"Can I see the proof of delivery slip?" Wolfe narrowed his gaze. "What about the period between eight and nine?"

"I was in my apartment, alone, having breakfast." Provine let out a long, aggravated sigh. "I'll make you a copy of the delivery note." He moved to the counter, took out a box crammed with paper, sifted through, then slid one into a scanner. He handed the document to Wolfe. "Is that all? I really need to keep an eye on the kids before they break something."

Jenna took the copy from Wolfe and read the information. As Provine had stated, the delivery arrived at nine. She folded the paper and moved her attention back to the storekeeper. "Thank you. Do you know Felicity Parker?"

"Yes, she comes in frequently with her friends."

Jenna nodded. "When was the last time you saw her?"

"Saturday, she was in with the usual crowd." Provine looked interested. "Yes, that was the last time. She didn't come by yesterday. I remember her friends asking me if I had sent her any bonuses because she wasn't answering her phone earlier in the morning. They thought she might be playing her game, and you know kids, they get engrossed for hours at a time."

"And did you send her any bonuses?"

"Yes, I sent out quite a few on Sunday, it brings the kids back into the store. You have no idea how keen they are to play the latest games. During summer break, Lucas and Chad are usually waiting outside the store for me to open. They catch the early bus into town." Provine smiled. "They always end up buying a game or one of the new gadgets, and the girls are great at grabbing my lunch. It saves me closing up for an hour like today."

*That proves where Chad and Lucas were on Monday morning.* "You send them out in emails?"

"No."

Jenna met his gaze and shrugged. "So if you don't use email, I gather you text them these game bonuses and… ah 'cheat codes', you would have to know their cellphone numbers? Exactly how many of these underage girls' numbers do you have in your contacts list?"

"Zero." Provine gave her an indignant glare. "They play online. Haven't you ever played a game on Facebook or one of the other interactive games sites? It's a community and people have player names. Most of the kids tell me their player ID so we can swap bonus cards online. I send the bonuses et cetera to their gift boxes."

"Okay." Wolfe flicked her a glance and closed his notepad. "That's all we need for now. I'll drop by and place an order soon." He turned for the door.

Jenna followed him into the street. "What do you think?"

"I'll have to unpack my equipment to discover if he is doing anything."

"I'm not sure I understand." Jenna opened the door to the cruiser and slipped inside. "What could he be doing?"

"I'm not sure yet but if he is chatting in an online games room, he could be dangerous, but Felicity and her friends seem to be playing online using their cellphones. If this is the case, without the phone, we have zip. I doubt I'll find anything via their computers." Wolfe dropped into the passenger seat and fastened the seatbelt. "I'll spend the rest of the day checking out Felicity's laptop and see if anyone has hacked it, but don't expect instant results—it takes time, maybe a day or two."

Jenna started the engine and headed back toward the sheriff's office. "Can you explain in plain English? I understand hacking but what relevance does that have to the case?"

"She might have been telling her friends on social media her plans for the day. Kids share everything and don't seem to worry who reads their posts or looks at their images. They friend anyone because the number of friends they have is a status symbol."

Jenna pulled the vehicle into her reserved parking space and turned in her seat to stare at him. "Is that possible? I mean, social media have privacy laws as a fail-safe. No one could find out where she lives for instance."

"There lies the problem. Once information is out there in cyberspace, it's too late. The kids post pictures of their locality and friends all the time and it wouldn't take a hacker to track them down." Wolfe gave her an intense stare. "In my line of expertise there is no such word as 'fail-safe' on the internet."

# CHAPTER TWENTY-SIX

Kane leaned over Rowley's desk and stared at the computer screen. "How did you get onto her Facebook page?"

"I did a search and found her easily enough via my own page." Rowley scrolled down the screen.

Felicity Parker's smiling face beamed out at him from her Facebook page. His stomach clenched at the sight of her looking so happy in the selfie taken the morning of her murder. "She looks like she doesn't have a care in the world."

"No, she mentions getting a game bonus on Sunday night and posted on her timeline fifteen minutes before her boyfriend called her." Rowley turned in his seat and looked up at him. "I've looked at all her posts leading up to her death, it's all normal chatter, plans to go to the dance, what she planned to wear, how many characters she caught in her game." He shrugged. "All the posts came via her cellphone."

"When Wolfe gets back, he'll go through her laptop and see what he can find. I'm not expecting him to get any information today—it's getting late, and with his girls at home, he won't be doing any overtime." Kane glanced up at the sound of voices at the front counter. "Ah, that has to be Mr. Rogers' lawyer. I'll speak to him. Go and collect his client from the lockup." He straightened and headed for the front desk.

"Deputy Kane, I presume?" The small, balding man wiped sweat from his brow with a gray handkerchief and glared at him. "I insist on seeing my client, Steve Rogers, this moment."

Kane folded his arms across his chest, which made the lawyer turn beet-red. "And you are?"

"Samuel Jenkins, Attorney at Law in the State of Montana." Jenkins fished a card out of his jacket pocket and waved it at him. "I insist on seeing the arrest warrant."

Kane noticed Rowley waving Steve Rogers into a seat at his desk and frowned. "You don't have to insist, we follow the letter of the law. I must insist you keep the details of this interview secret. We haven't released any details to the press and want time to investigate before we give out any information."

"Of course, I will instruct my client not to speak to anyone about the incident."

"Thank you. Your client is waiting for you at my desk if you'll come this way." Kane plucked the card from Jenkins' hand and ran his gaze over it then led him to his cubicle at the back of the room.

He took the arrest warrant from his desk drawer and handed it to Jenkins. "We had probable cause." He stuck the document into the lawyer's hand and waited for his reaction.

"You don't believe my client was involved in murder, do you?"

"What?" Steve Rogers' eyes bulged in astonishment. "Murder? Who has been murdered? Not Millicent?"

Kane leaned back in his chair and took a pen from the cup on the desk. "Who is Millicent?"

"My wife."

"And why would you think anyone would murder her?" Kane raised an eyebrow. "Is she missing?"

"You don't have to answer that question, it is not relevant to the arrest warrant, and in fact you don't have to say another word." Jenkins mopped his sweaty brow.

"If your client has nothing to hide and can account for his whereabouts between the hours of eight and ten yesterday morning, he is free to go; however, if Millicent is missing, perhaps we can help."

"She *isn't* missing." Rogers moved around in his chair. "We argued and she is probably at her sister's."

Kane made a few notes in an attempt to appear uninterested. "Maybe you should call to make sure she is safe?"

"Call her?" Rogers scowled and his eyes flashed with anger. "Trust me, if someone murdered her they would be doing me a favor."

"Mr. Rogers, I must advise you not to say another word." Jenkins pulled a horrified expression. "You are in custody as a suspect in a girl's murder. I suggest you refrain from uttering another word."

"I'm talking to him. I didn't murder a girl." Rogers turned his back on his lawyer and lifted his scowling face to Kane. "I like to walk in the forest and Millicent believes I'm meeting women." He let out a long sigh. "We argued and she left about ten minutes before you arrived. I was pissed, okay? I should have answered your questions. I haven't killed any girls."

*Girls?* Kane scanned the case file on his computer screen then turned his attention back to Rogers. "Do you take your dog for a walk with you?"

"I don't own a dog." Rogers gave him a quizzical stare.

"Did you see anyone or speak to anyone who can verify the time?"

"Yes, I spoke to Aimee Fox and Kate Bright at the traffic lights. It must have been around nine." Rogers cleared his throat. "It's not a crime to speak to my students."

Kane smiled. He had caught him in a lie. "You told them you had been in the forest looking for your lost dog but you mentioned you don't own a dog. Why did you need an excuse to be out for a walk?"

"I don't know." Rogers put his face in his hands and let out a mournful sigh.

"Can your wife verify what time you left yesterday morning?"

"No doubt." Rogers lifted his pale face and grimaced. "She watches my every move. It was around eight, or maybe eight thirty, I guess."

"It's a big forest. Do you have a trail you prefer?" Kane glanced back at the computer screen.

The lawyer had not said another word and looked as if he might explode.

"I walked to the rock pool, stayed there for about half an hour, then walked back."

Kane leaned back in his squeaky chair and bounced his pen on the desk between his fingers. If Rogers had told him the truth, he would have been at the rock pool at the same time as Lucky Briggs and Storm Crawley. "Did you see anyone in the forest or at the rock pool?"

"Maybe." Rogers avoided his gaze.

Kane pushed on. "Who did you see?"

"Lucky and Storm." Rogers looked down at his hands and appeared to wilt in the seat.

"They didn't see you." Kane cleared his throat. "Were you watching them skinny-dipping? Is this why you are being so defensive?" He glanced at Jenkins. "I suggest you explain to your client the difference between being charged with invasion of privacy and first-degree murder."

"I want to speak to my client alone." Jenkins placed one hand on Rogers' shoulder.

"Not a problem." Kane turned off his computer and walked to the coffee machine.

By the time he had poured the coffee into a mug, Jenkins waved him back to the desk. He returned and sat down, looking from one to the other. "Well?"

"My client was certainly not watching the cowboys at the rock pool nor is he interested in men in that way. He had an argument with his wife and took a walk to cool his temper. He was embarrassed seeing the two men swimming nude and didn't want them to know he had seen them. When he returned home, he discovered his wife had packed a bag and left. Mrs. Rogers can verify this, I'm sure. She is probably staying with her sister but she is known to take off for days without informing anyone." Jenkins dragged in a breath and wiped his damp brow. "Once you have spoken to Mrs. Rogers, I am sure you can release my client. You have not one shred of evidence to imply he was involved in a murder."

"Very well, I will speak to his wife, but if your client is innocent, I would like him to give a DNA sample." Kane reached into his desk drawer for a kit and raised a brow at the lawyer.

"No, I refuse." Rogers turned to his lawyer. "That's an invasion of privacy. I haven't been charged with anything."

"He doesn't have to comply." Jenkins bristled. "You'll need a court order and you don't have probable cause of any crime."

Kane rubbed his chin. "I have him coming out of the forest at the time of death and two witnesses to say he was in a distressed state."

"That's hearsay and from a couple of kids." Jenkins snorted in obvious disgust. "It won't stand up in court. You have nothing."

Kane pushed the notepad across the table. "I'll need your wife's cellphone number and your sister-in-law's name and number and a statement of your whereabouts between the hours of eight and ten." He waited for Rogers to write down the information then stood and walked to the kitchenette. As he turned his back to the counter, he noticed Jenna and Wolfe returning to the office and wondered what information they had extracted from Lionel Provine.

He pulled out his cellphone and found Mrs. Rogers at her sister's house. She confirmed that she and her husband had argued and that he'd left the house before eight. She left soon after and could not confirm what time he arrived home as she had gone to her sister's.

"Did you see anyone walking along Stanton Road on your way to your sister's? If so, can you describe them?"

*"Yes, a girl, maybe sixteen or so, wearing pink cowboy boots and a blue outfit. She had long black hair and those earbuds the kids all seem to have growing from their heads of late. She ran right across the road in front of me. I nearly hit her."*

"Can you remember which direction she was heading?"

*"Toward the forest."*

"Did you notice anyone else, any cars parked along the road or people out for a walk?"

*"Not that I recall."*

"I'll send a deputy out to take a statement, if that's okay?" Kane leaned against the counter and stared at Mr. Rogers hunched at his desk writing a statement. "Thank you for your help." He shut his cellphone.

He strolled into Jenna's office and closed the door behind him. "What did you get from Lionel Provine?"

When Jenna explained, he nodded. "He does makes money out of the high-school kids visiting his shop, but would they go there without his bonus cards?"

"We can't discount him as a suspect, although motive is a problem. We'll need a background check on him and all the suspects in case anyone has priors." Jenna sighed. "How did it go with the Rogers interview?"

"I have Mr. Rogers in my cubicle with his lawyer." Kane pointed over his shoulder with one thumb. "I think he is guilty as hell and I have a problem cutting him loose but I don't have enough evidence to charge him."

"What *have* you got?"

"Apart from the fact he was seen walking out of the forest at approximately nine this morning and the witnesses mentioned he looked agitated, his lawyer made a point of saying the information was hearsay. And Rogers has refused a DNA test." He shrugged. "Although at this stage it won't make a difference. From what Wolfe examined at the autopsy, he doubts they collected any viable DNA traces from the crime scene or the body. He checked all the samples personally under a microscope and found zip."

"Then we have to let him go." She lifted her blue gaze to his face. "We'll keep an eye on him, maybe park a cruiser near his house, so he'll believe we're watching him. He fits the age profile, arrived in town some months ago, but he is married. He was in the right place at the right time, and is on our suspect list."

"Sure, and I have a sighting of a girl matching Felicity's description heading toward the forest at approximately eight as well. I called Rogers' wife, and she said the girl dashed across the road and she almost hit her with her car." He raised both eyebrows. "So, we now know for sure she went to the forest alone. What we need to know is why."

"Yeah, what would make a girl of her age change her mind and dash across the road and head into the forest?" Jenna stood and added the name "Mrs. Rogers" under the "Last people to see Felicity" list then returned to her seat. "You have a positive ID."

"I'll follow up and send Rowley to get her statement but she described her and what she was wearing and even mentioned Felicity was wearing earbuds. No one has seen Joanne Blunt. It is obvious she went to the rock pool for a swim but how long was she there before the killer spotted her?"

"After the media release, I would have thought someone would come forward with information." Jenna chewed on the end of the pen. "Maybe just asking if anyone had seen the two girls in the vicinity of Stanton Forest was too vague."

"I don't think so." Kane rubbed the back of his neck. "I wonder if Felicity had a call to meet someone in the forest, her boyfriend perhaps?"

"Or she was playing that stupid game?" Jenna let out a long sigh. "I wish we had her cellphone."

"Hmm." Kane stared at the whiteboard, trying to let the clues percolate through his mind. "Or the boyfriend is lying. We know he called her, and was only at Mrs. Bolton's for five or so minutes. Although, the time Mrs. Rogers' saw Felicity is sketchy at best. We can't discount Rogers either. He was in the area and could have easily followed her."

"That's a possibility." Jenna tapped the board. "Right now, we have four suspects we can place in the area at the right time for both murders." She picked up the marker. "Derick Smith, the boyfriend, was delivering a car in the area and picking up the loaner; the teacher, Rogers; Lucky Briggs and Storm Crawley. Number five is the computer store guy, Lionel Provine, who can't account for his whereabouts at the time of the murders." She chewed on her lips as if trying to think. "The problem is we don't have enough solid evidence to charge any of them."

Kane's phone signaled a message. "This might be info from one of the other sheriff's departments." He stared at the screen and an icy chill ran down his back. "This came from Helena: 'Sending you information via email on eight similar cases recorded in the state of Montana. Same M.O. Victims are female, fifteen to seventeen, long hair. Murders escalated from months to one week apart. Local newspapers named him the Waterside Ripper. Nothing reported for six months, no suspects detained. Have checked state data bank. Please keep us informed of any suspects or arrests.'" A wave of doom washed over him. He lifted his gaze to Jenna and met her horrified stare. "It's confirmed, we have a serial killer in town."

# CHAPTER TWENTY-SEVEN

Kate Bright dabbed perfume behind her ears and grinned at her reflection in the mirror. She would leave the music channel on TV for the flashing lights, turn down the sound, and lock her bedroom door. From the hallway, the effect would be the same as if she had on her headphones and was playing games. No one would disturb her, not after helping all day and being the perfect daughter. Her parents were being way overprotective and would not tell her what had happened to Felicity. She had seen the news, the sheriff was asking for people who had seen Felicity and some other girl named Joanne Blunt near Stanton Forest. What could have happened to them? When she asked her mom, she had told her to stay home but she would say anything to prevent her from meeting Chad at night. *Adults think teenagers can only have sex at night. How stupid is that?*

She went downstairs into the kitchen and raided the refrigerator. Chad had a huge appetite and she would take him some energy bars and drinks. She stared at the stacked shelves for a few moments then grabbed a bottle of water. After the long hike to the campus, she would be thirsty. She heard her mother heading in her direction and darted toward the stairs. Once out of sight, she called out, "Mom? Do you mind if I play my game for an hour or so? I'll wear my headphones so I don't disturb you."

"You spend far too much time on the computer. It's not healthy. Watch TV with us and be sociable for a change. There's a good movie on tonight."

"I'll spend tomorrow night with you, I promise. Please, Mom?"

"I guess so but I'll hold you to that promise, young lady."

"Thanks." Kate bolted up the steps and back into her room.

She locked the door and stuffed a towel, drinks, and snacks into her backpack. Five minutes later, she slipped out the bedroom window and climbed down the terrace. The sun had dropped in the sky, casting long shadows, but she would get to the pool and back long before sunset. She doubted her parents would check on her before ten, and she should be home and tucked up in bed by then.

Not wanting anyone to recognize her, she pulled up the hood on her jacket, glad she had decided to cover her jeans and skimpy top. Although in Black Rock Falls the sun shone for over twelve hours a day, the temperature dropped in the evenings and her hair would be wet after skinny-dipping. She giggled at the thought of slipping into the heated pool naked. Sneaking out to meet Chad had become a naughty but exciting habit of late.

She rounded the last block of residential buildings and headed toward the wide road leading to the campus. Worried about someone driving by and seeing her trespassing, she kept to the shadows and walked along the tree-lined driveway to the entrance.

A jolt of apprehension tightened in her belly at the first sight of the buildings, empty with black windows and missing the usual welcoming illumination. Without the noise of students and vehicles, the campus resembled a ghost town. She moved on and the creepy sound the wind made rustling through the trees sent goosebumps running up her arms.

Back in the sunlight, her panic eased and she turned the last bend toward the main gate. She stopped and stared in disbelief at the massive gates blocking the entrance to traffic. With the number of cleaners and tradesmen coming and going during the summer break, they usually remained open. The only way inside would be through the wooded area. She hated the idea of running into a bear or a bobcat looking for its dinner, but she took a deep breath and plowed into the bushes.

The trees closed in around her, blocking the light, but she had taken this path before and hurried along. Nerves frazzled, she started at movements in the undergrowth and glanced in all directions. The woods seemed to be watching her with a thousand eyes. Branches snagged at her coat and tangled around her feet. Convinced roots would erupt from the earth and drag her down to hell, just like in the movies, she quickened her pace.

Gasping as waves of panic washed over her, she made her way back to the road, tripping over a sod of earth where someone had dragged wildflowers out by their roots. *Dang, now I have mud on my boots.* She could have avoided being scared to death if Chad had suggested meeting him closer to the main gate.

Loud rustling came from directly behind her as if something big had spotted her as their next meal. Fear grabbed her by the throat and she took off at a run. Moments later, she burst out of the woods on the other side of the gate and headed toward the gym. She checked the time on her cellphone. *Shit, I'm almost fifteen minutes late.* Chad should have been waiting for her but a peek through the gym window told her he had not arrived. Perhaps he'd walked to the pool to look for her. She messaged him but got no reply, and Chad usually answered in seconds. *I bet his dad still has his cellphone.*

Deciding to head for the pool to wait for him to arrive, she opened the cover of her cellphone and, engrossed in the game, wandered along the dark passageway. A few moments later, she reached the entrance. She heaved a sigh of relief seeing the gate slightly ajar. Chad must be waiting inside. She hurried along to the dressing room and disconnected from the game. The Olympic-sized pool stretched out in an expanse of blue, and the smell of chlorine drifted toward her.

She could see Chad swimming way down the far end and grinned. She would surprise him and sneak into the pool.

After stripping in the changing room, she wrapped a towel around her chest and stepped outside, slightly embarrassed at the idea of being naked in front of Chad for the first time. She peered at the empty pool and swallowed hard. *Where is he?*

A low chuckle came from behind her and she turned around, pulling the towel tighter, expecting to see Chad. A man walked out of the shadows, shaking the water from his hair. As he moved closer, she recognized him and her cheeks burned. "How embarrassing, I thought you were Chad."

"Chad couldn't make it."

Disappointment tinged with anger that Chad would do such a thing, she moved a step toward the dressing room. "If he is not coming, I'll get dressed and be on my way home."

A glint of metal drew her gaze to the knife glistening in his hand and she took a step backward. Panic closed her throat and she glanced around, looking for a place to run. The gate to the pool was not far and she could make it. She pivoted and sprinted between the dressing rooms and headed toward the gate. The black iron railings loomed up in front of her and she gaped in disbelief at the chain circling them.

Someone had locked the gate.

Gasping for breath, she grabbed the padlock but her trembling fingers refused to roll the combination. She stared behind her to see the man walking casually toward her swinging a red sock filled with something in one hand as if he had all the time in the world. Valuable seconds ticked by. She must concentrate before this lunatic changed his mind and ran at her. Turning back to the padlock, she spun the dial, locking in the combination.

One, click.

Two, click.

Three, click.

Four—nothing.

Frantic, she glanced over one shoulder. He was a few yards away and grinning like the Cheshire Cat. She spun the dial again and tried to lock in number four.

Nothing.

The evil, low, rumbling chuckle behind her made every hair on her body stand up.

"One, two, three, four ain't the combination no more."

*I have to escape.* If she took off now, she could run up the bleachers on the far side of the pool and jump the fence. Muscles bunched, she turned to run. Blinding pain smashed into her temple and her vision blurred. The ground appeared to rush up and hit her with incredible force. Air rushed from her lungs in a painful burst and, gasping, she tried to crawl away from the hideous laughter.

A shadow of the man passed over her and water dripped on her face from his wet hair.

"Going somewhere?"

# CHAPTER TWENTY-EIGHT

Jenna and her deputies had been working tirelessly to follow their leads, but by dinnertime on Wednesday, they had gotten nowhere. After eating dinner with Kane at Aunt Betty's Café, Jenna decided to have an early night. She slipped into her slippers and strolled into the kitchen. The moment she added cream to her mug of coffee, her cellphone sounded the nine-one-one ringtone. She groaned and stared at the constant vibrating interference in her life then swiped the screen to accept the call. "Sheriff Alton, what is your emergency?"

*"Oh my God, oh my God. You gotta send someone. I don't know what to do."*

Jenna snatched up the pad beside the landline and grabbed a pen from the bunch in the empty pickle jar on the kitchen counter. "Take a deep breath and give me your name and location."

*"Chad Johnson and I'm outside the gates of the pool at the campus."* He let out a mournful moan like an animal in distress. *"Something has happened to my girlfriend Kate, Kate Bright. I can see her lying on the diving board and her guts are hanging out. Send someone to help her."*

Jenna sucked in a breath to steady the rush of terror and forced her voice to remain calm. She moved swiftly to the landline and dialed Kane's number.

*"I can't get to her. She is inside the aquatic center and someone has locked the gate. I called out to her but she isn't moving."*

"Is anyone else there? Have you seen anyone in the area?"

*"No, please hurry."*

"Okay, stay on the line. I'm going to speak to my deputy, he'll call the paramedics and we'll be heading in your direction immediately." She muted the cellphone and heard Kane pick up. "Kane, it's Jenna, I have Chad Johnson on my cellphone. It sounds like we have another murder. Send the paramedics to the campus aquatic center but make them aware of the potential danger. Instruct them not to enter the area if the victim is deceased—he mentioned her guts are hanging out, so I think we have another murder. It's the same M.O. as Felicity."

*"I'm on it. Do you want me to drive you?"*

"Yeah, give me five to get dressed." She hung up the phone and went back to the cellphone. "You still there, Chad?" She poured her coffee into a takeout cup, filled another for Kane, then marched into her bedroom.

*"Yeah, but I think I'm gonna puke."*

She wriggled out of her nightgown and dressed quickly. "That's okay. Is there a garden bed or something close by you can use?"

*"Yeah."*

"Okay, vomit if you must but don't hang up. I need to know you're okay."

Trying to ignore the sounds of retching, she pushed her feet into boots and took her weapon from the bedside table. She slid her cellphone inside her pocket and attached the earpiece then went via the kitchen to collect the coffee. She set the house alarm and stepped onto the porch as Kane arrived at her front door.

"I've called Wolfe, he'll meet us there." Kane raised one dark eyebrow, waited for her to place the coffee in the console, then hit the gas. "What have we got?"

She buckled her seatbelt then glanced at Kane's profile as he engaged the new siren and lights he recently fitted to his personal vehicle. "I have Chad on the line but at the moment he is throwing up." She covered the microphone hanging midway on the earpiece from her cellphone. "He said little, only that we need to send someone because he found Kate Bright on the diving board at the campus with her guts hanging out."

"*Jesus.*" A nerve in Kane's cheek ticked. "It's only been two days since we found Felicity and Joanne. If this is the same guy, he is escalating fast."

The powerful vehicle roared along the highway, and green fields flashed by as it ate up the miles. They sped through town, lights flashing and siren blaring. Kane expertly maneuvered the vehicle through traffic, breaking then accelerating so hard, the G-force threw her back in her seat. Her deputy owned more than an SUV: Since the recent modifications, he had a bulletproof rocket on wheels. Reaching Stanton Road in record time, the SUV screamed along the edge of the forest and made it around the corner onto College Road seconds before the paramedics came over the rise from the other direction. She glanced at Kane. "Nice driving."

He flicked her a dark blue glance but dropped his lashes as if to hide his feelings. "Thanks."

She uncovered the microphone. "Chad, are you okay?"

"*Yeah, I can hear the sirens. Do you want me to wait here or walk back to the front of the building?*"

"Stay there. We are at the main gate now but it's locked. How did you get inside?" She turned as Kane leaped from the car and, in one smooth movement, pulled his weapon, took aim at the padlock on the front gate, and fired. The chain burst apart in a shower of sparks and hung like a dead snake trailing on the road. "Ah, never mind, we've found a way."

Muscles bunching under his cotton shirt, Kane ripped away the chain and dragged open one of the massive gates in an impressive show of strength. Jenna gaped open-mouthed at him but he shrugged then climbed back behind the wheel.

"Wolfe just arrived. Any idea where the aquatic center is in this place?"

Jenna shut her mouth with a click and pointed ahead. "Yeah, this one I know. I came to watch an event here last fall. It's out back of the sports center."

She gave him directions, and moments later they pulled up outside the gym. "The pool is down that passageway. Can you see the water glistening?" She uncovered the mic. "Chad, we're here."

*"I'm out front of the pool gate but it's locked too,"* Chad's voice came in her ear.

"Okay, you can hang up now, we are heading toward your position." She disconnected the call then slid from the car and walked over to meet Wolfe and the paramedics. "This is probably a murder scene. Wait here until we check it out and be aware there may be a threat in the immediate area."

"Did you see anyone on the street on the way here?" Wolfe's cold gaze moved over the paramedic's faces.

"Yeah, a white-haired old lady walking a poodle," one of the paramedics responded. "No one else. We didn't see any other cars except yours."

Jenna allowed Kane to take the lead and followed him along the darkened passageways then out into the clear night. A young man was sitting hunched on the ground, his back to the gates to the Olympic-sized swimming pool. Her stomach clenched at the sight of the girl stretched out, feet and arms dangling down each side of the diving board at the side of the pool. From the complete evisceration of the body, she knew it was too late to save Kate. She moved toward the young man. "Chad?"

He lifted a tear-stained face to her. "Yeah. Kate is in there." He indicated with his chin toward the pool but kept his eyes fixed on her face. "She hasn't moved and I've been calling her name. I know she's dead."

"Okay, come with me and we'll go and speak to the paramedics." Jenna led him away, taking a mental note of his pristine appearance. Apart from dust on his jeans from sitting on the ground, his clothes appeared clean. She turned to Kane. "I'll get him off the scene."

After leading Chad back toward the gym, she raised both eyebrows and shook her head at the paramedics. "Will you take Chad to the ambulance? I don't want him going into shock."

"Yes, ma'am. I assume the patient is deceased?"

"I would imagine but we'll go in and check. I'll call you if we need you."

One of the paramedics took Chad by the arm and they walked away. Taking a deep breath, she headed back to her deputies and peered through the gate. The sight of the girl, with her blonde hair blowing in the wind, presented in such a disgusting fashion appalled her. She turned her attention to Kane. "I *know* her. I spoke to her yesterday. She was so vibrant, so fun-loving. I'm not looking forward to informing her parents."

"When this sort of thing happens, I'm glad I never had kids. It must be hell for Wolfe to see her. All of our victims are the same age as his daughter."

"Well, we're not going to catch this animal unless we can get into the pool area to examine the body." She looked up at him. "Do your magic but if possible, try and hit the chain—we might get some prints off the lock."

"Yes, ma'am."

She turned to make sure Chad and the paramedics had not entered the immediate area and moved into the corridor between the changing rooms to avoid any ricochet but noticed Wolfe standing a few feet away from Kane, his bag of equipment in one hand. Having an expert shooter in her department sure made life easier. One shot and the chain fell away. She walked back to Kane's side. "Great job!"

"I think a good leader takes full advantage of all the assets on hand." Kane leaned closer. "In saying that, would you like to send Wolfe to check Kate and use me for a preliminary recon of the immediate area? With the gate locked, the killer might be close by watching to soak up our reactions, and we'll need to make a note of any possible escape routes from the scene and check them as well."

The offer of not listening to Wolfe describe the intimate details of Kate's demise would give her stomach time to stop rolling. "Good idea, and as I know her, I will be able to make a positive ID." She took out her notepad and pen. "You go ahead and I'll question Chad and find out how Kate happened to be here alone at this time of night."

"You okay?" Kane viewed her with concern. "Seeing that kind of carnage is hard for the most seasoned homicide team."

It was nice to have someone to worry about her but she had a job to do. She gave him a curt nod. "We wouldn't be human if we didn't react to seeing a young girl mutilated but thanks for asking. I'll be fine."

"Good." Kane turned away, swung open the gate and headed toward the body.

# CHAPTER TWENTY-NINE

Jenna walked back to the ambulance to speak to Chad. She had not asked Chad a single question before Wolfe moved to her side and lowered his deep voice to a whisper. "The victim is obviously deceased but I came to inform you I'll be handling the preliminary forensics on scene. I'll send the body to the mortuary and I'll do a post-mortem straight away."

"The M.E. will still have to preside over the autopsy."

"Not any longer, my state license came by special delivery and was there when I got home this afternoon. I'm now the official Black Rock Falls medical examiner. I've also been advised I have funding to set up a new laboratory and morgue. I would assume the mayor's office has sent you confirmation as well. I won't have to work out of the local mortuary for more than a few months."

She blinked a few times then cleared her throat. "So, I'll be losing you as a deputy?"

"No, I'll only be handling the suspicious deaths, so hopefully it won't interfere with my work too much." Wolfe's pale gaze moved over her face. "That is as long as you are okay with having in-house forensic investigations? I hope you agree. It means we can solve crimes faster."

"Yes, of course. I value your expertise and thank you for offering your services." She blinked. "Who is paying you? I can't imagine the mayor will offer any extra funding."

"All taken care of, ma'am. The letter I received from the mayor's office said Blackwater has offered funding to use my services as well and I'll have a full-time medical laboratory technician as an assistant to run the business side of things." He cleared his throat. "I've already been offered a suitable place. On the street behind the sheriff's office, there is an empty meat-packing plant. Mayor Petersham is going to push through town planning to have the building refurbished to suit our needs."

*All that and he's only been here a couple of days.* Astonished, she waved her hand absently toward the pool entrance. "Well then, get to work."

When he gave her a curt nod and headed back toward Kate's mutilated body, she went to the back of the ambulance and stood at the open doors. The two paramedics glanced at her with pale, drawn expressions, and Chad sat in the back, his hands wrapped around a bottle of water, tears streaming down his face.

She cleared her throat. "Do you want to call your parents?"

"And have my mom see Kate like that?" Chad dashed a hand over his swollen eyes. "She will be hysterical. Can you drop me off at home?"

"I should really call your parents. I'll speak to your dad if you prefer, and he won't be going anywhere near the pool, I can assure you. First, I need you to answer a few questions." She laid one hand on his shoulder and squeezed. "I need your help to find out who did this to Kate. How come you are here?"

"We planned to meet outside the gym at eight thirty." Chad took a sip of the water and his dark brown eyes rested on her face. "It was going to be six thirty then she changed the time. I got here about eight twenty and found the main gate locked, so I went through the woods and came out halfway up the driveway." He met her gaze. "Everyone cuts through the woods. If you look, you'll see the path, although you don't have to use it to get past the gate." He pulled a tissue out of his jeans pocket and blew his nose. "When she didn't show, I called her cellphone. I heard the ringtone she uses for me and thought she must be close by but some guy answered. I thought it might be her dad. I asked to speak to her and he told me she was waiting for me by the pool. I was worried then because her dad didn't know we were meeting in secret and if he was with her I would be in deep shit." He swiped at the end of his nose. "I found her, and when I couldn't open the padlock, I called you. The combination has been changed so I don't know how Kate got into the pool area."

Jenna frowned. "How did *you* know the combination to the lock?"

"Everyone does. It used to be one, two, three, four." His mouth turned down. "The janitor must have changed it recently."

*I'll need to speak to the janitor.* She made a few notes then looked at him. "You said you thought Kate's dad answered her phone. Did you recognize his voice? Does her father have an accent or anything that might distinguish him from anyone else?"

"I guess it could have been him but men around here sound much the same, most times. I mean he didn't have a Boston accent or anything. It sounded like her dad, a deep voice with a normal accent."

"What's Kate's cellphone number? I'll call and see if he answers."

Jenna jotted the digits down in her notebook then took out her cellphone and called the number. She received the "this number is out of service" message and disconnected. She chewed on her bottom lip, weighing up what to ask him next. "You didn't see anyone here at all, is that correct? Or on the way here, any cars, anyone at all?"

"No one, like I said before."

"Okay, how many people knew you had a date with Kate this evening?" She did not want to push him too hard. He was shaking so much he might go into shock. "Anyone you can think of at all?"

"I doubt anyone knew she had messaged me online to change the time. Unless she told Aimee. Aimee and Lucas both knew we made the date for six thirty. They knew she had to sneak out too so I don't think they would blab it all around town, especially as you warned us all to stay home and not go out alone."

"Do you know where Lucas is tonight?"

"Yeah, at home. I was playing games with him online from six until I left to come here, then I chatted to him on the phone on the walk here. His dad called him to do some chores just before I reached the gate." He looked stricken. "Holy shit, Lucas had nothing to do with this."

"I'm sure he didn't but I have to check the whereabouts of everyone she knows, it's normal procedure."

Jenna made a few notes then took down his parents' number. She walked some distance away and called his father. Not giving any details, she asked him to come and pick up his son alone. She would explain Kate's murder when he arrived, and insist he not discuss the homicide with the media.

Leaving Chad with the paramedics, she sucked in a deep breath, and conscious of every shadowed doorway she passed, she strode toward the crime scene. Kane had finished his search of the immediate area, had marked all possible evidence with yellow circles, and was assisting Wolfe with his examination. Gritting her teeth, she dragged her feet toward the body and forced her gaze to move over the mutilated body of Kate.

The young, vibrant woman now resembled a mannequin in a waxworks recreation of a torture chamber. The skin on her face stretched like thin parchment over her cheekbones, stark white against her crude red lips and cheeks. She had cuts across both eyelids as if to prevent her closing her eyes but she lacked the defensive wounds found on the other two victims' arms and legs.

Bile rushed up her throat at the sight of the vicious yet competent, almost surgical-like cuts in her torso. The killer had taken his time with her and the fact Chad had heard Kate's ringtone close by proved he had remained to witness Chad's distress at finding her mutilated body. The monster must have lapped up the young man's horror and remained long enough to wallow in his grief.

Boosted by the professional calm of Kane and Wolfe, she gathered her wits and stared at the scene, noting the similarities, the lack of blood, the flowers. The killer had planned this murder too. She had seen no flowers anywhere close to the aquatic center but a wooded area ran along the roadside leading to the campus. The hairs rose on the back of her neck and she had the strange feeling someone was watching her. *I bet the killer is still here—watching us.*

The sound of Kane's voice made her jump and she lifted her gaze to him. "Sorry, what did you say?"

"He killed her in the recovery spa. It's a small pool the divers use to warm up during competitions." Kane wrapped one large hand around her arm and led her toward a covered area. "He probably raped her here as well." He narrowed his blue gaze at her and a worried expression crossed his face, then as if making up his mind, he cleared his throat. "This murder is significant. It proves the killer is looking for more sadistic ways to kill and needs a bigger fix to satisfy him. He has experience in killing, as in military or has medical training. As you know, in combat training they teach us where to stick a knife to kill or disable. He cut her spinal cord and paralyzed her from the neck down but didn't cut her throat like the others. Wolfe is under the impression the lacerations on her eyelids cut the muscle preventing her from shutting her eyes. The bastard made her watch him until she bled out." He shook his head. "He feeds on suffering, likes seeing fear, and it turns him on. He craves the power he has over his victims."

*This is way out of my comfort zone.* Jenna swallowed hard and shuddered in disgust. "So, we might find trace DNA or something in the recovery spa?"

"Not a hope. There is blood in there and we can pull out the filters and pumps, but being summer vacation, it has so much chlorine in the water nothing will be viable. Hundreds of people have used the pool, we wouldn't find anything conclusive. However, there are a few fibers attached to her nails. Wolfe placed bags around her hands to preserve any latent DNA. He is collecting samples from every possible area and we might hit pay dirt." Kane rolled his wide shoulders. "Did you get anything out of the boyfriend?"

Jenna went over the conversation she had with Chad. "If the janitor changed the combination to the padlock, how did Kate get in here?"

"I believe the killer had the combination to the lock and opened the gate before she arrived. This guy is smart. He knows how to cover his tracks but anyone watching a crime show would know chlorine destroys DNA." He pointed up to the CCTV cameras. "Every one of them is disconnected but the janitor could have disabled them to save power during the break."

"We'll need to speak to the janitor. For now, he is on the suspect list as well." Jenna raised one eyebrow. "Go on."

"Maybe as she was meeting Chad, she went to change. I found her clothes in the women's dressing room, folded neatly on the bench. Where I've marked over there close to the gate is where I believe a struggle took place. There is a towel by the gate as well, and as it is still there I would say the killer hasn't touched it—he is far too clever to risk leaving any traces of DNA." Kane pointed one gloved finger toward the gate. "I think she came out of the dressing room, saw the killer, and bolted for the gate. The killer ran her down and disabled her there—" he pointed to a yellow circle on the ground "—and then he dragged her by her hair to the recovery spa. I found a few hairs on the ground, and from the color they could be Kate's, but Wolfe will make a positive ID later. Once he has finished his preliminary examination, he'll go over the area with luminol to look for blood or tissue. The victim, I mean Kate, has marks on her back and legs consistent to being dragged across the cement."

Jenna pushed down the need to puke and swallowed a few times to gain some modicum of control. Her hands trembled and she thrust them deep into the pockets of her jacket. She had an investigation to run, and falling to pieces would not find the animal who killed the girls. Moving closer to Kane—because having him there, solid as a brick wall, kept her mind firmly on the job—she lifted her chin. "Do you need to question Chad? I think I covered everything and I would really like to get him home with his family."

"Maybe, but if the killer sounded like Kate's father, it would be prudent to call him and put him on speaker so Chad can hear his voice then we would know if the killer is local by his accent."

"I'm not informing him by phone that some lunatic sliced up his daughter." She snorted in disgust. "I'm not that damn heartless."

Kane stared up at the sky as if seeking divine intervention then dropped his blue gaze back to her. "*You* don't have a heartless bone in your body. A tongue like a viper, maybe but—" he tapped one long finger gently on her chest "—in there is a kind, considerate, and loving woman. Don't you think I know how these murders affect you? I'm not blind." He sighed. "I spent five years killing people for Uncle Sam. I can turn off my emotions when I have to, and Wolfe, well he would have a body farm if it would further his knowledge of forensic science."

Embarrassed by his gentle words, she looked away. "So why call Kate's father?"

"Ask him if he'll be home this evening as we need to speak to him and will explain when we arrive." He shrugged. "Then if Chad recognizes his voice, you'll know if her father was involved."

Straightening, she nodded. As usual, he made sense. "Okay. I'll do that now and wait with the paramedics to speak to Chad's father when he arrives."

"Could you ask the paramedics to transfer the body to the funeral home? Wolfe should be finished in about ten minutes. I called ahead and they'll be waiting. Wolfe will follow and get the autopsy underway tonight."

"Sure." More than happy to leave her deputies to the unpleasant task of moving the victim into a body bag, she headed toward the ambulance.

After speaking to Chad, she made the call, making sure the young man could hear Kate's father. "I'm sorry to bother you, Mr. Bright, this is Sheriff Alton. Would it be possible to drop by in about twenty minutes? I need to speak with you."

*"Katie hasn't got herself into any trouble, has she?"*

Jenna hedged, not wanting to discuss anything over the telephone. "I'll explain when I get there. I would like to speak to you and your wife if possible."

*"Yes, of course. Come right over."*

Disconnecting, she took in Chad's haggard appearance. He was close to breaking point. "Was that the voice you heard?"

"It was similar but the man I spoke to referred to her as Kate." Chad wiped a sleeve across his red-rimmed eyes. "I didn't think it was strange because we all call her Kate, but now hearing his voice I remember her dad always calls her Katie." He sniffed. "The man who answered her cellphone said I would find *Kate* by the pool, not Katie. I am 100 percent sure."

She heard a car engine and glanced toward the sweeping driveway. "That is probably your dad. I'll speak to him and then you can go home and rest." Thinking ahead to the dreadful task she had of informing Kate's parents and the support they would need, she squeezed Chad's shoulder. "I'll catch whoever did this and get justice for Kate."

Her calm exterior covered the rage she had festering inside for the demented lunatic murdering at will on her watch. She could feel his presence and almost taste the evil lurking in the air. She turned to see Kane walking grim-faced from the pool area beside the paramedics pushing a gurney carrying the body bag. Had a military-trained super-soldier arrived to help her by divine intervention or was it just dumb luck? The "do things by the book" sheriff part of her wanted to arrest the killer and take him to trial to pay for his brutality, but deep down inside, the woman in her wanted Kane to put him down like a rabid dog.

# CHAPTER THIRTY

Kane watched Jenna walk with Chad toward a car parked at the front of the complex and let out a long sigh. The sleepy town of Black Rock Falls had become a playground for crazies of late, and he wondered how much more stress she could take. Six months earlier, Jenna had suffered near death at the hands of two psychopathic murdering brothers who had befriended then stalked her. The brutality of the murders those lunatics had committed turned his stomach, and now six months later, Jenna was dealing with another potential serial killer.

He waited for Wolfe to join him and cleared his throat. "I'm worried about Jenna. I know she is strong but it wasn't long ago she was held captive by a couple of killers herself."

"She won't let her guard down in front of us or anyone else. Maybe you need to get closer to her. I'm not saying *sleep* with her but she needs a shoulder to lean on. We all have our breaking point—even you."

"She respects I have feelings for my wife and the job makes it difficult." He grimaced. "You wait until you feel the lash of her tongue the moment you step on her toes at the office."

"I'll make a point of keeping well clear of her toes."

Kane rubbed his chin. "I admire how feisty she is. She can fight with the best of them."

"Well, Jenna is never going to be the quiet type, is she?" Wolfe placed his bag at his feet and huffed a weary sigh. "Forget Jenna for a moment. I'll need to give my girls a call then I'm heading to the funeral home. I'd like to get the autopsy out of the way ASAP. The time of death could be out by some time, depending on how long the killer kept her in the hot spa before laying her out on the diving board." He waved a hand toward Jenna. "If you're worried about her, offer to go with her to see the parents. If they ask, I'm afraid they won't be able to view Kate until I've finished. Probably in the morning. Once I release her body, I'll let you know."

"How do you cope when you have to do autopsies on kids?"

"It doesn't matter who I have on my table; they all need my help. I'm the voice who tells their story and brings their killer to justice." Wolfe's gaze was cold and steady. "They deserve dignity and a name. To me they are never 'the victim.' If they are a Jane Doe then that's their identity in my mind until proven otherwise." He shrugged. "Does it make me angry or sad? More than you'll ever know. I've seen what man is capable of doing in war to protect his country but when someone tortures for enjoyment, it churns my guts the same as the next man." He nodded toward Jenna. "Do as I say and keep her company tonight; she is walking a tightrope right now and needs a friend."

"I'll do my best." He strolled toward Jenna and waited some distance away as she spoke to a man he assumed to be Chad's father.

When the car drove away, he went to her side. "I would like to come with you to see Kate's parents, then I need to escape from the horror of the last couple of days. I'm going home to switch off for a while. Maybe watch a cheesy movie or something."

She gave him one of her "Jenna has left the building" stares and ignored him, but her gaze moved around the complex and a tremble went through her. "I can feel the killer here, as if he is watching us—what if it's two men? I've been wrong before, haven't I?"

Considering she could be suffering from undiagnosed PTSD, Kane took her by the arm. "What makes you believe he is watching you?"

"Chad called Kate's cellphone when he arrived and heard her ringtone somewhere nearby." She looked up at him and fear flashed in her eyes. "He was here watching to see how Chad would react to seeing his girlfriend gutted."

When she did not shrug off his hand, he gave her a gentle squeeze. "I checked the immediate area. All the passageways have locked doors. He may have been inside the pool area at that time but left before we arrived."

"How? Chad didn't see anyone and the gate was locked." She glanced around at the woodland along the opposite side of the driveway. "I bet he is over there watching us."

"Then we'll take a look. Get in the car." He opened the door of his SUV and slipped behind the wheel.

The engine of his powerful vehicle roared into life. He backed up then hit the spotlights, and two beams of white halogen light pierced the dark woodland for fifty feet or more. Bats flew out of the trees in a cloud of confusion but nothing else moved. "He's long gone and wouldn't have risked hanging around to be identified." He turned to look at her pinched expression. "We'll talk to the parents then I'm taking you home. Grab your stuff and come over to my place, and we'll watch a movie."

"Why?" She gave him a long, confused stare.

He shrugged. "I need to leave the job behind for a few hours and I need some company before I lose it big time."

"*You* lose it? Give me a break." Jenna snapped back into sheriff mode and snorted with mirth. "Between you and Wolfe, I don't need to wait for winter for the room temperature to drop to subzero." She turned in her seat, her expression hidden in shadows. "But I will take you up on the offer of wine and a movie. I can't wait to tell Maggie a tough guy like you enjoys watching romcoms."

He spun the SUV around and headed for the gate. The task ahead would be depressing to the max and he needed to keep the banter between them light-hearted. "I've created a monster." He smiled at her. "No, I take that back, once Maggie spreads that news around town, everyone will know I'm really a sensitive guy."

"Good luck with that." Jenna placed one small hand on his arm. "I think we should close the gate once the ambulance has left."

Kane pulled up at the curb. "Yeah, and I'll wrap some tape around it to keep the kids out of the area until I notify the dean. Although, he is likely vacationing somewhere." He glanced at her. "Have you called a support person for the Brights?"

"Not yet, and I can't find any other people with the last name Bright in the local phone listings. It's late and someone local would be ideal." She frowned. "Apparently Reverend Jones has been very helpful for the Parkers. I know they go to the same church, and as it happens, I have his number in my contacts list." She pulled out her cellphone. The light from the screen illuminated her worried expression. "Do you think I should call him?"

"If you don't have the contact number of a family member, I guess a reverend would be the next best person."

"Okay, I can at least ask him." Jenna shook her dark head then called Jones and asked him to meet them at the Brights' residence.

Once the ambulance and Wolfe had left, Kane went to shut the gate and noticed a squashed flower on the driveway not far from the entrance. Moving back inside, he bent to examine it; noting the resemblance to the ones left with Kate's body, he dropped the plant into an evidence bag and pushed it into his pocket. He straightened then headed into the trees adjacent to the long driveway, using his flashlight to search the area of woods close to the road.

He noticed a small patch of disturbed earth as if someone had wrenched the flowers out by the roots then broken the stems and scattered the remains. "So that's where he collected the flowers." He did a visual scan of the area.

On closer inspection, he found a clear, small footprint in the disturbed soil. He pulled out his cellphone and took photographs using his boot beside the imprint to give a size comparison. If the footprint belonged to Kate, which he imagined it did, he had a clear sequence of events. He strolled back to the gate and after wrapping crime scene tape around the bars, he climbed back behind the wheel.

"Did you find something?" Jenna's dark gaze fixed on his face.

"A flower. The killer took them with him, which proves intent; going on how he left flowers at the last two crime scenes, this has to be the same person. Somehow he *knew* she would be at the pool and at what time."

"What makes you think he didn't follow her?"

"There is a patch of disturbed earth where someone pulled out the flowers and a small footprint in the upturned soil. If the footprint matches Kate's shoes, then she had to have walked through the woods *after* the killer collected the flowers. I wouldn't mind betting she arrived at six thirty as originally planned."

"I guess the time of death will give us a better idea but Chad did say he planned to meet her at eight thirty and found her minutes after."

"What the killer did to her takes time and he wanted to savor every second." Kane shook his head in disgust. "You mentioned Chad received a message via his online game room changing the meeting time from six thirty to eight thirty. How the hell did the killer have time to inflict so many injuries?"

"I have no idea."

Kane drummed his fingers on the steering wheel and stared toward the woods. "We have proof the killer was close by because Chad heard the ringtone of Kate's cellphone. When we arrived, there was no one else in the pool area. Trust me, I had a good look around and found zip. My guess is he watched Chad, then took off into the woods to take Chad's call, then made his escape."

"Just a minute." Jenna turned and wrinkled her nose, something she did when sorting out a problem. "This all sounds reasonable but you have missed the main point. *How* did the killer *know* she would be at the campus in the first place?" She tapped her bottom lip. "We'll need to ask Chad when and where he asked her on the date. Chad mentioned Aimee and Lucas knew about the date. The killer must have been near them at the time to have this information but we can rule out Lucas. He has an alibi for Felicity's murder and Chad was in contact with him around the time of the murder." Jenna let out a long sigh. "If the killer is the same person Helena Police Department is looking for, he is a very smart cookie."

"If this lunatic is the same man, this changes everything. Up to now everything pointed to him being local. We have to think outside the box. Who works in a job that would get them close to young people in a short time and be privy to their private information?"

"Just about everyone on our list of suspects." Jenna worried her bottom lip, making it cherry-red. "Rogers started at the school in January; both cowboys come and go; the computer guy, Lionel Provine, took over the store around December, I think. The only suspect who has lived in town all his life is Felicity's boyfriend, Derick, *but* he moves around with the team playing football and they do stay at least two nights in each town." She shrugged. "I'll be interested to find out if they all have alibis for tonight."

"Then there is the janitor." Kane turned to look at her. "Kids of this age use Facebook and give out intimate details of their lives. I mean we have no idea if her friends told anyone else she was meeting Chad. It could be all over social media for all we know." He sighed. "It looks as if we have a lot of work to do."

He started the engine and headed toward the main road. On the corner of Stanton Road, the headlights picked up a blue sedan parked alongside the forest. He slowed his vehicle. "That's a strange place to leave a vehicle. Did you notice it parked there when we arrived?"

"I'm not sure. You drove like a bat out of hell."

Pulling to the curb beside the car, he slipped from behind the wheel and, using his flashlight, examined the vehicle. Something inside moved and his heart raced. He reached for his weapon. "Sheriff's department. Put your hands where I can see them."

Angling his Glock along the flashlight, he approached with caution and the beam of light fell on Steve Rogers' face. "Get out of the car, hands on head."

In his periphery, he noticed Jenna moving toward him, weapon drawn. He kicked Rogers' feet apart and patted him down. Finding no weapons, he spun him around, noticing his disheveled appearance and the circles of sweat marking the underarms of his shirt. The top button of his mud-spattered jeans was unfastened and he was barefoot. He glanced inside the car and noticed a laptop on the passenger seat. "What brings you out at this time of night, Mr. Rogers?"

"I heard sirens and thought there might be something going on, so I came down here to take a look." Rogers refused to meet his gaze. "No crime in sitting in my car is there?"

Kane flicked a glance at Jenna and shrugged. "No, but you appear to be a little hot and bothered. What else have you been doing tonight? Jogging in the forest perhaps? And do you usually run with bare feet?"

"I haven't been doing anything. I heard gunshots and forgot my shoes when I dashed out to see what was happening. There's no law about not wearing shoes is there?"

"No." Kane glared at him. "What gunshots are you talking about?"

"I heard them but I checked the local news on my cellphone and nothing has been reported." His thin lips twitched. "What *did* happen?"

Kane shrugged. "Kids broke into the college and set off a few fireworks is all. Nothing for you to worry about." He opened the car door. "Why don't you head on home."

Kane waited for him to drive away and turned to Jenna. "He had a laptop on the front seat and did you see the way he was dressed? He was sweaty and looked out of breath as if he'd been running." He sighed. "Man, I'd love an excuse to look at the history on his cellphone."

"Look over there. I think I see tire marks on the edge of the road."

He moved the flashlight over the grass and they followed the track into a clump of trees. "Someone parked here, and if he is our killer, he could have run here from the college, but although Rogers had splashes of mud on him, his feet looked clean but he could have removed his shoes. Perhaps he wanted to watch the people coming and going to the scene. Maybe he planned to leave, saw our head-lights, and stopped then ducked down to pretend the car was empty."

"Yeah." Jenna stared blankly at the empty road. "Especially as Chad can place the killer at the scene between eight thirty and eight forty-five. Maybe we should have arrested Rogers?"

Kane gave her a sideways look. "On suspicion of murder? Finding him in a car in the local area half an hour at least after the fact without a shred of evidence to prove our case, his lawyer will have us up on harassment charges. We could seize his computer with suspicion of child porn or money laundering. Take your pick." Exhausted, he rolled his shoulders and headed back to the SUV. "How do you want to proceed?"

"We'll leave him for now but he has moved up the suspect list. I wish we had enough on him for Wolfe to access his computer to see what he was doing."

"Again, the judge will laugh the paperwork out of his office." Kane raised an eyebrow. "Where to?"

"I'll enter the Brights' address in the GPS." Jenna took out her notebook and went to work. "First we inform the parents some maniac has murdered their daughter."

"Yes, ma'am." Kane slid behind the wheel and started the engine.

# CHAPTER THIRTY-ONE

After informing the stunned and shocked parents of Kate Bright, Jenna decided to leave them in the capable hands of Reverend Jones. The reverend had solemnly informed them he would go with them to the mortuary and help arrange the funeral once Wolfe released Kate's body. Glad to have the awful business over, she stood. "You have my card if you need to contact me."

"Dear God, how did this happen?" Mr. Bright gave her a blank look and stared at the card in his hand. "I thought she was safe in her room. Why didn't I check on her?" He glanced at Kane and anger replaced devastation. "I want to be there when you catch this animal. I'll tear him apart with my bare hands." He raked at his tear-filled eyes and body shook with grief. He clasped Kane's arm. "Tell me you'll catch this son of a bitch."

"We'll catch him, sir." Kane turned his concerned gaze on her. "Ma'am?"

A flashback of being tied, helpless and in the hands of two killers, hit Jenna like a train. The conversation swirled around her like water flowing down the drain in the sink. The next moment someone gripped her arm. She panicked, wanting to run away, then Kane's voice broke through the buzzing in her head.

"I think we should call back at another time. We need to leave these people to get some rest."

She focused on his face and nodded. "Yes, of course. I'm so sorry for your loss."

"Just catch the man who did this to my little girl." Mr. Bright mopped at the tears welling in his red-rimmed eyes. "I want to see her."

Jenna cleared her throat. "Yes, of course. I'll contact you the moment the M.E has released her."

Relieved to be leaving the pain and misery behind, Jenna followed Kane to his SUV. "I hope the reverend will be able to help them cope."

Jenna noticed Kane stiffen and the tick in his cheek.

"I don't *do* religion." Kane shrugged then his blue gaze moved to her face. "I *kill* people, maybe in the line of duty but I don't expect a welcome at the Pearly Gates. I'm paying for my sins every day of my life."

"It's not a sin to protect your country or to save a life." Astonished her iceman had vented his innermost feelings, she gaped at him. "I thought you *liked* living in Black Rock Falls?"

"*Like* is a pretty strong word." Kane snorted in derision and his lips turned down. "A new life maybe, and having you as my boss is a bonus, but I watched my wife die and I live in pain. I'll probably be stuck here for the rest of my life."

"*Oh my God.*" Jenna punched him hard in the bicep and pain shot up her arm. Dammit, she had got close to breaking her knuckles, and Kane only looked at her with one raised black eyebrow. He had not moved an inch. "What the hell is wrong with you? *Poor* boy, are you feeling sorry for yourself? Want me to buy you a pacifier?" She glared at him. "Pull yourself together."

When Kane flashed her a brilliant white smile, she gaped at him, speechless, rubbing her throbbing hand.

"That's the Jenna I know." He mussed up her hair with one big hand and chuckled. "I thought you had checked out on me for a while before—and next time, punch me in a soft area, or knee me in the groin if you want to get my attention, or you'll hurt yourself." He sauntered toward the car.

Running her fingers through her hair, she followed him. "What do you mean by that comment? Are you saying I'm demanding?" She climbed into the passenger seat and turned to see him trying to hide a smile. "What's so funny?"

"Not a thing, ma'am." Kane's full mouth twitched at the corners. He started the engine and turned the SUV for home. "The last few days have been horrific and I'm glad to have you back."

"I haven't been anywhere." The meaning to his words dropped into place and she shrugged. "Okay, yes, I had a few flashbacks. It's hard not to relate to what the victims went through. I've been there, and if you hadn't arrived, the Daniels brothers would have raped and murdered me. I *know* they are dead and can't hurt me. What's happening to me?"

"We all have a breaking point and you need time to unwind. We have done everything we can for tonight. We can't compare cases until we get the autopsy results on all the victims. If you want, I'll write up the case file when I get home and send off an email to Helena to keep them in the loop."

Jenna sighed. "Thanks. It has been a very long day and I do need to turn off for a while."

"I'll take you home so you can take a nice hot shower then why don't you come over to my place and watch a movie?"

She turned in her seat and looked at him. "No shop talk."

"I promise."

The SUV slowed outside Aunt Betty's Café and Kane held up one long finger then headed inside the store. She glanced up the street and a wave of unease slid over her yet the brightly lit street had a number of people strolling by. Music drifted out the door of the café, and through the storefront window, she noticed Lucky Briggs and Storm Crawley at a table in animated conversation. She waited in the car but try as she may, she could not drag her mind away from the murders. There had to be something, some clue she had overlooked.

She turned on the overhead light and took out her notepad, scanning each page with care. She read the interview notes she had taken with Aimee and Kate. Allowing the girls' replies to her questions to percolate through her mind, she focused on what they had said. Their attraction toward Lucky Briggs and Storm Crawley had included Felicity. Would they make a secret rendezvous to meet the men of their dreams? She had to admit she would have walked on hot coals to meet the members of her favorite band at the same age, and these men just happened to be locals. They would have the girls' trust, and after her unnerving interview, she would not put rape past either of them—but murder?

Cowboys worked on ranches when not traveling the rodeo circuit; they likely butchered livestock. And most men hunted in the region, and blood and guts came with the sport. She had failed to look deeper into the cowboys' lives. She made a note to ask Rowley to ask the locals. People gossip and he would be the best person to pry information loose.

What else had she missed during the interview with Aimee and Kate? Had she overlooked a small but crucial reference or had she failed to ask the correct questions? She rubbed her temples in an effort to force her mind to work harder. Her attention moved to the computer store sitting in darkness, and a spark of memory ignited like a Roman candle on the Fourth of July. *Aimee and Kate said they communicate online.* She had the impression they would not use the term if they meant called each other by phone. She assumed the games room they used had a live feed; people often played games against each other. *Is it possible the killer is hacking their video calls?*

# CHAPTER THIRTY-TWO

Kane dropped onto the soft leather sofa beside Jenna and handed her a bowl of popcorn. She had been distant on the drive home, and after taking a shower, she had called him to walk her over to his cottage. The murders had spooked her more than she was prepared to admit and spending the rest of the evening watching a romantic comedy seemed the right thing to do. He hit the play button on the remote, and to his surprise, she sniffed and he noticed her eyes fill with tears. "Relax for a while. It has been a tough few days. Don't take everything so personal; you're human not a machine."

"But I'm the sheriff." Jenna swiped at a single tear streaming down her cheek. "I need to crack the whip and act tough."

He grabbed a handful of tissues from the box on the coffee table and handed them to her. "You are tough. In fact, you've surprised me many times. I think you are a great sheriff and so do the townsfolk. They voted you back in for another term, didn't they? What more proof do you need?"

"That's because no one had the guts to stand against me." Jenna dabbed at her eyes. "What if I missed something and Kate died because of it?"

He let out a long sigh. "Then we all missed a clue, didn't we? You have to stop blaming yourself for everything that happens in town. People commit crimes, and nothing we do can change anything. It's called free will: People decide to keep the peace or break the law, their choice. Our job is to catch them and send them to jail."

"In the car, I remembered Aimee and Kate mentioned they spoke online." She lifted her tousled head and looked at him. "They *spoke* online. I didn't put that in my notes. If the killer is stalking them online, and I missed that crucial part of the conversation, I could have saved Kate."

"No. The killer is to blame. You have to stop doing this to yourself, it's not healthy." He reached for his cellphone, called Wolfe, and put his device on speaker. "Just a minute. I'll clarify your worries with Wolfe." He placed the cellphone between them. "Ah, sorry to bother you. I need some info. How long would it take you to trace a Black Hat's IP address?"

*"Dammit, Dave, you know that's impossible. They bounce the signal off so many towers in so many countries, it could take weeks, and they change computers all the time. I'm good but if you are alluding to our killer hacking the girls' computers, it's possible but highly unlikely. One, maybe, but not all of them. Is that all? I need to finish up here and get home to my kids."*

"Yeah, thanks, man." Kane disconnected and looked into Jenna's distraught face. "See, it made no difference, plus the fact Wolfe already considered the idea. Now blow your nose, drink your wine, and watch the movie. We said no shop talk."

"Okay."

Sleep had crept up on Kane way before the end of the movie, and he woke with a stiff neck sometime in the early hours. The temperature in June dropped considerably overnight, and Jenna was the only thing keeping him warm. He glanced down at her in the blueish light from the flat screen. She had fallen asleep against him. Her long black lashes brushed her pink cheek and one hand gripped his T-shirt. Dressed in soft, white pajamas and her pink slippers, she had a vulnerability that tugged at his heart. If she needed him as a friend, he would be there for her. Soon the darkness and self-doubt would slide away and she would be back in control of her emotions.

Edging carefully away, her long fingers tightened in the fabric of his shirt and she made a disgruntled moan. He lifted her onto his lap, gathered her into his arms, and stood then carried her into his bedroom. He stared at his reflection in the mirror and shrugged. *What am I doing?*

Right now, Jenna needed him as a friend. Holding her would ease the nightmares and ensure she enjoyed a good night's sleep. He lowered her gently to the bed, pulled back the blankets, and rolled her onto her side. When she moaned and her hands trembled, he let out a long sigh. *I'm going to pay for doing this in the morning.* Shaking his head, he strolled back to the living room, turned off the TV, and made a quick trip to the bathroom to brush his teeth then crawled into bed beside her.

It had been a long time since he had spooned, and the thoughts of Annie, his wife, hammered his mind. They had discussed the fact he might not survive a tour of duty and he insisted she should move on with her life. He could still feel her hands cupping his face as she made him promise he would do the same. *I'm trying, Annie, but I'll never forget you.* He touched the scar covering the metal plate in his head then allowed sleep to claim him.

Since his first tour of duty, he could not fall into a deep sleep. His mind remained on constant alert and woke him at the slightest threat. He opened his eyes a crack, remembering with a rush of apprehension he had taken Jenna to his bed. Under his arm, her muscles tensed but she kept her breathing steady. *She is pretending to be asleep.* He let out a long sigh, abstained from farting, and rolled onto his back. "I know you're awake. I woke up about two this morning and carried you in here because you were freezing. That's all that happened."

He heard her snort of derision and rolled out of bed then headed for the bathroom. "It's too late for a workout this morning. I'm taking a shower and heading for Aunt Betty's Café. I'm famished. I'll see you at work, ma'am."

As he reached the bathroom door, he heard swearing he would regard as classic with a touch of the macabre. Heavy footsteps followed by the front door slamming hard enough to loosen it from its hinges. *Not a happy camper this morning?* He grimaced at his reflection, pulled out his shaving gear, and started to get ready for work.

After a hearty breakfast at Aunt Betty's Café, Kane drove to the sheriff's office and parked in his usual spot beside Jenna's new SUV, the replacement for the old cruiser she had been driving since her car wreck last winter. When she had a bone to pick with him, she usually arrived well ahead of time, and he gathered his day at the office would be one he would remember for some time to come. He pushed through the glass doors and into the sheriff's department, surprised to see a young blonde-haired girl at the front desk with Magnolia. He strolled toward them and smiled. "Good morning. Lovely weather today."

"Well, aren't you all sunshine and roses, and the sheriff rolled in here like a thunderstorm with threatening hail." Magnolia's brown eyes flitted over him. "Know what's going on?"

He shrugged and kept his expression blank. "I have no idea. She hasn't spoken to me this morning. The cases we're dealing with are complex and she is under a lot of pressure right now."

"Dreadful is the word I would use." Maggie's expression changed to sadness. "Is there anything I can do to help?"

He frowned. "Did the sheriff ask you about the janitor at the college campus? We need his name and address."

"Hmm, she stormed in here without a word but you won't find anyone up at the campus for the first two weeks of the summer break. That's when all the staff, cleaners and the like, take their vacation, then they all come back and the maintenance crew comes in to fix up the place for the new semester. The janitor is back by then. I'll get his name and address for you and I'll give his house a quick call just to see if he is at home." Maggie raised both dark eyebrows. "Oh, have you met our intern for the summer? This fine young lady is Emily Wolfe." She waved the young girl forward. "Meet Deputy Dave Kane."

"Nice to meet you. My dad mentioned you called last night." Ice-gray eyes an exact replica of Shane Wolfe's gave him a once-over.

He shook her hand and smiled at her haughty air. "Yes, Shane has mentioned you too but I wasn't aware we were getting an intern. Are you planning on becoming a deputy or are you here for the administrative experience?"

"Neither." She tossed a lock of white-blonde hair over one shoulder. "I'm planning on studying forensic science like my dad then I can work with him. The school likes seniors to do some type of internship during the break, so here I am. It will be interesting to watch the process of the law in a small town. Of course, I'll need to be aware of such things if I plan to work beside my dad."

The idea the young girl had Wolfe's almost ghoulish predilection for examining the cause of death in murder victims surprised him. "I'm sure you'll be a great asset to the team." He noticed Jenna's door swing open and, wanting to avoid her fury, turned toward his desk. "I'd better get to work. It's fifty lashes if I'm late." He grinned at her astonished expression and strode to his cubicle. *Of her tongue.*

# CHAPTER THIRTY-THREE

Jenna read the horrific details of Kate's death from Wolfe's autopsy report and reached for her coffee. Exhausted, she needed the caffeine to keep on her toes. Breaking down in front of Kane was unforgivable, and waking up in his bed a total disaster. All her years of training to withstand torture had vanished and she had fallen to pieces in front of him. Everyone has a breaking point but she had woken up angry with herself—in Kane's arms. Worst of all, Kane felt sorry for her. *Sorry.* Holy shit, he had held her all night. She had to pull herself together before he lost confidence in her leadership.

Her rudeness after waking was inexcusable, especially as she had forced her problems on him. She had seen a different side to him, a gentle, caring side he kept well-hidden. He had treated her with the utmost respect and tried to help her rationalize the situation. In the last six months, he had become a close friend but she needed to remain in control at work. She had to think about how best to handle the situation. *Later. I have murders to solve.* She pushed to her feet and strode to the office door. "Wolfe, Kane, in my office now!"

Dragging down the whiteboard, she stared at the notes she had listed under each photograph. When the deputies entered the office and the door clicked shut behind them, she turned slowly and regarded them down her nose. With the two massive men in the room, the area appeared filled to capacity. She cleared her throat and moved her attention to Wolfe. "Are you 100 percent sure there are only two sets of prints on the pool padlock?"

"Yes, it was wiped clean but I found Kate's and I collected Chad's this morning on the way here and they are a match." His blond eyebrows rose. "The gate must have been open when Kate arrived, and Chad admitted trying to open the padlock to get to her." He rubbed the stubble on his chin, the sound like sandpaper. "I don't think Chad can be classed as a suspect. When I went to his house this morning, I asked what time he left and his father confirmed the time as eight fifteen. What the killer did to Kate took, I would say, fifteen to twenty minutes but I would say he took his time and made it last as long as possible. Add the fact Chad was clean and wearing the same clothes his father described him as wearing when he left home puts him in the clear."

"I agree." Jenna sucked in a deep breath. "You are certain Kate was alive most of the time?"

"Affirmative. The injuries inflicted to her eyes prevented her from closing them. The killer wanted her to see what he did to her. She died from blood loss and shock."

"So, different from both the other murders?"

"Only in a few instances." Wolfe's gaze narrowed. "He planned Felicity's and Kate's murders. They were calculated and he took his time. Joanne's murder was different, rushed. It was a quick thrill-kill and messy, proving he didn't have his tools of the trade with him. If we had released Felicity's murder to the media, I would have considered Joanne's murder a copycat."

She moved her attention to Kane, who had his secret-agent blank expression in place. "In your opinion as an expert on psychopathic behavior, when do you believe he will strike again?"

"He is escalating and could strike again anytime." Kane rolled his wide shoulders and his blue gaze rested on her. "If he is still in the area. So far there have only been two murders of the same type in each town, and he has done three here. He might think it's time to move on."

"Yes, but those murders were spread all over the media, and they called him the Waterside Ripper. Here we have the local newspaper's consideration to keep the main details of the murders under wraps until we close in on the killer." She pushed her hair out of her eyes. "I'm wondering if this is the best thing to do—maybe he'll escalate even more to see himself in the press and on TV?"

"I don't agree. Feeding his ego by releasing the details of the crimes is a mistake. Killers love to relive every moment, and seeing this on TV makes him feel powerful. He'll kill again and again until we stop him, media coverage or not. The parents of the victims know we are working on the cases and all agree they would rather not see the intimate details of their kids' rapes and murders splashed all over the news. Saying we suspect foul play is good enough for now." Kane's mouth turned down at the corners. "My guess is if he is in the area he'll be watching everything we do and planning his next move."

Jenna stared at the whiteboard. "I'll need one of you to speak to the janitor."

"The janitor is on vacation." Kane raised a dark brow. "He left the first day of the summer break, so you can rule him out. The dean and his family are in Europe for the duration. I found out at Aunt Betty's this morning. Susie Hartwig is a good source of information."

"So it would seem." She turned to the list of suspects. "We have Steve Rogers in the area and I noticed Lucky Briggs and Storm Crawley in Aunt Bettys Café last night as well. We have two positive sightings of suspects from Felicity's murder in the area the night of Kate's murder. I suggest we find out when the cowboys arrived at the café. I want to re-interview the suspects in Felicity's case and see if they have alibis for the time of Joanne's murder. Get Rowley to call them and check on their whereabouts. If they seem in any way suspicious, we'll follow up." She turned to Wolfe. "Rowley picked up Kate's laptop last night and it is in the evidence locker. Maybe you can cross-reference their logs or something and see if anything matches. There has to be a connection."

"I'll get on it straight away but you can be sure the same killer murdered the three girls." A flash of worry crossed Wolfe's face. "It is a case of who is next. If we take Joanne out of the equation, the killer has chosen two friends. I think we need to be keeping a close eye on Aimee Fox and the rest of the group who hang out together." He gave her a long, considering stare. "This has now become a personal problem for me because apparently yesterday, Aimee and another girl, Julia Smith, came by my house with their mothers as a welcoming committee. Emily takes after me. She is not a social butterfly and more of a nerd, so the opportunity to be accepted into a group of girls who spend a great deal of time at the computer store was attractive to her." He let out a worried sigh. "She is meeting them at Provine's store after her shift this morning."

Her mind re-ran a photoshoot of the victims' mutilated bodies and she blinked to force the images away. Maybe she was suffering from PTSD after all. She cleared her throat. "You should take the time to walk her to the store and pick her up when she is ready to leave."

"Thank you for your concern but I'm not sure that would work, ma'am." Wolfe raised one blond eyebrow. "She would lose face in front of her friends if her daddy treated her like a two-year-old. I have a fail-safe in play with my kids and they understand the meaning of stranger danger. I'm obviously telling you this in the strictest confidence. Each of my daughters carries a number of tracker tags, much like the ones I gather Kane made for you, but mine are lightyears ahead of the simple device he used in your earrings."

"I'd like to know what new technology you have developed." Kane stretched out his long legs and folded his arms. "I agree what I gave Jenna was a simple tracker much like the ones available for luggage and the like, *but* it worked."

"Not good enough though, was it? These days, people are more aware of technology and criminals will be looking for anything suspicious. Jenna couldn't contact you because the men who kidnapped her knew about the device." Wolfe's pale gaze moved over her face. "My girls have something similar but installed in their earrings and necklaces, and if all else fails one that looks like a teddy bear pin. I made them waterproof as well, so they never have to remove them. The difference with my invention and the one Kane placed inside your earrings is the devices have a mic, and once activated, not only am I alerted but I can hear what they are saying. I decided not to include a speaker because if any of my girls are in danger any communication might be detected."

Astounded by Wolfe's abilities, she smiled at him. "Absolutely brilliant. I think if I had kids I would have a permanent tracker installed under their skin."

"Ah, I think that is going a bit too far. I had a subdural one to allow HQ to track me and it felt like a huge invasion of privacy." Kane's long fingers clenched and unclenched. "But I would recommend allowing Wolfe to make something similar to his kids' devices for all of us. He can make the tracker so only the wearer can activate it, so at other times privacy is assured."

Needing to be in control, she straightened. "I gather the earbuds and power packs have arrived? We will implement them during any suspicious callouts but if you believe a tracker alert button or whatever you call the damn thing is advisable, then I'll agree, but I want mine placed in a ring this time. I have a tight one at home and it's very difficult to remove. Will that suffice?"

"Yes, ma'am." Wolfe's lips lifted at the corners. "But it will have to be opaque, like a cameo or similar?"

"Fine." She sat in her chair, placed her elbows on the table, and rubbed her temples. "Emily is a very intelligent girl and not the clique-type, I assume?"

"She is very independent and thinks for herself." Wolfe gave her a worried look. "Good Lord, you're not asking her to go undercover and report on her friends, are you? Absolutely not, she'll have a hard enough time finishing her final year here without ratting out her friends."

Jenna lifted the phone and asked Maggie to ask Emily to join them. When she stepped into the room, head high and confident, Jenna could certainly see her father in her. "Take a seat. I would like to ask you a few questions. I gather your father has informed you in confidence about the murders this week?"

"Yes, and I haven't told anyone." Emily shot a gray gaze at her father. "I do understand the meaning of confidential."

Jenna folded her hands on the table and smiled at her. "I'm sure you do. If your father agrees, I wondered if during your time with your new friends, you would take note of any interaction you have with any of the men listed on the board over there." She pointed to the whiteboard and the photographs of the suspects lined up under their names. "Lionel Provine is the man who owns the computer store, Derick Smith was Felicity Parker's boyfriend, and Steve Rogers is the teacher at the high school. Lucky Briggs and Storm Crawley are local cowboys currently in town for the rodeo." She raised an eyebrow. "I don't want you to get involved other than making a note of the time and name of the person you notice hanging around or speaking to the girls, then report to your dad."

"I can do that, no problem at all." Emily's attention moved to Wolfe. "If it's okay with you, Dad?"

"Absolutely no interaction. Any one of those men could be the killer." Wolfe narrowed his pale eyes. "Understand?"

"Yes." Emily's hair fell over one shoulder as she nodded in agreement. She took out her cellphone and snapped a picture of the suspects. "Don't worry. I'll crop the image so the other information is not visible, just in case I lose my cellphone." She smiled and patted Wolfe on the arm. "I'll message you if we go to Aunt Betty's Café and when we leave and return to the computer store. As far as I know the girls are restricted to those areas the same as I am." She frowned. "Since Kate's murder they are scared but no one knows what happened to them. They are sticking together but no one seems to know anything about Joanne Blunt."

Jenna leaned back in her chair. "Joanne was a visitor to town and we believe she was in the wrong place at the wrong time. She has no connection to the other victims or any of our suspects, which makes our killer all the more dangerous. Take care this afternoon and I will look forward to your report."

She waited for Emily to leave the room and turned to Kane. "I want to keep a close eye on her. Is the new CCTV camera system installed near the computer store?"

"Yeah, it gives a clear view of the computer store and Aunt Betty's Café and there are six others along the street. The interview room I converted into a command center also gives the ability to move the cameras, zoom in, et cetera."

She tapped her pen on the table. "How long do the discs run? Do we have to change them or do they re-write every twelve hours or so?" She heard Wolfe make a strange sound halfway between a snort and a chuckle. She glared at him. "Okay, what's so funny?"

"Everything is digital now, ma'am. We have terabytes of storage and keep them for six months, then if no crimes have been commit-ted, we overwrite them." Wolfe's mouth twitched into a half smile. "The hard drives have approximately ten years' life before we need to replace them but well before that no doubt they will be able to hold enough data for a year or more." He raised one blond brow. "I can add an app to our cellphones to allow us to view the footage in real time. It might come in handy."

She nodded. "Do it as soon as possible. I'll get Rowley on phone interviews with our suspects but I gather we'll have to chase up Lucky Briggs and Storm Crawley. It's unlikely they will have their cellphones on hand if they are competing. The events at the rodeo did start today, I believe?"

"I can take a ride over there if you like?" Kane leaned nonchalantly back in his chair, his large hands resting on the arms. "I've organized four deputies from Blackwater to patrol the fairgrounds from Thursday through Sunday as we'll be there undercover, so to speak. The new mayor is paying them so we don't owe them our time."

Annoyed he had taken charge again, she narrowed her gaze at him then a memory dropped into place. She *had* asked him to speak to the mayor about spending money on the town's safety. He had informed her about funding for the CCTV cameras but not the extra help. The anger she had for him melted like last winter's snow. "Yes, I remember asking you to speak to him. Thank you."

"We can hire another full-time deputy as well, but a rookie. The mayor said the budget won't stretch to another ex-marine." Kane's blue eyes searched her face. "Would you like me to place an advertisement once we have caught the killer or go ahead and start looking for someone now?"

She shook her head. "No, you have enough to do at the moment and a rookie to watch as well will be more trouble than he is worth. In any case, we have Maggie to do the grunt work. I can't expect you to do her duties as well."

Last night, he had let down his guard by showing her his gentler side. Rather than push him away she should encourage him to relax with her in their downtime. Their evening together had been natural as if they fit together, and the fact he cared enough to cuddle her all night meant a lot to her. She smiled and caught his relieved expression. "Thanks for handling the mayor, I find him a bit condescending. Then most of the old-school types in town think being a sheriff is a man's job."

"Trust me," Kane smiled at her in a slash of white, "everyone knows who is in charge."

# CHAPTER THIRTY-FOUR

Kane noticed the color rise in Jenna's cheeks and stood ready to leave. "If it's alright with you, ma'am, I'll head out to the fairgrounds and speak to the cowboys."

"Just a minute, Kane. I need a word with you before you leave." Jenna tucked a strand of raven hair behind one ear then turned her attention to Wolfe. "If you need a quiet area to search through the laptops, use the control center, and you can keep an eye on Emily at the same time via the CCTV cameras."

"Yes, that would be a good idea." Wolfe rubbed the blond stubble on his chin and looked at Jenna. "I'll need Chad's IP address as well, and Kate's other friends. It will give me a better idea of who was interacting and when. If I see someone we can't identify, we will know it's our bogey. Do you mind if I call the parents for the information?"

"No, go ahead and do what's necessary."

Unsure of Jenna's mood or motive for keeping him behind, Kane dropped back into the chair and rested one boot on the knee of his other leg. After Wolfe left the room, closing the door behind him, instead of going back to her seat, Jenna stood between him and the desk and stared down at him with a confused expression. He gave her his brightest smile. "What can I do for you, ma'am?"

"Last night—*okay*. I *know* I checked out for a while." Jenna rubbed both small hands over her face then peered at him through her fingers. "Before you ask, the flashbacks are a bitch but I'm coping, and swearing at you this morning was unforgiveable. I shouldn't have had a drink or bothered you with my problems. It wasn't a fair thing to do in the circumstances and I'm sorry, it won't happen again."

Kane leaned back in the chair and looked up at her. The memory of her snuggled against him came back in a rush. He frowned. "What circumstances?"

"You've recently lost your wife and ending up in your bed was unforgivable."

"Her name was *Annie* and I lost her eighteen months ago." He regarded the sorrow in her eyes and frowned. "You're my friend and last night we both needed a little comfort. Trust me, sleeping alone after having Annie beside me for five years is hell. Just knowing she would be waiting for me to come home after a mission kept me alive. It's been a long time since anyone needed me or cuddled me." He reached for her hand and rubbed his thumb over her smooth skin. "Sometimes you'll need a shoulder to cry on and I'll need a cuddle or we'll stop being human."

Her dark blue eyes moved over his face and she gave the tiniest of nods. "I agree. I value the friendship we have outside the office. I think not allowing personal life to get in the way of the job is part of being a professional."

He looked at her for a long moment. His dream of a wife, a white picket fence, and a bunch of kids had died with Annie but he had found a kindred spirit in Jenna. "I enjoy your company too and with all that's happened lately, it's not healthy to be alone every night to dwell on murder. Come over for a steak tonight and we can finish watching the movie."

"Sure, let me know how you get on with the cowboys."

He dropped her hand and touched the brim of his hat before heading for the door. "Yes, ma'am."

\*

Pedestrians dressed in their best fringes and sparkles filled the sidewalk. With the first day of the rodeo underway, the local businesses in Black Rock Falls were doing a roaring trade. Most of the stores had stalls out front carrying local souvenirs, preserves, pottery, and other interesting items. The boldly colored bunting draped on every available surface gave the main road a carnival atmosphere. Speakers set high on the lampposts vibrated with country and western music, the latest tunes interrupted by the local radio station with the results of events at the fairgrounds. The noise in the "quiet" town had increased to a constant babble of voices.

As Kane walked to his SUV, he returned the smiles on the faces of the people and friendly greetings but the memories of the mutilated bodies remained at the front of his mind. He slid behind the wheel ever vigilant, his gaze moving over the people, taking a mental note of men close by or speaking to young women. Somewhere in the happy crowd lurked a monster waiting to pluck another victim from existence.

His attention moved to a couple of girls heading into Aunt Betty's Café, chatting animatedly with the computer science teacher Steve Rogers. When he noticed one of the girls was Aimee Fox, his worry meter hit the bell. He pulled to the curb and observed the trio for a few minutes, noting how different Steve Rogers acted with the girls. All charm and smiles, not the henpecked husband he had tried to convey to him during the interview. The man could easily fit the profile of a killer. Kane had seen more than two faces of evil displayed in a man who took pleasure in murder. He had an inbuilt dislike for Steve Rogers, and his gut instinct told him he was not what he seemed.

Needing to take a closer look, he climbed out of the vehicle and headed inside the café. He went to the counter and ordered a coffee to go then wandered over to the table where the two girls sat with

Rogers. The trio had their heads together looking at one of the girls' cellphones and making excited comments. He wanted to make it quite clear he had seen the teacher in the company of the girls. "How are you today, Mr. Rogers?"

"Enjoying a coffee with two of my pupils in plain sight." Rogers gave him a condescending stare. "Am I breaking the law?"

"Nope." Kane leaned down to look at the cellphone. "I noticed Aimee's attention was fixed on something on her cellphone and was wondering what is so interesting. I've seen quite a few young people running around as if their lives depended on it."

"It's the new game app. See, it interacts with the camera." Aimee held up the screen. "The idea is to collect the characters or whatever to go up a level. The final level apparently unlocks a bonus game."

Kane glanced at the screen and saw the interior of the café, and right in the middle was a green character waving at him. He looked at the room then back at the screen. "That is incredible, digital interaction via the camera and the navigation system on the cellphone." He glanced at Rogers. "You'd know all about this type of game, wouldn't you?"

"My skills are not quite up to this standard or I wouldn't be teaching, I'd be a billionaire." Rogers gave a sarcastic laugh. "But I do have a few tricks up my sleeve."

"I bet you do." Kane smiled at Aimee. "Remember what your mom told you about going straight home."

"You don't have to worry, Julia's mom is in town and Mr. Rogers will make sure I get back to my car, he is parked right behind me." Aimee smiled sweetly. "We had to use the parking lot at the library, everywhere else is packed today."

Deciding to make Rogers aware someone would be watching his every move, Kane nodded. "That's a good place to park. The library has a CCTV camera in the parking lot and a security guard keeping a close watch on everything over the next few days. You should be safe but stay alert just in case someone is lurking about."

"I thought it was your job to keep the townsfolk safe, Deputy." Rogers' mouth turned up in the corners into almost a smirk.

Kane rolled his shoulders and noticed Susie Hartwig waving at him to collect his coffee. "Yes, but I'm sure these young ladies know not to go out at night alone during the rodeo especially as three young women have been found dead in the area." He plucked cards out of his shirt pocket and gave them to the girls. "If you need help anytime day or night, that's my cellphone number." He smiled. "Stay safe."

"Don't I get a card?" Steve Rogers glared at him. "Or don't you think *all* Black Rock Falls citizens are in danger during the influx of the rough types?"

"You don't look like a teenage girl to me, Mr. Rogers." Kane bit back a smile and bent down so only Rogers could hear him. "Trust me, I'm the last person you should call. I've met men like you before and I see who is lurking behind the mask." Satisfied by seeing the color drain from Rogers' face, he strolled toward the counter. *You're up to something, you smug son of a bitch.*

# CHAPTER THIRTY-FIVE

Back at the car, Kane pulled out his cellphone and contacted Jenna to explain his observations. "We need eyes on Steve Rogers. He stinks on ice right now."

*"I agree he should know better than to hang around with his students."*

"He tried to make me look like an incompetent idiot." Kane sipped his beverage and sighed. "He makes my skin crawl, he is up to something. My gut is never wrong."

*"Okay, I'll give the info to Wolfe and he'll keep an eye on our Mr. Rogers. I think we need to do a bit of surveillance on him too. I'll ask Rowley if he will take the afternoon off and spend a few hours this evening keeping an eye on Rogers' movements. I'll call Rogers' house and see if his wife is back from her sister's yet. She might tell me when he went out last night. She was very cooperative the last time I spoke to her."*

"Good idea." Kane started the engine. "We'll talk later, ma'am. I'm heading for the fairgrounds now." He disconnected and turned his SUV toward the fairgrounds.

As he approached the Black Rock Falls Motel, he noticed a cowboy dressed in fringed chaps leaning against the wall outside one of the rooms, smoking. Kane pulled into the driveway and slid out of the car. He approached the man with a friendly wave and a smile. "Morning. Is Lucky around?"

"Nope, he has a steer-roping event about now." The cowboy dropped the stub of his cigarette and extinguished it with a twist of one well-worn boot. He tipped back his hat and his brown eyes narrowed. "You can't be a friend of his, Lucky don't like cops."

Kane chuckled. "Sometimes we do good deeds, like finding the owners of valuables. I'm pretty sure the ring handed in to the sheriff's department this morning belongs to him but he'll have to prove he was at the right place at the right time to claim it."

"He was out last night with Storm. They went to the Triple Z Bar, left 'bout six, came back sometime after ten." His mouth turned up into a cocky grin. "Tell Lucky Zeke expects a reward."

Not familiar with the place in question, Kane nodded. "Sure. I'll go and find him at the fairgrounds. Thank you for your time."

On the way back to his SUV, he called Rowley to ask about the Triple Z Bar. Raised in Black Rock Falls, the young deputy was a fountain of local information. "What else can you tell me about the place?"

*"It's off the main highway, past the campus, and open Monday through Saturday nights. It's a dive, serves beer and hard liquor, probably moonshine, but not everyone can pay the Cattleman's Hotel prices. Cowboys from the local ranches go there, and there are usually brawls. It's not a place I would go to pick up a woman. Let's say they are a little free with their favors, if you get my meaning."*

He rubbed his cheek. "How come nobody has mentioned this place before now?"

*"No one is going to put in a complaint, are they? Trust me, they don't want the law showing up there. If the mayor closes the Triple Z, there isn't another bar for miles. The owner of the Cattleman's Hotel runs the bar at the fairgrounds and the Lark's arena. He has a dress code, and smelly, hard-working guys straight off the ranch are not permitted."*

"How far is the Triple Z from the college campus?"

*"Three miles, I'd guess."*

"Which places Lucky Briggs and Storm Crawley in the area of Kate Bright's murder at the right time. Sheriff Alton saw them at Aunt Betty's Café on our way back from the murder scene." He sighed. "I'm going to speak to Briggs and Crawley now, tell the sheriff what I've discovered."

"*Okay.*"

Kane disconnected and climbed behind the wheel. As he drove toward his destination, his thoughts centered on the investigation. Following his profiling, the cowboys had moved down a few slots in his personal suspect list but the new information made things complicated. With little concrete evidence and suspects coming out of his ass, he had to narrow the field before the maniac struck again.

Although the cowboys appeared to stand out like sore thumbs, he doubted either of them had the brains to hack a computer, but both men moved around a lot and attracted young women. He could not discount that their meetings with both victims could have been verbal. After discovering Felicity and Kate loved the rodeo cowboys, it would not have taken too much persuasion to convince the girls to meet them at a secluded spot, but he doubted the men would be stupid enough to murder Joanne and leave her in a place they admitted to frequenting.

It would be conceivable to believe Kate had changed the time to meet Chad *because* she had made a date with Lucky Briggs. Jenna had mentioned Kate and Aimee had been star-struck by the two cowboys. If Wolfe had discovered one tiny shred of DNA, he would not be chasing his tail in endless circles.

At the fairgrounds, Kane maneuvered through the masses of people and checked the running sheet for the day's events. His suspects had events for most of the day, and from the announcement, Lucky Briggs had won the bull riding. He ambled toward the group of cowboys leaning on the fence waiting for the next event, and

Lucky Briggs climbed over the railing and landed two feet in front of him. Covered in sweat and dust and with a smile as big as Texas, he swaggered through the group of men. Kane moved to block his path. "Congratulations! May I have a word?"

"Most people want an autograph." Lucky pushed a hand through his sweat-soaked hair then replaced his black Stetson. "Mind if I get a drink? It's mighty dry work." He strolled inside a shed milling with men wearing numbers pinned to their shirts and took a bottle of water out of a cooler, popped the cap, and drank the contents. "What can I do for you?" He dropped the bottle into a trashcan, reached for another, and wiped a filthy, gloved hand over his mouth.

Kane pushed his hat up and leaned casually against the doorframe. "The last time we spoke to you, did you go back to the rock pool that afternoon?"

"Nope." Lucky wiped a rag over his sweaty face. "The local media was holding interviews all afternoon."

"I hear you went to the Triple Z Bar last night with Storm."

"So?" Lucky raised both black eyebrows. "No law in drinkin'. I'm over twenty-one."

"Did you come back to town via Stanton Road?"

"Ain't no other road back to town from the Triple Z, so I'd be lyin' if I denied it, wouldn't I?" Lucky's brow crinkled into a frown. "Now I have a question for you. Why?"

"There was an incident at the campus, and as you and Crawley were in the area, we are speaking to everyone." Kane straightened and took out his notebook and pen. "What time did you leave to go to the bar?"

"We left the motel just after six, I guess." Lucky scratched at a drip of sweat, leaving a wet line on his dusty cheek. "We got back to town around nine and had dinner at Aunt Betty's Café. I saw you come in and buy some takeout, it must have been closer to ten."

"Did you see anyone walking along Stanton Road or cars parked in the area on the way to the bar or on the way back?"

"Hell, man, do *you* notice cars or people when you're driving? Sexy chicks maybe but that's about all I see." Lucky snorted with mirth then held up one hand. "Hang on a minute. Yeah, I *do* remember seeing a chick, long legs, wearing tight jeans, cowboy boots, and a hoodie heading toward the college." He stared into the distance for some moments. "That's all I remember."

*He saw Kate.* "What time did you see the woman?"

"It was on the way to the Triple Z, close to six thirty, I guess."

Kane opened a clean page on his notebook and handed it to Lucky. "Write what you saw, the girl's description, and time, then sign it. If you do this for me now, I won't have to haul you into the office for a statement."

"Sure." Lucky took the pen, rested the book against the shed wall, and wrote the statement, signing it with a flourish. "Here you go. Anything else?"

Kane read the statement, signed as a witness, and pushed the notebook back inside his pocket. "Yeah, thanks, where can I find Crawley?"

"In the tack room, where you spoke to us before."

Kane nodded and headed across the crowded venue, weaving around people and avoiding the piles of horse and cattle dung. Fairgrounds had the same smell no matter what state or country: fried onions, horses, sweat, and cow shit. He wiped the sweat from his brow and strolled into the stables. As Lucky had predicted, Storm Crawley was in the tack room cleaning his saddle for the following day's events. He took the same line of questioning and he remembered seeing Kate as well.

"Do you remember the time?"

"Must have been around six thirty." Storm's lips thinned into a line. "She was on Lucky's side of the car. I didn't get a good look at her but I remember long legs and a hoodie. I didn't see her face at all." He rubbed his chin. "I did see a dark sedan heading off the road into the forest, some ways along Stanton Road. I thought it might be a couple looking for some privacy, if you know what I mean." He smirked.

*Holy shit!* "What time would this have been?"

"I'm not sure, but it was still there when we went by later. We only stayed at the Triple Z for a couple of hours. Lucky was hungry and we got to Aunt Betty's Café around nine." His mouth slashed into a white smile. "Saw you there too picking up some takeout for the sheriff."

"We all have to eat." Kane smiled and pulled out his notebook.

He asked Crawley to write a statement and then thanked him. Dodging kids with balloons on sticks or eating huge hotdogs dripping with ketchup, he headed for the car then reached for his cellphone and called Jenna. "I have a witness that puts Steve Rogers within walking distance of the college around six thirty and two eye-witnesses who saw Kate walking on Stanton Road at the same time."

*"With what we have, that's enough to arrest him on suspicion. I'll start the paperwork."*

# CHAPTER THIRTY-SIX

The man's mind was on the task of choosing his next girl. The thrill of killing Kate thrummed through him and the smell of her still lingered in his nose. He moved into the entrance to an alley and slid into the shadow of the bank then took out his cellphone. The images of his girls, all his girls, were a touch away, hidden in a special folder. He had to take a quick look and enjoy the surge of pleasure, seeing his work at its best.

The images of Kate lit up the screen and his heart pounded at the memory of a knife pressed in his palm. The fear in her eyes and the taste of her. He flicked through the images, and sweat trickled down his spine. Each time he looked at them, he wanted to add another to his collection. Breathing heavily, he relived every tiny detail.

So many girls, so much exquisite fun.

He lifted his head to gaze at a group of girls chatting close by and smiled. After the thrill of finding a girl in the forest and taking her, his skill had proven invincible. He would snatch a girl off the street soon and display her for all to see, then the media would not ignore his art. He bit back a groan, remembering the intense satisfaction of killing his forest gift. Oh, she had fought well but none had ever escaped his knife.

No one ever would.

His mind shifted to the sheriff. A pretty woman and worthy of his art but she would take the brunt of his anger. He would have her soon and enjoy every second. The way she strutted around as if she owned the town made him more determined to tame her. *They all beg in the end.* Her deputies were no match for his skill, and he would be able to deal with them one at a time in his own special way.

Reluctantly, he closed the file on his cellphone. He had plans to make. He ran the faces of his chosen girls through his mind and trembled with anticipation. *Who will be next?*

# CHAPTER THIRTY-SEVEN

With the statements from Aimee Fox and Kate Bright plus Steve Rogers' account placing him in Stanton Forest around the time of Felicity Parker's murder added to the signed accounts from Lucky Briggs and Storm Crawley, Jenna's application for an arrest warrant went through in minutes. She arrived back at the sheriff's department to find Kane waiting in anticipation. Waving the document, she smiled at him. "Good work. I think we have our killer."

"Just in time too, he was in town chatting to Aimee Fox and one of her friends, Julia Smith, earlier. I wouldn't mind betting he is still in town. Wolfe is going through the surveillance footage for the last hour or so. I know he parked his car in the library parking lot, so he would have to return there eventually." Kane's mouth turned down and he cracked his knuckles. "I can't wait to arrest him."

"I *know* where he was about five minutes ago." Wolfe strolled out of the back room. "He was buying a newspaper from the stand near the church."

"It sounds like he is searching for information." Kane's blue gaze rested on her face. "That's typical behavior for an exhibitionist psychopathic killer, he wants to read about the murder in the newspapers so he can relive the thrill. Not seeing his kills on the news must be driving him crazy."

"Okay, I'll handle the arrest with Kane." Jenna checked her weapon and tucked a couple more zip cuffs into her pocket. "Let's go." She headed out the door and made for her SUV with the department's insignia on the doors.

She drove the vehicle down the main street, noting the way Kane drummed his long fingers on the dashboard in an agitated fashion. She flicked him a glance. "We'll find him, he has no idea we're coming for him."

She headed straight for the church, and seeing Steve Rogers strolling toward the computer store, she pulled the vehicle into a bus stop and leaped from the car. Before she had taken two steps, Kane had reached Rogers, spun him around, shoved him face first into the brick wall, and cuffed him. She gaped in surprise, then seeing the crowd gathering, she stepped forward. "Steve Rogers, I am arresting you on suspicion of murder." She read him his Miranda rights then nodded at Kane. "Put him in the car."

"Clear the way. There is nothing to see here." Kane's large frame cut a gap through the spectators on the way to her vehicle.

Jenna followed close behind and waited for Kane to secure their prisoner in her SUV. To her surprise, Rogers had not resisted arrest or uttered a word apart from agreeing; he understood his rights. She slid behind the wheel and headed back to the office. The moment she stepped inside, Rogers gave her a cold look.

"I want you to contact my lawyer. His number is in my wallet."

She nodded. "Very well, and what about your wife?"

"She left me, and don't go looking for her, I have no inclination to speak to her." Rogers gave her a belligerent glare. "I know you have been talking to her behind my back, I heard the messages you left."

*That's why she didn't return my call.* "As you wish." She glanced at Kane, who had a firm grip on Rogers' arm as he handed him over to Deputy Walters at the counter. When he returned, she straightened. "Take Wolfe with you, book him, and lock him up."

She gave Kane a long stare. "Don't give him any reason to make a complaint—understand?"

"Yes, ma'am."

She had not missed Kane's grim expression and the flash of anger in his eyes or the way his knuckles had whitened around Rogers' arm. When Wolfe strolled out the back room, she touched his arm. "I know you both want to pulverize him but he is innocent until proven guilty and right now all we have is circumstantial evidence. I have a warrant to seize his car and I'll arrange a tow truck to collect it now. Where is the best place for you to do a search?"

"We need a clean room but I guess the garage at the funeral home will have to do. I can set it up with plastic sheets. We don't want to give the defense any reason to suspect we tampered with evidence." Wolfe's blond brows narrowed. "Make sure no one opens the car or touches anything without suiting up first. Maybe I should go and supervise?"

"Sure, but get Rogers processed first. The car can wait for an hour or so; it's not going anywhere and I have to call his lawyer."

Anxiously, she stared after Kane, hoping he would keep his cool. The number for Steve Rogers' lawyer was in her daybook from the last time Kane had questioned him. She went into her office and made the call. After disconnecting, she contacted the tow truck company and asked them to wait for Wolfe in the library parking lot. She heard a tap on the door and Rowley strolled into the room.

"I guess you won't need me to watch Mr. Rogers' house tonight?"

"Ah, but I *will* need you to do a midnight until seven shift overnight. I'll ask Walters to cover the early shift. I'll need someone here to keep an eye on our prisoner." She smiled at him. "You and Walters won't have to pull a shift over the weekend; the Blackwater deputies will be on duty until Sunday. We can all go to the dance." She smiled at him. "You and Walters can take the afternoon. I'm guessing Mr. Rogers' lawyer will try to get bail, which will be denied and he'll be taken to the jail and held until the hearing."

She heard Kane's voice in the hallway and glanced at the door. He strolled in and his dark eyebrows met in a frown.

"Rogers' lawyer will be out for blood. We'll need to have every shred of evidence with the prosecutor or he'll walk out on bail. Wolfe has left to supervise the pickup and search of his vehicle. We have probable cause to search his house as well and need to ASAP. I have his house key."

Jenna took a sheet of paper from a folder on her desk. "I have everything ready but I'll need to be here when Rogers' lawyer arrives." She handed him the search warrants. "Take Rowley and head over to the funeral home to search the car with Wolfe, then go to Rogers' house. It will be quicker with three of you working the scenes."

"Yes, ma'am." He raised both eyebrows. "Are you sure you won't need me here?"

She waved him away. "Yes, now go, then once you have written your report, send Rowley home, he is covering the graveyard shift."

"I would advise you to ask the lawyer to interview Rogers in the cell." Kane flicked his blue gaze over her. "Don't give him an inch. He may be acting passive now, but don't trust him."

"I'm sure I know how to handle a dangerous prisoner. Get out of here, Kane." She followed the deputies out of the room and headed for the coffee machine. *There's that overprotective streak again.*

After collecting her coffee and a muffin then informing Walters of the change of shift, she had made it back to her office when Samuel Jenkins, Rogers' lawyer, stormed into the department and appeared at her door doing a great impression of a raging bull. She gave him her sweetest smile. "Good morning." She glanced at her watch. "You made it here in record time. Not speeding, were you?"

"Exactly what evidence do you have against my client to arrest him on suspicion of murder? Who is he supposed to have murdered?"

Jenna inhaled her coffee then took a sip. She needed to stall for time. What she had was circumstantial, but with luck, her deputies would find something else to use against Steve Rogers. "Close the door and take a seat." She placed her mug on the table and leaned back in her chair. "I have copies of the witnesses' statements but you'll need the background information."

"Witnesses to what?" Jenkins gave her a look to freeze hell, and placing his briefcase on the floor, he sat in the chair before her desk. "I am very close to making a complaint about harassment, but I doubt you would take much notice so I intend to take my complaint straight to the mayor."

"I see." Jenna met his gaze and collected the copies of the statements from the folder on her desk. "Three girls have been brutally murdered: Felicity Parker, Joanne Blunt, and Kate Smith. These witnesses—and I might add here that Kate Smith was a witness and I have her signed statement, which as she is also a victim is suspicious in itself." She took a breath. "These witnesses can place Mr. Rogers at or close to the scene at the time of death. He knows two of the murdered girls and, as we believe the killer hacked their computers to discover their whereabouts, is an expert in the field."

Jenkins' mouth dropped open but he remained silent.

"At the moment, we are conducting searches of his car and house, and any computers he has in his possession will be examined for evidence." She reached for her coffee and eyed him over the rim of the mug. "I read your client his rights and he has remained silent. If you would like to speak to him, I will take you to him now."

Jenkins made a great show of reading the documents, punctuated by huffs and puffs of annoyance. "You have nothing. This is all supposition. I will speak to my client—alone, as is his right."

Jenna pushed to her feet, eyeing the muffin on her plate with a sense of loss. "I'll take you to him now but we need to interview him as well." She called to Walters to follow and left him on guard outside the cells.

Delivering Jenkins to his client, she offered him a smile. "You should be aware I am issuing a statement to the press this morning, and with luck we'll have more witnesses coming forward. I'll send the evidence we discover to the prosecutor; I'm sure under full disclosure he will forward the details to your office in due course." She turned and headed back to her muffin. *I sure hope my deputies find something.*

# CHAPTER THIRTY-EIGHT

After dressing in protective coveralls, booties, and mask, Kane pulled on a pair of latex gloves then popped the trunk of Steve Rogers' dark blue sedan. A waft of sewerage hit him in the face and he whistled. "Ah, Wolfe, I think we have something here." He waved Rowley over to take photographs. The camera clicked twenty or more shots and he waved to get his attention. "That's good enough."

He stood to one side to allow Wolfe, dressed in blue coveralls with only his eyes visible, to peer into the recess. "Muddy boots and a shovel. What do you think he was doing in the forest?"

"Your guess is as good as mine, but from the smell and what looks like blood and definitely hair, he wasn't up to anything good." Wolfe's pale eyes peered at him over the top of his mask. "I've collected an assortment of hair and fibers from the interior and swabbed any suspicious areas. If you could collect fingerprints, I'll work here. Rowley is in charge of the samples—it's best we have one man doing that job so we don't step on each other's toes." He removed the boots from the trunk and dropped them into an evidence bag held open by Rowley. "Cover both ends of the shovel then roll the entire thing in plastic."

"Yes, sir." Rowley juggled the huge evidence bag as if it had a severed head inside, gave a snort of laughter, then complied.

Kane nodded. "Right, I'll leave the logging of evidence to him. I'm interested to see what shows up under luminol."

"Yeah, me too."

After dusting the car and running the scanner over the prints, he returned to watch Wolfe. The meticulous way he collected evidence impressed him. The man was so methodical and nothing escaped his attention. One hour later, satisfied he had everything he needed, Wolfe expertly sprayed the trunk with luminol. Kane extinguished the lights and gaped at the bloodstains showing under the UV black flashlight.

"I know it's blood but I have yet to determine if it's human blood. He could have killed a dog and buried it in the forest. If it is human, I'll run a DNA test to see if it matches any of our victims." Wolfe's blond eyebrow rose. "If it doesn't fit the genetic profile of any of the victims here or interstate, and it is human blood, then we'll have another mystery on our hands." His gaze moved to Kane. "We should search the house first and grab his laptop. If this blood is human, we'll have to backtrack from where you saw his car parked in case he buried a body close by. It won't be easy to do a grid search of the forest on our own. We'll need cadaver dogs. If the test is positive, I'll make a few calls when we get back to the office and see if we can get a team down here first thing in the morning."

Mind reeling with the implications of Wolfe's statement, Kane frowned. "I'm confused. If Rogers is our killer, burying a body is a complete turnaround in behavior. I have yet to hear of a psychopath who enjoys exhibiting his kills one day then burying them another. I've read about killers burying their victims and digging them up later but not both fetishes at the same time." Every hair on his body stood on end at the idea of two killers in town. "What if Rogers isn't our man?"

"Don't get sidetracked. There is no evidence of another murder and we have no one else reported missing in the area." Wolfe's stern gaze got his attention. "We don't know if he kidnapped Felicity. We are assuming he killed her in the river. What if he disabled her and transported her to the river in the trunk of his car? When you caught him beside the forest the other night, he could have been burying his trophies. Felicity's clothing or the knife he used to kill Joanne."

Wolfe made a lot of sense and Kane's hackles went down. "How long before you know if the blood is human?"

"I'll check it now. I can do a precipitin test. It distinguishes between the blood of humans and animals. I have a kit in the lab." Wolfe let out a long, tired sigh. "It will take time to run the DNA tests. I have purchased the latest equipment but we're looking at three days at least before I'll get a result."

Kane followed Wolfe from the garage and into a small laboratory Wolfe shared with the previous M.E. The room was cramped yet sterile and he wondered how Wolfe managed to juggle so many jobs at once. He waited for the result, and when Wolfe held up the test tube and his ice-gray eyes met his over the mask, his stomach dropped to his boots. "It's positive, right?"

"Yeah, it's human blood, but until the DNA results come back or we find concrete evidence in his home or on his hard drive, we can't assume he killed the girls—or in fact anyone. The blood could be his, for all we know." Wolfe's blond brows met in a frown. "In forensics it's baby steps, not rushing to conclusions. What comes out of my lab, I'll need to verify with proof in court. I know it's frustrating but as you only have circumstantial evidence, the blood work has to be conclusive."

Kane stripped off his gloves, blue coveralls, and booties. "You get the tests started and we'll search Rogers' home. If I find anything of interest I'll call you, and if not I'll bring any computers I find back to the office."

"Okay." Wolfe's pale gaze remained on his face. "Take your time. If this is our man, we need to do everything by the book."

He gave him a wave and headed for the door with Rowley on his heels. "By the book it is."


The drive to Steve Rogers' house took longer than usual. Traveling through town with the hustle and bustle of the rodeo crowd was bad enough but jaywalkers streamed across the road dodging vehicles as if they had a date with the Grim Reaper. They took no notice of the blue flashing lights on Kane's SUV, and waved or grinned at him as if he had turned them on to join in the celebration. "Is it like this every year?"

"Every *year*?" Rowley flashed him a cheeky grin. "We'll have a least another four events at the fairgrounds this summer. Right now, it's tame; wait until later, they go a bit crazy after the dance and once they get the drink into them. The park becomes party central and Aunt Betty's Café stays open twenty-four hours to keep the food coming."

Kane hit the siren a couple of times to move a bunch of teenagers from blocking the road, and rather than quiver with fright at his stare of death, they made a cacophony of grunts. He shook his head, biting back the laughter threatening to break his austere façade. "The Blackwater deputies are going to have their work cut out for them. I might see if I can borrow a few extra men from Durum County. With all of us covering the murder cases, we don't have time for this shit."

"Sometimes when it's tough with murders and the like, I look forward to normal times like these." Rowley's mouth turned down at the corners. "How do you handle the nightmares?"

Kane fell back on his cover story; only Jenna and Wolfe knew the truth about his past. "I don't have nightmares. At first, yeah, it was difficult working homicide and seeing up close what people are capable of doing. The kids' murders got to me but when I shot my first killer, I sure as hell didn't lose any sleep over it."

He turned out of town and doused the lights as they hit Stanton Road ten minutes later. He turned into Rogers' driveway and parked. "Full gear, same as before, we don't want to contaminate a possible crime scene." He slid from the car and opened the back door to pull out his bag. "Here, help yourself."

Using Rogers' keys, they entered the premises, and just in case Mrs. Rogers was at home and thought blue-suited aliens had invaded her house, he pushed the door open slowly. "Sheriff's department. Are you there, Mrs. Rogers?"

At no response, he moved inside the family room, placed his bag on the floor, and glanced around. The room smelled like cleaning products and mildew. "The Chinese rug is missing. I remember seeing it when I came to interview him. It was bright red and blue, very distinctive." He strolled across the room and flung open the drapes. "Turn on the lights, start this end of the room, and check every surface for blood spatter or hair. I'll take a quick look through the house. If you see anything, mark it and photograph it. I'll take samples when I return."

His gut gave a small twist; something did not ring true with the home. When he had looked inside the last time, the home was as neat as a pin; now the kitchen had dirty plates stacked on the counter but the sink was empty. *Why?*

Most people would pile plates in the sink if they did not have a dishwasher, and he could not see any appliances other than a stove and refrigerator. From the state of the house, Mrs. Rogers had not returned to collect her belongings. Takeout cartons littered the trashcan overflowing onto the floor, and the smell of spoiled food was disgusting. He peered down the sink, surprised to find the smell of cleaning products missing. Returning to the family room, he collected a specimen jar from his bag of tricks and headed back to the kitchen. After removing the p-trap under the sink, he carefully tipped the contents into the specimen jar then bagged the pipe. He might find trace evidence if Rogers had washed blood from his hands in the sink, and by the color of the water in the trap, he had hit pay dirt.

# CHAPTER THIRTY-NINE

Kane took the samples back to the family room and, leaning against a dresser, labeled each one then stashed them in a main evidence bag. He turned to Deputy Rowley. "I'm labeling these specimens 'Rogers House,' then the room and numbering each one."

"Sure thing."

Kane watched as Rowley collected a couple of what looked like fingernails and bagged them. "When you spoke to Mrs. Rogers at her sister's house, did she say when she would be returning home?"

"When hell freezes over, I believe."

Kane glanced around. "No wonder the place is such a mess."

Taking his time, he moved through the house, doing a preliminary search. Most of the rooms appeared undisturbed but the main bedroom had clothes on the floor, and on the unmade bed sat a laptop. He bagged the device then did a quick search of the area. Taking photographs of each section, he opened the cupboard doors and peered inside. The couple had a his-and-hers built-in wardrobe, and from the amount of clothes hanging on Mrs. Rogers' side, she had not taken much with her. The racks appeared full and the neatly lined-up rows of shoes undisturbed. He had known frightened women to walk out with just the clothes on their back, but she had not mentioned her husband had abused her. *Something isn't right here.*

He turned a full circle, examining the room in small sections, then noticed the purse tucked down beside the bed. His wife, Annie, had kept her purse next to the bed and her cellphone on the bedside table;

maybe all women did the same—except Jenna, she kept a loaded Glock 22 beside her bed. He smiled at the conflicting memories and bent to retrieve the purse. Inside he found the normal array of female necessities but goosebumps prickled his flesh at the sight of a wallet and credit cards.

He reached for his cellphone and dialed Mrs. Rogers' number. A ringtone blasted, sending his heart racing. He slid open the top drawer of the nightstand and the bright light from the screen illuminated the contents. The cellphone sat beside a carved wooden box containing an assortment of gold jewelry.

He disconnected and stared at the cellphone in disbelief. Sure, a woman might leave in a hurry during an argument but not without her purse, jewelry, and cellphone. Mrs. Rogers had been at her sister's when Rowley had taken her statement. She had made a point of saying she would be staying with her sister, and his gut screamed that something did not gel. A pang of worry curled in his gut as he stared at the cellphone sitting in the drawer. He called Jenna and waited for her to pick up. "I've found Mrs. Rogers' cellphone here at Rogers' house and her purse but before we jump to conclusions we'll need to check if she is still staying with her sister."

*"I'll ask Maggie to give her a call. Perhaps she wanted to break all contact with her husband?"*

Frowning at the open purse, he sighed. "I hope so but I don't know many women who would leave home without their purse, credit cards, and cellphone. The entire situation isn't sitting right with me. I'll keep looking around and see what I can find."

*"Bag and tag and I'll try to find her. You might want to check her calls and see who she contacted. If I find her in the meantime, I'll get back to you."*

"Roger that." He hung up, removed the cellphone from the evidence bag, and finding it unlocked, scrolled through the list of recent calls and texts.

He found the usual banter between two sisters and a few references to her husband being a pig, meeting other women, and spending too much time in town with his students. He recognized the number of her last call and, replacing the cellphone in the evidence bag, pulled out his own device and scrolled down his contacts. He blinked in confusion. The last person she called was Jake Rowley.

*What the hell is going on here?* He jogged down the stairs and came close to colliding with Rowley as he came through the family room door. "Did you receive a call from Mrs. Rogers after you'd interviewed her?"

"Yeah." Rowley gave him a bemused stare and pulled out his cellphone. "I must have been calling someone because she left a message. When I returned the call, she didn't pick up." He hit a button and replayed the message.

*"Deputy Rowley, this is Millicent Rogers. You said to contact you if I remembered anything and I have. I will call you back in the morning."*

"With all that has been going on, I completely forgot to mention the call to you." Rowley looked chagrined.

"I understand, it has been hectic and it sure doesn't sound like she was in trouble or worried about her husband. If the sheriff locates her, we'll follow up on what she remembered." Kane headed upstairs to search the bathroom.

The dirty laundry hamper overflowed onto a pile of wet stinking towels on the floor. Photographing everything as he moved through the area, he noticed the neatly lined-up beauty products on the shelves. The mess was certainly not usual for Mrs. Rogers and again, women who come back to pack take everything; hell, he had a good idea how much money women spent on face cream alone. Glad of the face mask, he bagged all the dirty clothes and pushed the towels into a separate bag. Concern for Mrs. Rogers' welfare became a priority. He collected the hairbrush and toothbrushes in case Wolfe could find a DNA sample. *Something stinks and it isn't the dirty laundry.*

Mind reeling with confusion, Kane went downstairs and back into the kitchen. He noticed a few dark spots on the ceiling and took samples. The idea Rogers had murdered his wife flashed in his mind like a neon sign but the practical side of his brain insisted a psychopathic killer capable of dissecting three young women and putting them on display would be unlikely at best to risk murdering his wife. Add the fact he had searched every damn inch of the place and so far had found nothing in relation to the three victims. Psychopathic murderers keep trophies, and if Rogers had hidden them somewhere, they would be easily accessible. The need to touch and relive the thrill was a common trait. He met Rowley in the hallway. "I've found nothing relating to the victims. You?"

"Nope, mostly dust and a few smears of something on the hall floor. I've marked it and taken samples." Rowley's dark eyes moved toward the hallway. "If it is blood, then it's feasible something or someone was wrapped in the Chinese rug and dragged out the back door. I found a couple of dark spots in the laundry; the back door leads to the garage."

A tingle of worry crawled up Kane's spine. "Wolfe gave me a test kit. If it's blood, we need to call Wolfe." He strolled into the family room and retrieved the kit from his bag.

The test was simple enough: drop a swab into a small test tube and shake. He flicked a gaze at Rowley, who watched him with interest. "Yeah, it's blood. I'll call Wolfe then I guess I'll have to check the cellar."

"You must hate checking cellars?"

After finding two bodies and Jenna fighting for her life in various cellars six months previously, he understood Rowley's worries. "Yeah, I do. Let's hope this one's empty."

He contacted Wolfe and gave him the rundown on the situation and Wolfe had offered to take over. He sighed with relief—once he cleared the cellar, he could get back to the office and go over the facts and timeline with Jenna. As he had not heard back from her on Mrs. Rogers' whereabouts, the possibility something had happened to her shouted loudly in his head.

After a quick search, he found the cellar door in the laundry room and, ignoring the morbid anticipation rushing into his mind, headed down the steps. The overhead lights flooded the room but he found nothing but a boiler and a few storage boxes. With Rowley working beside him, they went through each carton and found Christmas decorations and old clothes. The light coating of dust on the floor and his and Rowley's footprints gave him the impression no one had been down there for some time.

"Okay, this is a dead end. Did you check every nook and cranny, any place someone might hide something?"

"Yeah, when you went upstairs I checked the kitchen cupboards, opened all the containers, and found nothing." Rowley's Adam's apple moved up and down. "I did find porn but nothing illegal. No young girls."

"Okay." Kane collected all the evidence bags, placed them inside one large bag, sealed it, then headed toward the front door. "I need some air."

On the porch, he pulled down his mask and frowned at Rowley. "The sort of women who arouse a killer doesn't mean it's the kind he prefers to murder. Some types trigger a response—say, for instance, a blonde skinny girl at school made him look stupid in front of his friends then the killer would more likely marry a curvaceous brunette and murder blonde skinny girls. To a psychopath, rape and murder are punishment. Child abuse can trigger a psychopathic response, which remains semi-dormant until something happens, and as kids, they usually take it out on their pets. The cat scratched him, so he killed it because he has power over the cat, the power he didn't have as a kid."

"I see, so Rogers could still be our man?"

Kane's attention moved to the arrival of Wolfe's SUV. "Yeah, we just need to build a case, and so far, apart from being in the same location at the time of two of the murders, we have zip." Wondering why Jenna had not contacted him about Mrs. Rogers, he rubbed his chin. "I just hope he didn't murder his wife."

# CHAPTER FORTY

Jenna picked up her cellphone to call Kane then heard his voice in the hallway outside her office. He loomed at the open door, his Stetson low over his brow, elbows out like a huge bat, and an expression of complete exhaustion on his handsome face. She looked at him for some moments then realized the pink cat's whisker-like markings on his face came from wearing a paper face mask for some hours. "You look exhausted, sit down and take the weight off."

"Being a bit OCD about cleanliness—having to sift through the filth at the Rogers' house was disgusting, especially when I found nothing to tie him to the murders." Kane placed a holder with four cups of coffee on her desk and two takeout cartons. "I have food and coffee. I left Rowley at Aunt Betty's to have something to eat. He plans on devouring the entire menu then he is going home before he takes the graveyard shift to watch our prisoner."

"He'll be fine." She smiled at him and peered into a carton. "Yum. Bagels and cream cheese. I've been stuck in the control room watching Emily, just in case something happened to her while Wolfe was out. She is currently at Aimee Fox's house and Wolfe is dropping by to pick her up on his way here. He'll find out if she has any information then drop her home."

"I'm glad she's okay. I can't help noticing Wolfe's protectiveness. I take it he isn't convinced Rogers is our man."

A sliver of worry crawled in goosebumps up her arms. "What do *you* think?"

"I'd like to go over the timelines again with you because we have nothing to tie Rogers to the murders apart from circumstantial evidence." Kane removed his hat and dropped it on the chair beside him then ruffled his tangled mass of black hair. "I'm not convinced he is our man but my gut tells me he is hiding something."

She leaned back in her chair, fingers wrapped around her coffee, and sighed. "Apparently, he will talk to us later this afternoon. His lawyer is trying to get him released but so far our arrest warrant is holding." Sighing, she sipped her beverage. "The story of the murders will hit the news this evening. All I said in the statement was we found the bodies. I asked for anyone in the locations who had seen the girls or noticed any person or car in the area at the time to contact our office. No other details."

"Let's hope we don't get a heap of crazies calling." Kane's brow furrowed. "Any luck finding Mrs. Rogers?"

Pulling the wrapping from a bagel, she shook her head. "No, her sister said she went home to get her things and hasn't heard from her since. This behavior is apparently quite normal. Mrs. Rogers only calls her sister when she wants something or has an argument with her husband. She said her sister often takes off for days alone."

"I hope so." Kane's blue eyes met hers over the rim of his takeout coffee cup. "I have the awful feeling she's dead. Most people won't leave home without their cards and wallet and I doubt if I could find anyone who willingly leaves without their cellphone." Kane raised one black eyebrow. "Even you."

She frowned. "For me it's weapons then cellphone, and I usually stuff some cash into my pocket." She sipped the coffee, easing the soreness in her throat. "But I admit I *do* keep essentials here in my office."

"Exactly." Kane flashed her a white grin. "So, unless Mrs. Rogers has a hideout somewhere with a stash of cash and clothes, I think we should be concerned about her safety. Especially as we found evidence of blood on the hall floor and the Chinese rug is missing."

"She is not at her sister's and I've contacted all the friends on the list she gave me. No one has seen her." She rubbed her temples in slow circles. "If you add the muddy boots and shovel… It's not looking good, is it?"

"Nope." Kane's blue gaze slid over her face. "Wolfe is bringing in cadaver dogs. Stanton Forest covers miles in all directions. We'll need to set up a search party and spread out in sections from where Rogers parked his car." He wiped his mouth with a paper towel. "The problem I have is if he isn't our killer, we are counting down the hours for the next victim to turn up." He sighed. "If he has escalated, we would expect him to hit over the weekend."

A cold chill shivered down Jenna's spine. "My guess would be while everyone is occupied at the dance at the showground on Friday night."

"That was my thought as well."

Trying to push past the horror of finding another mutilated victim, Jenna stood and went to the whiteboard. "Okay, while we're waiting for Wolfe to finish his tests and for the K-9 team to arrive, the best course of action would be to remove Rogers from the suspect list then run through the timeline of each victim and see if any of our suspects match the murders." She glanced at him. "As we have absolutely zero suspects or information concerning Joanne Blunt, I'm treating her death as a random thrill-kill by the same killer. We have nothing to tie her in with the other victims and we can discount a copycat."

Taking the black pen, she made two separate sections at the end of the whiteboard and titled them, "Felicity, Kate other suspect options."

**Felicity.**

*Movements prior to death:*
*Last seen alive: Monday morning approximately seven fifty*

*By whom:*

*A.  Parents*

*B.  Mrs. Rogers at approximately eight*

*What was she doing?*

*A.  Leaving home to visit Aimee Fox*

*B.  Mrs. Rogers witnessed her walking toward Stanton Forest –
opposite direction to Fox home*

*Location: Stanton Road*

*What was she wearing? Blue shirt with butterfly, blue skirt, pink
cowboy boots, earbuds.*

*Boyfriend: Derick Smith*

*Friends: Aimee Fox, Kate Bright, Chad Johnson, Lucas Summerville*

*Recent social interactions: Online gamer, Aunt Betty's Café, computer
store*

*Suspects:*

*A.  Lionel Provine: interacted with Felicity and unable to verify
whereabouts*

*B.  Derick Smith: Felicity's boyfriend, cannot account for time missing
during a car delivery*

*C, D. Lucky Briggs and Storm Crawley: seen in forest at time of death*

**Kate:**

*Movements prior to death:*

*Last seen at home: Wednesday evening at approximately six*

*By whom: Parents*

*What was she doing? In her bedroom playing online games*

*Last seen alive: six fifteen by Lucky Briggs and Storm Crawley*

*What was she doing? Walking toward college*

*Location: Stanton Road.*

*What was she wearing? White top, blue denim jeans, cowboy boots,
dark blue hoodie, earbuds.*

*Boyfriend: Chad Johnson*

*Friends: Aimee Fox, Lucas Summerville.*

*Recent social interactions: Online gamer, Aunt Betty's Café, computer store*

*With: Lionel Provine and Aimee Fox, Lucas Summerville and Chad Johnson in computer store*

*Suspects:*

A. *Lionel Provine: unable to account for whereabouts*

B. *Lucky Briggs and Storm Crawley: Seen in town at Aunt Betty's Café approximately nine on Wednesday night*

"What about Derick Smith?" Kane stretched out his long legs. "We haven't really considered him, have we?"

Jenna chewed on the end of the pen. "Okay, I'll add him with a question mark until you can speak to him again." She sighed. "Take out Rogers, and all the others look pretty weak."

"Nah." Kane's long fingers closed around his second cup of coffee. "I think we need to take a closer look at Lionel Provine. You have him as a key player in both cases. Both victims played online games and interacted on a social level with Lionel Provine. He lives alone and can't prove his whereabouts during either murder."

"Yes, I agree." Jenna made some notes on the whiteboard. "The kids regard him as a gift horse. He has gotten close to them by giving them gift cards or whatever they use to obtain bonuses in their games. He could be skulking online and pretending he is a kid."

"That's a possibility. Those games rooms are open to everyone who purchases the game." Kane peered at her with a worried gaze. "Pedophiles use them all the time to get close to kids. The fact they are able to swap bonus cards should be a red flag to any parent. Wolfe has been so busy with the forensic investigations he hasn't had time to look at the victims' laptops, and their cellphones are missing. He did a trace and couldn't find any of them, so I would say they've been destroyed."

"That fact alone makes me wonder if the killer has left a trail to him on their cellphones. Maybe not Joanne but the other victims." Jenna went back to her seat. "He must be close to the local girls; this is why Rogers fits the profile as well. Computer-savvy, knows the girls, hangs around the computer store with Provine, was in the area *both* times the murders were committed. You said they must have known their killer to be lured to their deaths, or someone had up-close and personal information about their whereabouts." She picked up her second coffee and sipped. "Rogers could be in the damn games room acting as if he is one of the kids."

"So what is your next move?"

Jenna tapped her fingernails on the desk and considered his question. "I'll wait here for Wolfe to return. I can't leave at the moment. I sent Walters home as he is doing the six until midnight shift." She rubbed her brow. "Go and lean on Lionel Provine and drop over to Miller's Garage and have a chat with Derick Smith about where he was last night. I'll call you if Wolfe has come up with any startling new evidence."

"Sure." Kane stood and towered over her. "What time is the lawyer due to arrive? I would like to be present for the interview if that's possible, ma'am."

"Three, so you have an hour." Jenna looked up at him, way up, and smiled. "Would *you* like to interview Rogers?" She noticed his eyes flicker as if in surprise. "You are my expert of psychopathic behavior and if he is not the killer of our victims, we need to know. Although, dragging him across the table and beating a confession out of him is out of the question as he'll have his lawyer in the room." She bit back a snort of laughter.

When Kane's dark gaze narrowed, she caught a flicker of the man who killed for his country without one shred of remorse.

"Yeah, I'll be happy to interview him." Kane inclined his head and examined her face. "If you order me to do anything else, it will have to be after the lawyer has left." He turned to leave.

Appalled he had taken her joke seriously, she gaped at him. "Kane, I—"

His large frame pivoted in the doorway and he grinned at her. "Gotcha."

# CHAPTER FORTY-ONE

As Kane walked through the jostling crowd toward Miller's Garage, he noticed Emily Wolfe strolling beside Aimee Fox ahead of him, the pair stopping occasionally to check out the rows of stalls cluttering the sidewalk. After Jenna had informed him both girls should be spending the afternoon at the Fox residence, he pulled out his cellphone and called Wolfe. "Hey, I'm not sticking my nose in your business, man, but I'm heading toward Miller's Garage and Emily is ten feet in front of me. Jenna mentioned she was at the Foxes' house this afternoon."

*"Thanks, I'll give her a call. Keep your eye on her for a few minutes—for her to break one of my rules, she must be onto something. I'm leaving the lab now, ETA ten minutes."*

"Roger that." Kane disconnected and ambled along the sidewalk as if he had all the time in the world.

He stared into storefronts, keeping his attention locked on the girls. Aimee, it seemed, had a lot more friends than they had anticipated. The girls wore serious expressions as they stopped to speak to a few different teenagers, but when they strolled into Miller's Garage, he noticed they went straight into the workshop. *Stupid! Of course, they know Derick Smith.* He had failed to add him to their list of friends.

He purchased a bag of cookies from a stall then spent so long gazing into the window of the bakery that the proprietor came out to speak to him. Embarrassed by the huge box of donuts pushed into his hand, he came close to missing the girls heading out of the garage. He dropped the carton into the plastic sack with the cookies and slipped it over one arm. Following a discreet distance away, he made a mental note of the girls' interactions. They checked all the stalls, bought cookies, then met Lucas Summerville outside the computer store.

Kane's cellphone vibrated in his pocket and he found a fuming Shane Wolfe barking into his ear.

"Yeah, hold on, what's wrong?"

*"Emily isn't taking my call and I'm stuck in traffic."*

"I'm eyeballing her now. She is with Aimee and Lucas Summerville outside the computer store. They are deep in conversation." Kane cleared his throat. "I'm heading over there; whatever he is saying to them is upsetting Aimee but Emily is taking it in her stride."

*"My daughter is tough, probably too tough for her own good. She would probably slip into your old occupation without blinking an eye. She thinks outside the box."*

"I'll hang with the kids and wait for you."

*"Do me a favor. Tell her you need her back at the station. She won't appreciate me hauling her ass out of there."*

Kane bit back a laugh. As tough as Wolfe was, his daughter had him tied around her little finger. "Roger that." He disconnected and crossed the road.

As he approached the group, he could hear Lucas telling the girls to be careful of strangers if they planned to go to the rodeo dance. Walking up behind him, he slapped him on the shoulder. "Afternoon."

"What's going on, Deputy Kane?" Lucas's mouth turned down. "It's all over town you arrested Steve Rogers this morning and searched his house. Is he involved in the deaths of our friends?"

Kane rolled his shoulders and looked down at him. "I'm afraid I can't discuss ongoing investigations with members of the public."

He sighed. "Now if you'll excuse me, I need to speak to Emily. She is needed back at the sheriff's office." He walked out of earshot and she followed him. "What is going on? Your father is frantic."

"Not now, I think I'm onto something. One thing for sure, the teacher didn't do it."

"How could you possibly know that? He is our prime suspect."

"Because, *I know.*" She crooked one dainty finger and beckoned him to bend down, then lowered her voice to a whisper. "Dad told me the victims were raped, and I overheard Mrs. Fox speaking on the phone about Mrs. Rogers. She was saying she didn't know why Mrs. Rogers believed her husband was seeing other women because he couldn't get it up and hadn't been able to for five years. He'd seen a specialist and tried everything. How could he have raped those girls if he was impotent?"

Swallowing the lump in his throat from Emily's candidness, he rubbed his chin. "So, I'm guessing you have a suspect of your own?"

Emily gave him an ice-gray stare. "Aimee has been speaking about their online friends, and Lionel Provine is closer to the group than you realize. Apparently, he asks some of the girls to go upstairs to his room to show them 'stuff.'" She wiggled her blonde eyebrows at him as if to exaggerate the word. "I'm in the inner sanctum now. Give me ten minutes and I'll see what he is doing. Tell Dad if Lionel invites me upstairs, I'll hit my security tag so he can listen in."

Astounded, Kane shook his head. "No way, he'll go ballistic if you act as bait. It's a stupid idea. It takes seconds to kill and no one would get to you in time."

"Oh, *doh*, I'm *not* stupid. I have a can of mace in my pocket and I'll use it if I have to." Emily's gaze bore into him. "Not even a mass murderer would risk killing me with twenty kids in his shop, and Aimee will be there too. I'm the best bet to find out if he is the killer. I'm doing it and that's final."

Hackles rising, Kane glared down at her. "Not one hope in hell. You haven't seen what this monster can do."

When she nodded slowly and met his gaze, his stomach did flip-flops. He shook his head in denial. "Nah, I don't believe Wolfe would show you his files. It would be unprofessional."

"He didn't *show* me anything. I examined the file this morning at the sheriff's office. You really need better security on your filing system." She tossed her fair head and her hair fell straight down her back like a silk scarf. "I looked because I've been studying forensic science for two years; not officially, but I have completed two online courses." She glanced over one shoulder at her friends. "I have to go. Call my dad and tell him what's going down."

He watched her move into her circle of friends and they headed into the computer store. Grabbing his cellphone, he relayed the information to Wolfe, who went ballistic as predicted but moments later broke through the crowd and joined him. He shrugged, feeling useless. "Sorry, she refused to listen to me."

"Yeah, *I know*. She has been a handful since she could speak. I think she has the fear gene missing, unlike me. Right now I want to march in there and slam the pervert into the next life." Wolfe rubbed his blond whiskers and sighed. "We should get out of sight away from the computer store." He led the way down an alley between the stores and leaned against the wall. "I did a sweep of the entire Rogers house and have reason to believe someone was struck on the head or had their throat cut in his family room. After spraying luminol, the amount of blood would indicate the victim would have little chance of survival. The carpet you mentioned was missing correlates with the evidence. I found drag marks consistent with a woven fabric, carpet fibers, and blood traces. The luminol highlighted a path leading from the family room to the backdoor through to the garage."

"So he killed *someone*, but from what Emily said it's doubtful he murdered Felicity or Kate. Although, we can't rule out that killing might be a cure for his impotence. We'll need a court order to obtain medical records to prove the extent of his impotency but his lawyer might persuade him if we threaten to charge him with murdering both girls." Kane looked at his strained expression and caught a flash of apprehension in his eyes. "We can't locate his wife and we know they argued, plus I found her purse and cellphone in the house."

"That's not good. In my opinion, Rogers murdered someone, wrapped them in the Chinese rug, and buried them in the woods." Wolfe raised both eyebrows and his mouth thinned. "I have a team with cadaver dogs arriving at sunup to search Stanton Forest from where you saw his car parked, but right now my priority is keeping Emily safe." He pulled out his cellphone, activated an app, and stared at the pulsing red dot on the screen. "I hope she knows what she is doing."

# CHAPTER FORTY-TWO

The cellphone made a noise like a siren, and with lightning speed, Wolfe's long fingers moved over the buttons. He lifted a concerned gaze to Kane. "Here we go. It's on speaker and I'm recording. They can't hear us."

Kane rested his hand on his Glock; one move in the wrong direction and he would be inside the computer store before Lionel Provine took his next breath.

A man's voice came through loud and clear.

*"Oh, come now, don't be so shy. Ask anyone, you can trust me."*

*"My daddy told me never to trust strangers, and I don't know you, Mr. Provine. I think we should stay right here in the shop."* Emily was working like a pro, giving her location and the name of the person speaking to her.

*"Come upstairs and see my collection of figurines, I'll give you some gift cards."*

"I'll kill the asshole." Wolfe shook with anger. "The pervert is grooming her."

*Oh, Jesus.* Concerned, Kane gripped his shoulder. "If anything happens, I'll take him out. Remember my motto: one shot, one kill. For now, she is okay. Just listen. If he touches her you can go in and tear him a new asshole."

When Wolfe pulled his weapon and moved closer to the edge of the building, a wave of foreboding hit Kane. He needed to contain the situation. Wolfe was not like him, cold and in control in a life-threatening situation, especially when his daughter was the target. "Stand down. That's an order. *Listen*, Emily is more sensible than you believe."

*"Come on now."* Provine's voice had dropped to a coaxing tone. *"I don't bite."*

*"I don't think so."* Emily's voice quivered a little and Kane noticed Wolfe's muscles tense under his shirt. *"I'll agree to go to the door of the storeroom but I'm not going anywhere else with you."*

*"Okay, but remember not to tell anyone. It's my secret club. Only a few people are involved, but as you are new in town and a friend of Aimee's, you can join too. Here, this is for you."*

*"What do I need that for?"* Emily sounded confused. *"Is it a thumb drive?"*

*"Not exactly. Just insert this toggle into the back of your laptop and we can communicate secretly online, which means outside of the games room. I can place bonus cards directly into your gift box so you'll be able to jump levels and beat the boys."*

*"That all sounds interesting, Mr. Provine, but nothing is free. What do you want from me or any of the girls you have in your club?"* Emily's voice came through loud and clear. *"I mean, if you're looking for a BJ or sex, I'm out of here."*

"Say it and I'll punch your teeth down your throat." Wolfe's threat came out in a growl.

*"No, nothing at all like that, heaven forbid."* Provine chuckled. *"No, just ask your parents to buy the latest devices from me. I'll help you and you'll help me."*

*"Okay, I'll do it."* Emily cleared her throat. *"I have to go. My daddy is waiting for me."*

*"Our little secret then? I don't think your father would understand."*

*"Sure."*

"I'll give him 'our little secret,' the asshole." Wolfe's face paled and his eyes flashed with rage. "I'll insert his damn toggle where he'll never find it again."

Trying to control his own anger, Kane grabbed his arm. "Cool it. What's the bet the toggle is a remote access device? I guess you have the know-how to discover just how often he is interacting with the girls online?"

"Oh, yeah. I'll go deep and find out all his dirty little secrets, he won't be able to hide anything from me. I'll conduct the search via Kate's or Felicity's laptops, then we won't need a court order. I already have written permission and what I discover will be admissible in court." A shudder went through Wolfe and he clenched and unclenched his big hands. "It might take some time but I'll be able to monitor him."

"So, remote access means he can control their computers?" A wave of disgust washed over Kane. "What about their webcams?"

"I'm not sure yet but if he has, just leave me alone with him for two minutes." Wolfe shot him a glance of cold fury. "Filthy little pervert. We'll need to keep a check on him. When I get back to the office, I'll set up a tracker and attach it to his car because we don't have the manpower to put someone on surveillance."

Emily's voice interrupted their discussion.

*"Daddy? I'm safe and walking toward Aunt Betty's Café. Did you get all that?"*

Kane slapped him on the back. "Go, I've got this. I'll see you back at the office."

After Wolfe took off at a run, Kane strolled back onto the street and walked into the store. He moved close to Lionel Provine and spoke softly but in a tone that demanded his immediate compliance. "I need to speak to you—alone."

"Yes, of course." As if Kane had just asked him about the latest technology, Provine led the way into a storeroom off the main shop floor. He waved at a screen displaying the entire store. "Can't be too careful."

Seeing a way to track Provine's movements, he acted dumb. "So, do you keep the disks and check them each day in case something is stolen, or are they automatically written over every few hours?"

"I have the latest technology, so unless something is missing, I re-write the hard drive weekly." Provine gave him a haughty stare, then, as if seeing him as a potential customer, smiled. "I see you've been shopping—is there anything I can help you with today?"

Kane slid the plastic sack up his arm, took out his notepad and pen, then inclined his head. "Can you account for your movements between the hours of six and nine thirty yesterday evening?"

"Yes, I was here as usual but I was online. Playing a new game called *Thunder Clap*. My online user name is Geek Twenty-Four. The kids meet me in the online games room and we often play against each other or on the same team." His small eyes narrowed behind his glasses and he held out his hand for Kane's notepad. "I can write down the games room's URL. It's easy to check the logs. In fact, I'm sure your new deputy will be able to find it okay."

"Just tell me the address, I'm not computer illiterate." Kane took down the URL then frowned. "I also know anyone can log on and not play or have some type of remote player. You'll need a better alibi than that, I'm afraid."

"Let me see, I went into Aunt Betty's Café around nine thirty to buy some snacks. Tilly the older waitress served me." Provine gave him a concerned stare. "Two of the rodeo cowboys were there as well and one of them was Lucky Briggs. He could have seen me but he was in deep conversation with the other waitress, the young one who does the late shift... ah, Sally, I think."

"Nine thirty, huh? Must have been hungry work playing that new game."

"With the store filled with kids during the school breaks I don't get time for lunch most days, let alone shopping for groceries. I'm lucky to have a group of the older girls who'll run errands for me."

"Why don't you make your lunch and bring it downstairs with you?" Kane looked down his nose at the man and noticed sweat forming on his top lip. He had rattled him. *Good.*

"I do sometimes, it depends on the weather." Provine wiped a hand over his mouth, the nails bitten down to the quick. "I wouldn't expect them to run around for me in the rain or snow."

"I *see,* and what do the girls get from you for running these 'errands'?"

"I receive piles of merchandising, game cards, free downloads for promoting the products, and I hand them out like candy." Provine made an exaggerated head bob toward the flat screen. "I really should get back to the kids." He wet his thin lips. "I'm sure you can check my alibi."

*Alibi is a word used by a guilty man.* "Aimee Fox mentioned you closed the store for over an hour on Monday afternoon. Did you have to go somewhere?" *Did you just happen to murder Joanne Blunt while you were out?*

"I had to update my server and the computers were down. I closed the shop to get some peace and quiet."

Kane made a note then turned to go. "Okay, thank you for your cooperation." *Not good enough, Provine.*

He headed toward the garage with the intention of speaking to Derick Smith again but wanted to relay the afternoon's information to Jenna in person. He had spent far too much time already and wanted to interview Steve Rogers at three. The interview was crucial for him to profile the man in a controlled situation. At this point, the charges they had against him did not hold water and he would be out on the street again. Rogers had killed someone, without doubt. He flicked through his notes, found the number of Smith's mother, and called her. Discovering Derick had been home playing pool with three of his friends yesterday evening, he took him off his list and headed back to the office. He wondered how Jenna would take the news; he doubted if the man locked in her jail had killed the girls, which meant their killer was still on the loose.

# CHAPTER FORTY-THREE

Jenna glanced at the clock in her office; in less than fifteen minutes Steve Rogers' lawyer would be walking into her office and demanding an interview. Kane was MIA and Wolfe had flashed past her door ushering Emily before him, face in a permanent frown and looking like a Viking berserker. *What the hell is happening now?* She closed the open file on her computer then pushed to her feet. The smell of coffee brewing was driving her crazy and if she snuck out to the kitchenette now, she had time to grab a cup of Joe before the interview. In the hallway, she could hear the rumble of Wolfe's deep voice; not loud but if her father had spoken to her in such a way, she would have shriveled up and died on the spot. Feeling a little sorry for Emily, she reached for the freshly brewed pot of coffee.

"Pour one for me, will you?"

As usual, Kane had walked up behind her without making a sound. She turned her head a little to watch him drop a large box of donuts on the counter then turn away and stash something in his desk drawer. "Been on a shopping spree? You do remember Rogers' lawyer is due in about ten minutes?"

"Yeah and I haven't been shopping." He raised one dark eyebrow and piled his coffee with sugar and cream. "I was undercover, so to speak, keeping an eye on Emily. The baker had the strange idea I was staring so long in his window because I couldn't afford to purchase a cake. He came out, thrust the donuts into my hands, and gave me the best 'get lost' look I've seen in ages. I guess having me hanging around outside his shop was bad for business." He grinned. "The cookies I stashed are *mine*. A guy my size needs a lot of cookies, especially chocolate chip ones made by his boss."

Jenna grinned at him. "I'll bake some more this weekend." She waved her cup toward the control room. "Wolfe is in there with Emily, and from his face, she is in trouble with a capital T. What happened and why did you have to watch her? I thought she was at the Foxes' place." She reached for a sugar donut.

"You have no idea." Kane cocked one dark eyebrow. "Let's say the situation was more than tense. You had two deputies ready to throw law out the window and throttle the little weasel."

Amazed Wolfe had agreed to Emily's plan to discover Lionel Provine's secret dealings, she gaped at him as he explained. Her mind went into freefall at the revelation Steve Rogers' doctor could prove he was innocent of the girls' murders. She stared at Kane, trying to process the fact Rogers could have killed his wife. She shook her head slowly, realizing the magnitude of the problem she faced. "*Oh my God.* The arrest warrant for Rogers was specific to the girls' murders and is useless. We can't hold him on suspicion of murdering his wife; as far as we know, she isn't missing." She leaned back on the counter and sipped her coffee. "We are in deep shit." She glanced at him. "I hope you can help me figure a way out of this mess?"

"I'll do my best." Kane's blue eyes moved toward the front door. "I'll need to think quickly, here is the lawyer now."

"Dammit." She flicked a look at the door. "Rogers is going to walk, and if we've made a mistake, he'll kill again."

"Someone will kill again. The clock is ticking." Kane rolled his wide shoulders. "All we can do is stretch our resources and watch these suspects."

Jenna sighed. "Take Mr. Jenkins down to the interview room then get Rogers. I'll ask Wolfe to place trackers on our suspects' vehicles. I doubt we'll be able to use any evidence gathered in court but between you and me, I wouldn't mind knowing if either of our suspects leaves home tonight."

"Neither would I."

She strolled toward the lawyer and fixed a smile on her face. "Right on time. If you will go with Deputy Kane, we'll have your client in the interview room in a few minutes."

"Interview room?" Jenkins adjusted his tie, his buffed, manicured nails glistening as he moved his soft hands. "Why was I forced to speak to Mr. Rogers in his cell last time?"

"Because we didn't have a room available and now we do. Deputy Kane will be conducting the interview and he will bring your client."

After speaking to Wolfe, she strolled across the main floor, down the passageway, and through the door to the steps leading down to the cells. To her delight, Wolfe had made a few changes in the days since his arrival. He had changed a storage area into an interview room. It had an electronic lock complete with card entry, turning it into a secure area. She flashed her ID card over the scanner and held the door open.

She glanced at the lawyer seated at the large wooden table and sat opposite. "Before we begin, how open do you believe Mr. Rogers would be to waive the doctor–patient privilege?"

"It is not something we have discussed but from my dealings with Mr. Rogers, I can assure you he is of sound mind." Jenkins' thin lips turned down as he fussed with his leather briefcase. "This trumped-up charge is just that—pure fabrication and indication of more harassment from your deputy."

The door opened and Kane's blue gaze rested on Jenna for a few seconds before he ushered the handcuffed Rogers into the room.

She took in the prisoner's disheveled appearance and the smell of unwashed sweat filled her nostrils. Her attention moved to the lawyer. "I would like to make it very clear, it is a prisoner's choice to use the facilities or not. Mr. Rogers was offered a shower this morning but he refused."

"After four days, we usually hose them down." Kane dropped his huge frame into the chair beside her and his mouth quirked into a slight grin. "Health reasons, you understand?" He placed a folder on the table.

Jenna glared at him then cleared her throat. "I am switching on the recorder now; the interview will be sound- and video-taped. The time is five past three. In the room is Sheriff Jenna Alton, Deputy David Kane, attorney for the prisoner, Mr. Samuel Jenkins, and the prisoner, Mr. Steve Rogers. Deputy Kane will start proceedings."

"Mr. Rogers, we have determined your whereabouts during the murders of Felicity Parker and Kate Bright." As he slid three graphic crime scene photographs of the victims across the table, his expression turned to granite. "We have signed statements from witnesses who can place you in the area at the time of death of both these girls."

"I didn't do that. My God, do you think I am some kind of animal?" Rogers' eyes bulged and a blue vein throbbed in his temple. "I *know* those two girls, they are my students. I'm a teacher at the high school, for God's sake." He pointed at Joanne's image. "I've never seen her in my life."

"The girls were savagely raped." Kane's hard gaze did not leave his face. "Then displayed to make them look like prostitutes. Animals might tear a person to shreds but I've never heard of one raping their victims first."

"I couldn't rape anyone." Rogers' cheeks pinked.

Jenna wanted to interject and ask about his potency; it seemed the perfect time but as she opened her mouth to speak, she caught Kane's disapproving stare and leaned back to observe. He was using his skills to lead Rogers into confessing his virility.

"Really?" Kane's large fists clenched on the table. "What is your opinion on prostitution, Mr. Rogers?"

"That question is totally irrelevant." Jenkins' dark eyes flashed in anger.

"Is it?" Kane moved his dark head slowly toward the lawyer then back to Rogers. "In my opinion, the killer has had dealings with prostitutes, perhaps suffered abuse as a child. Did you suffer abuse as a child, Mr. Rogers, is that why you killed these girls as revenge against your mother?"

"I want to answer the question." Rogers' face paled but he lifted his chin. "I don't have an opinion on prostitutes. I wouldn't go to one but how they live is their business." He let out a long sigh. "As to my childhood. *My* mother is a compassionate, gentle, God-fearing woman."

"So, nothing like your wife?"

"My *wife?*" Rogers scratched his head, making his hair stick up in all directions. "My wife could shred a man's dignity with one lash of her tongue."

"You mentioned you 'couldn't' rape anyone and that's normal, but most people would find a beautiful young woman attractive. Of course, the majority would not dream of touching an underage woman but to deny the victims were attractive has to be unusual." Kane's cold stare moved over Rogers' face and Jenna could almost see the prisoner squirm in his seat. "Are you impotent?"

Jenna moved her attention toward Jenkins and waited for him to halt the interview but to her surprise, he was regarding his client with interest. Perhaps he had gleaned the notion if Rogers could prove he was impotent then he was innocent of murdering the girls.

"Why would you ask such a personal question?" Rogers' cheeks glowed. "That is none of your business."

"Ah, but it is a very relevant question." Kane's blue gaze narrowed. "Did you rape these young women?"

"Good Lord, no." Rogers' eyes filled with tears that ran down his cheeks. "I would never do such a thing."

"Wouldn't or couldn't?"

"Both, okay?" Rogers wiped at his red-rimmed eyes. "I've been seeing specialists for years. Since moving here my records are with Doctors Littleman and Peters at Black Rock Falls General Hospital. I had an appointment two weeks ago. I had a skiing accident three years ago, damaged my lower back, and since then zip. My wife insisted there was nothing wrong with me and I was ignoring her and having sex with every woman in town."

"If you will give permission for your doctors to verify the condition, we will be willing to drop the charges." Kane leaned his wide shoulders back in the chair, making it creak alarmingly.

"I would advise you to comply and I can get you out of here this afternoon." Samuel Jenkins gave his client a look of pity. "I'll collect the information personally so nobody else need know."

Jenna leaned forward. "I'm afraid the DA will need to be notified of the reason we are withdrawing the charges against Mr. Rogers."

"Very well, draw up the papers and I'll sign them." Rogers dabbed at his tear-glossed cheeks with the end of his shirt.

"Just one more thing before I return you to your cell." Kane leaned his muscular forearms on the table and stared at Rogers with near violent intensity. "Where is your wife?"

"I hope she is rotting in hell." Rogers' Adam's apple bobbed. "After all I've been through she refused to believe I wasn't seeing other women. Stupid me was faithful to her for four long ugly years, and trust me, I had plenty of offers. She threatened to leave me on a daily basis. Now she's gone and I'm free of the witch."

"That's all I have for now. Sheriff, do you want to question the suspect?"

"No, I have nothing to add." Jenna turned her attention to the lawyer. "Is there anything you would like to say?"

"No."

"Very well, the interview is terminated at three-ten" She turned off the recording device. "I have the paperwork ready for signature." She removed documents from Kane's manila folder and passed them to Mr. Jenkins. "If you'll check these, ask Mr. Rogers to sign all copies, we can obtain the information without delay."

"I will take the documents personally and return them as soon as possible. I have some sway and will go directly to the hospital." Jenkins gathered up his copies with a flourish and stood. "If you'll open the door, I'll be on my way." He patted Rogers on the shoulder. "I'll have you out of here soon."

Jenna looked up into Kane's worried expression and chewed on her bottom lip. In a few hours, a potential murderer would be walking the streets of Black Rock Falls and there was not a damn thing she could do about it.

# CHAPTER FORTY-FOUR

After spending an hour setting up his trap, the man stepped from the shower and grinned at his reflection. Law enforcement in Black Rock Falls was a joke. He examined his body, making sure he had not one hair on his flesh, and chuckled. Watching the deputies running around chasing their tails was amusing, and he could remain in Black Rock Falls undetected for a long time. Sheriff Alton was gullible and her trained dogs as useless as tits on a bull. He had stolen a large pair of used crime scene coveralls and booties from the garbage outside the sheriff's department right under their noses. This time he would wear the coveralls inside out. Imagine the face on the M.E. when he discovers one of the deputy's hairs or DNA on another dead girl. He would watch the sheriff arrest her deputies and laugh himself stupid.

He craved a higher risk and a more thrilling kill each time. Having a couple of hours to plan his next kill had been challenging but he was smart. In Evansville, he cut his timing so damn close, the sheriff walked straight past him on the way to investigate the screams.

Kate had been his best work so far. He enjoyed the fear in her eyes as he cut. He moaned at the memory, loving the way his reflection remained in her eyes. Her terror of seeing him as his true self. He hated muffling her screams but noise echoed in the tiled room and he wanted to spend a lot of time with her.

The cuts on her eyelids had been a stroke of genius. Oh yes, his amazing skills shone though again, so underestimated for so long. Kate's big blue eyes had followed his every move and the way her lip trembled with each incision had been a delight. Oh, she tried to scream, but the sound had been like the moaning of a whore.

Just as well, he had time to think. He needed to plan his next move. How could he pry Aimee Fox away from her parents? Then he remembered Thursday night in the Fox household was parents' date night, which usually meant a visit to the Cattleman's Hotel Restaurant and a movie. Aimee would expect her boyfriend—oh what was the boy with the greasy hair's name? Ah, yes, *Lucas Summerville*—to visit her, but by sending him a bonus round in his new game, Lucas would forget all about Aimee and be in the online game room.

Wrapping a towel around his waist, he ambled into his bedroom and dressed quickly. If his plan worked, he would need to leave soon, and he went into the office to finish the final steps to gaining his prize. Seated at the desk, he opened his laptop. There she was, Aimee Fox, ripe and ready for the picking. She was chatting with Emily, Deputy Wolfe's daughter. He grinned at the thought of plucking her right out from under her father's nose. He placed the girls on a split screen then relaxed to listen to their conversation.

He wanted Emily. He craved to fist his hand in her long blonde hair and see the life slip away in her eyes. He shook his head to dispel the images. *I must follow the plan.* He entered the online games room and sent a message using Julia's username. As a new member of the Aimee Fox clique, she would be trying to gain points from her esteemed leader. He heard the pinging as the message arrived on Aimee's computer.

"Just a minute, I have a message from Julia." Aimee held up a finger to stop the conversation. "I've got to go out."

"Where? Didn't your parents tell you to stay home tonight?" Emily tossed a strand of long blonde hair over one shoulder. "It's not safe to go out alone, not after three girls have been killed. Who knows who will be next?"

"I won't be alone, silly. Julia has located three rare characters on the edge of Stanton Forest. She'll be there in fifteen minutes. I only need two more characters, then if I find the Golden Wizard, I'll get to the bonus level."

"It's a stupid game and only an idiot would risk their life going out alone. The game is not worth it." Emily's pretty face crinkled into a frown. "Wait until Lucas arrives then you can go together—or why don't you drive?"

"I've already said I'll meet her. I can't just leave her hanging and I'm not driving. It's a few minutes' walk and there are houses all the way. It will be okay." Aimee chuckled. "Remind me not to invite you the next time we go to a haunted house on Halloween."

"There's no such things as ghosts." Emily frowned at her. "That's different, there's a killer running around Stanton Forest. A real person."

"So why isn't there cruisers driving up and down the street every five minutes?" Aimee chuckled. "If you're that worried, I'll find Julia and bring her back here then drive her home later. Okay?"

"I guess so." Emily chewed her fingernails. "Maybe you should call me and stay on the line until you find her?"

"Great idea, then I won't be able to hear the killer creep up behind me."

"I'll tell my dad you've gone out alone." Emily glared at her. "You're being irresponsible. He'll call your mom and you'll be grounded for life."

"Jesus, how old are you?" Aimee grinned at her. "Stop acting like a baby. I'll be fine and if you tell your dad, don't bother calling me again. I don't like people I can't trust with secrets. I've got to go get dressed now or I'll be late." She disconnected.

Tingling with excitement, he pulled on his gloves and bent to pick up his bag. "Yes, Aimee, come and find me. I have a *very* special treat for you."

# CHAPTER FORTY-FIVE

A ringtone Jenna recognized as Kane's woke her from a deep sleep. She glanced around. Oh Lord, she had fallen asleep at Kane's again but at least this time she was in his spare room. *Where is he?* She frowned at the persistent beeping then heard his voice speaking softly.

"Okay, I'll let Jenna know. We'll be there at six thirty."

When he strolled into the bedroom, showered, shaved, and dressed for work, carrying two steaming mugs of coffee, she pushed the hair from her eyes and sighed. "You shouldn't have let me sleep. Are we late for work?"

"Nope." He handed her a mug and sat on the edge of the bed. "Wolfe was calling to remind me the cadaver dog team will be waiting at the spot we found Rogers' car at six thirty. As it's five, we'll have plenty of time." He gave her a long, considering stare. "Are *you* okay? Are we still good?" He cleared his throat. "You fell asleep again and I didn't want to wake you."

Glad to see a touch of color highlight his cheeks, she smiled. "Yes, I'm fine, but right now I need to shower and get ready for work." She sniffed the delicious brew. "Maybe *after* I've had my coffee." Her stomach growled. "I doubt we'll have time to eat before we leave."

"Sure we will. I'll make breakfast then you can go and get ready." He stood and smiled down at her. "Scrambled eggs okay?"

It felt good to have someone to care and be there when she needed a friend. How long had it been? Maybe three or four years since she could trust anyone. She returned his smile. "Scrambled would be bliss, thank you."

At six thirty on the dot, they arrived at Stanton Forest in Kane's SUV to find Wolfe and Rowley chatting with a team of dog handlers with barking dogs. Jenna and Deputy Rowley had left their SUVs outside the sheriff's office, to minimize the police presence, and had instructed Deputy Walters to hold the fort until they arrived back at the office. With the extra deputies from Blackwater running double shifts in town and at the fairgrounds for the next few days, she had time to concentrate on the murders. She glanced up at Kane. "You know, I could get used to having six extra deputies."

"Mayor Petersham seems to be far more approachable than Rockford used to be—maybe he'll stretch the budget to three, if you ask him." Kane smoothed back his black hair then pushed on his buff-colored Stetson.

Jenna strolled beside him toward the men. "I can only try." She turned her attention to the men and waited for Wolfe to join them before giving introductions. "Okay, so you have your gear with you in case we discover a body?"

"Yeah, Kane has his backpack as well and we have three shovels, just in case." Wolfe's blond eyebrows rose as he handed one to Kane. "The dogs have been going crazy since they arrived, so I guess we follow the dogs?"

"Okay, move out." She dropped into stride beside Kane, glad to have his solid strength beside her.

Not twenty paces along the well-trodden pathway, the unmistakable reek of death came on the wind and rustled the pines. The whining groans as the large branches swayed back and forth raised goosebumps on her arms. She peered ahead in a strange wave of the morbid fascination, expecting to see a grave disturbed by animals. The dogs' barks reached a crescendo and the men stopped in front of her, blocking her view.

"Dear Lord in heaven." Wolfe turned his cold stare in her direction. "Suit up." He slipped the backpack from his broad shoulders. "Get those dogs back to the vehicles. We'll need to secure the scene."

Jenna pushed forward, ignoring the dogs' wet noses pressing against her hands. "What have you fou—*oh*, shit."

Bile rushed up the back of her throat and her heart raced so fast, she leaned against a tree to stop the dizzy spell. Hanging between two pines to one side of the trail, arms and legs spread, was Aimee Fox. Head bent with her chin resting on her chest, her tawny hair fell in a silk curtain on each side of her face to frame eyes wide open and fixed. Red lipstick smeared on her lips and cheeks made her look like a horrific clown. Ants covered her mutilated young body, hardly recognizable as human. She dangled above a shallow grave scattered with wildflowers. Jenna covered her mouth and swallowed, not fully comprehending the horror before her. A face peered out from the soil, blue and swollen with her eyes wide open as if watching Aimee.

"Oh, Mother of God, that's Mrs. Rogers." Rowley turned an ashen face toward her. "And—" He turned away covering his mouth.

Retching followed, and Jenna turned to see Rowley run away from the scene and vomit behind a tree. The sound made her stomach twist into knots but she turned and took the protective equipment Kane thrust into her hands. When he gave her a searching look, she met his gaze. "Don't worry, *I'm fine*. It's a dreadful thing to say but I'm getting back into the swing of turning off my emotions."

"You don't have to turn them off." Kane's expression was compassionate. "Just turn them around. We have to help her by discovering her killer, so look past the horror and find the evidence."

"Yeah, I remember the training speech." She swallowed the lump in her throat and blinked away the tears threatening to show her weakness. "Go and help Wolfe."

"Yes, ma'am."

Wanting to suck in deep breaths, she walked some distance away to compose herself. She dressed in coveralls and booties, placed the mask firmly over her nose, then moved back to the scene. She stood to one side to allow Kane and Wolfe to examine the area, placing markers beside evidence and recording each find. The camera whirred as Kane moved expertly, filming the scene before taking individual images by the hundreds. Gathering her professional façade around her like a shield, she tried to push away the fact she knew these women and examined the area with cold detachment.

"I see two sets of footprints. One looks like the person was wearing socks." She gestured to the soft indentations in the disturbed soil. "The M.O. is slightly different. He did not wash Aimee like the others but he murdered them by water. By the blood congealed on the ground beyond the grave, he murdered her here."

"We haven't released any details for this to be a copycat." Kane had adopted his professional granite expression. "This has to be the same person who killed Aimee and the other girls but someone else murdered Mrs. Rogers. The uncovering of the grave to show the face is part of the exhibitionism the lunatic has displayed before. He wanted someone to watch. If we have two suspects, how Aimee's killer knew Mrs. Rogers was here is the question." He looked at her. "May I suggest you ask two of the K-9 officers to go with Rowley and haul Steve Rogers back in for questioning? The tracker on his car has remained stationary, so we may be in luck." He indicated with his chin toward the main road. "He only lives a few hundred yards away and I think we have cause by the bucket loads."

Jenna swept her gaze over the scene then nodded, walked to Rowley, and issued orders. In the background, she could hear Wolfe speaking into his voice recorder and listened, amazed at his on-the-spot deductions. It was as if he could re-enact the crime in his mind.

"The homicide victim is known to me as Aimee Fox, seventeen years old, female, Caucasian, brown hair, brown eyes. Time of death according to current body temperature is between twelve and fourteen hours, which would be between six and eight last night. Killer attached a green commercial cord made from synthetic fiber to stretch the body between two trees. Initial findings would suggest incapacitation by a blow to the back of the skull. Laceration across throat from left to right would suggest the killer is right-handed. The angle of the wounds to the torso would suggest evisceration occurred after the victim was suspended. Bruising around the genital area and thighs would suggest rape. Lipstick on mouth and cheeks consistent with previous victims." Wolfe moved around the body, his gaze intently scanning the remaining flesh. "There is a fabric pattern on a blood smear to the right side, extending from under the armpit to the thigh. I have taken a sample of fibers attached to the skin. From my initial examination and the unusual footprints surrounding the area, I would presume the killer was wearing forensic coveralls and booties. Lack of bloody fingerprints on the body would suggest gloves." He turned off the microphone, his eyes void of emotion. "That's all I can do for now. We'll have to cut her down and bag her. I'll drop her feet-first into the bag then we'll lower her in, keep the cords in situ. I need to check them very carefully for evidence."

"Sure." Kane turned and his blue gaze slid over her. "Ma'am, do you want me to call it in first and ask Maggie to arrange transport for the bodies?"

The way he deferred to her constantly of late made her wonder if he had finally gotten used to having a woman as his superior. She gave him a curt nod. "Go ahead."

"We can handle the exhumation, if you agree." His full lips turned down at the edges. "Digging up Mrs. Rogers won't be nice."

A wave of revulsion clutched her. She shot a glance at the staring blank expression peering out of the grave then hurriedly looked away. "No, it won't, but I expect Wolfe will find it more than a little interesting, since his interest in decomposition is his main topic of conversation of late. Carry on. I'll make casts of the footprints." She turned to head toward Wolfe's bag of crime scene supplies and heard his voice behind her.

"Excuse me, ma'am."

Glancing over one shoulder, she met Wolfe's gaze. "Yes?"

"No one has reported Aimee missing, so her folks don't know." His steel-gray eyes narrowed. "They'll be frantic once they find her gone."

Jenna sighed. Being the bearer of bad tidings had become a nasty task of late. "I'll go and speak to them but if I had a choice, I'd dig up the body." She took the key fob Kane offered her. "Thanks, but I *could* walk, it's not far." She dragged off her protective gear and rolled it into a ball.

"Drive. We have potentially two killers roaming the immediate area." Kane's dark eyebrows met in the middle in a frown. "Either of them could be in the forest and waiting for their next victim."

She straightened, unwilling to show the trepidation his words had produced. "Okay. I'll be back as soon as I can." Turning away from the gruesome sight before her, she headed along the narrow trail.

Icy fingers of dread walked a path up her spine. She glanced into the picturesque forest of tall, majestic pines. Packed so close together, their dark zebra shadows had become a backdrop for brutality and could hide a man or a bear from sight. The morning usually brought a cacophony of birdsong rejoicing in a new summer's day, yet not one bird watched her from the branches, not even a crow waiting to pick at the rotting flesh. Stillness surrounded her as if nature mourned the loss of beauty.

# CHAPTER FORTY-SIX

Jenna stood in the Foxes' hallway, enclosed in a shroud of dread. It took every ounce of her strength not to break down at the sight of the faces contorted with grief in front of her. Aimee's parents had returned from date night and, seeing their daughter's door closed, had tiptoed to their bedroom without checking on her. Arriving at their front door at eight forty-five on a Friday morning, they stared at her in disbelief after discovering a monster had murdered their daughter.

"It can't be true." Mrs. Fox turned around and ran up the stairs. Moments later a scream of anguish echoed through the house. "She's not here and hasn't slept in her bed. Oh my God." She stared down from the top of the stairs, her face pale and eyes wide with shock.

"Are you sure it's Aimee?" Mr. Fox ran a shaking hand down his face.

Jenna laid one hand on his arm and guided him into the family room. "I'm sure. *Please* take a seat."

"What happened to her?" Mrs. Fox stumbled into the room and collapsed on the sofa beside her husband. "I need to know. You have to tell me." She burst into uncontrollable sobbing.

Wanting to be compassionate, Jenna pushed the images of mutilation to the back of her mind and fell back on the usual answer. "Cause of death is yet to be determined, although the M.E. at the scene has determined it is homicide. I am so sorry for your loss."

"Who would kill Aimee?" Mr. Fox stared at her with a blank, unseeing expression. "I can't understand why she left the house. I thought Lucas was coming to keep her company. I told them not to leave the house, not after the girls went missing."

Jenna cleared her throat. "I take it you missed the news last night? We believe the same killer murdered Felicity, Kate, and Joanne Blunt."

Two sheet-white faces stared at her in disbelief. She needed information and had to ask the questions. "When did you last see Aimee?"

"When we went out for dinner around six last night." Mr. Fox looked at her bleakly. "We ate early then caught a movie. We dropped into Aunt Betty's Café for coffee and cake around ten then came home close to eleven, I guess."

"What was she doing at the time?"

"Online with the new girl, what's her name?" Mr. Fox wiped at the tear streaming down his cheeks and glanced at his distraught wife.

"Emily, the new deputy's daughter." Mrs. Fox pleated her skirt with trembling fingers. "You should call Lucas, he might have asked her to meet him somewhere."

Assuming Chad would have informed his best friend about finding Kate's body after the news story aired, Jenna shook her head. "I doubt he would risk asking her to leave home alone. He is a friend of Chad, isn't he? Kate's boyfriend?"

"Yes, but what does that have to do with anything?" Mr. Fox gave her a puzzled look then reached for a cellphone on the coffee table. "I'm calling Lucas now." He leaned back on the sofa. "Lucas, this is Mr. Fox. Did you drop by to see Aimee last night? No? Oh, she mentioned you planned to keep her company." He stared into space, listening. "Okay, thanks." He disconnected and met Jenna's eyes. "He received a bonus game card and played online until way past midnight. He forgot about calling Aimee to tell her he wouldn't be coming, and asked me to tell her he'd call her later."

"Would Emily have asked her to come over?" Mrs. Fox wiped her wet cheeks with a tissue then straightened.

Jenna pushed to her feet. "No, she is aware of the danger but I'll go and speak to her now. The M.E. will contact you if you wish to see Aimee. Is there anyone I can call?"

"No, no thank you." Mr. Fox pushed unsteadily to his feet. "I'll contact our family. When will we be able to see her? She is all alone, we should be there."

"Later today, perhaps tomorrow morning." Jenna walked with him to the front door. "She is in safe hands, Mr. Fox. I promise I will find the person who did this and bring him to justice."

Out in the open, Jenna took in a few deep breaths to steady her nerves then walked toward Kane's SUV and reached inside her pocket for the keys. The idea of returning to the crime scene churned her guts. She fired up the engine, swung the powerful SUV around, and headed back to the crime scene. The K-9 team had left by the time she arrived and paramedics were loading the bodies into the back of two ambulances. She pulled to the curb and met Kane walking out of the forest. "Find any evidence at all?"

"Yeah, a few fibers and a couple of hairs." A trickle of sweat ran down Kane's face. He appeared hot and exhausted. Mud caked his coveralls. "It looks like Mrs. Rogers was hit over the head then strangled." He pulled off the booties, unzipped the coveralls, and rolled them into a ball. "Wolfe is convinced we are dealing with two different killers."

Unease slid over her. "Dammit, *two* killers and we let one walk right out of the door yesterday." She walked around in circles. "We look like incompetent fools. I don't suppose Rogers is waiting at home for us to arrest him again either?"

"Nope. I sent Rowley to his house to look. Steve Rogers is on the run. His car is in the garage but we have to assume his wife's car is missing, and it looks like he left in a hurry. He must have hidden her car close by but we have the license plate. I've contacted the state police and put out a BOLO plus told Maggie to give his photograph to the media and inform them he is wanted on suspicion of murder." He gave her a long, compassionate look. "It's not our fault. At the time, we had no evidence to keep him in custody. Think about the evidence. We didn't have a missing person, only blood smears and a missing carpet. No judge is going to allow us to keep a suspect under arrest without proof of a crime." He squeezed her shoulder in his large palm. "If it makes you feel any better, I doubt he'll murder again. I think by the number of blows he inflicted, it was a crime of passion. Nothing like what happened to the other victims."

Her stomach rolled and she stared up at him. "What about Aimee? Did she suffer like Kate?"

"Wolfe will be able to tell us more after the autopsy. Her murder was close to the street and he would worry about someone hearing her screams. The blow to the back of her head would have knocked her out cold. It looks like the killer uses the same method to subdue his victims each time. He attacks from behind, stuns the victims with a blunt object, then rapes them." Kane's mouth turned down in a grimace. "It seems too much of a coincidence he stumbled over Mrs. Rogers' grave as he was killing Aimee. I've been wondering if he was hiding in the forest after killing Kate and saw Rogers bury his wife."

Trying hard to concentrate, Jenna rubbed her temples. "Going on what we know, Rogers was in the forest at the time of Kate's death, and it's more than likely Kate's killer was as well, so it's possible. Why uncover Mrs. Rogers' face? It seems so macabre."

"Not if you look into the mind of a psychopath." Kane removed his hat and massaged his head as if he had a headache. "When he knocked Aimee out, he didn't have the thrill of the fight, so I think he uncovered Mrs. Rogers' face to watch him."

Sick to her stomach at the memory of Mrs. Rogers' blue face surrounded by blood-stained carpet, she gaped up at him. "That is so gross. What kind of human being does such a thing?"

"You can't think logically when dealing with a psychopathic mind. They don't have emotions like we do; they are narcissistic and have no compassion, so trying to talk them out of murder never works. You can't reason with them because they see a victim as an object not a person." Kane's forehead wrinkled into a frown. "It's all about them, their needs, and their desires. As an example, think how we would regard soda in a can—once consumed, we toss away the can, it has no value. That's how a psychopathic killer regards their victims."

"So why display them, what does he get out of the shock value?"

"It's a 'look at me' syndrome in the narcissistic part of their personality. I would say he feeds off the girl's terror and gets some sort of extra thrill with the shock value he generates. This killer is making a point." Kane's blue eyes settled on her face. "It all goes with the makeup on the face and the mutilation. Each girl he kills is a symbol of the person who damaged him so bad it triggered his behavior. He is punishing a woman and sending a message to others. It's not over, he is escalating, but it looks like he is sticking to the same group of friends. We have to figure out which one of them will be next."

The interview with Aimee's parents slammed into her brain. "*Oh, Jesus*—she was speaking to Emily online last night."

# CHAPTER FORTY-SEVEN

Kane met Wolfe coming out of the forest. "Is Emily at home? Jenna told me she was talking to Aimee online last night around six. As this lunatic seems to be moving through a group of friends, we need to be worried about her safety."

"I'll call her." Wolfe tore off his face mask, displaying a grim expression. "Not that she would go out again alone." He removed his protective gear and pushed it into a plastic bag Jenna held out for him.

"She is a sensible girl. I wish she would join the sheriff's department once she has finished school." Jenna's smile reached her eyes. "I need a female deputy."

"She has bigger plans, I'm afraid. She will walk through a forensic science degree and will be joining me here as an M.E." Wolfe's tone made it clear Jenna's suggestion would never happen. He dragged out his cellphone and turned his back, displaying a large patch of sweat. He paced up and down then turned to face them. "I'm sorry but there is no easy way to say this to you. Aimee is dead and I understand you spoke to her last night?"

Kane observed the changes of expression on Wolfe's face during the conversation. The man was blunt and did not pulled any punches with his daughter. When Wolfe finally disconnected, Kane waited expectantly. "What did she say?"

Wolfe held up one large hand as if halting traffic and stared at the ground for some moments as if considering what to say. His large frame expanded as he drew in a big breath then let it out slowly. "I *know* how the killer lured the girls to the murder scene."

"What?" More than a little interested, Kane moved closer to Jenna and stared at him. "How?"

Wolfe's steel gaze swept over Kane and he grimaced. "He is manipulating the damn game they play on their cellphones. Emily said Aimee rushed off to meet Julia. Emily tried to stop her and threatened to tell me but Aimee pulled the peer-pressure card. She said Julia had apparently left Aimee a message to say she'd found three rare characters on the edge of Stanton Forest." He gave him an agitated look when he opened his mouth to ask a question. "The game involves collecting digital images of characters projected in real time through a cellphone's camera to move forward in the game." He rubbed the blond stubble on his chin, making a rasping sound. "Emily tried to contact Aimee about eight thirty this morning to smooth things over and when Aimee didn't pick up, she assumed she wasn't speaking to her, so she called Julia." His stone expression met Kane's gaze. "Julia *didn't* send Aimee a message last night."

"How is he impersonating the girls?" Jenna's blue eyes widened. "*I mean*, a phone number comes up to identify people in messages."

"Emily mentioned the group of friends use an online messaging system via the games room to contact each other. Aimee told her it stopped her parents from snooping." Wolfe raised a blond eyebrow. "I assume they made a habit of checking her cellphone messages. This means the killer is hacking the online games room. My guess is he is using the kids' usernames to post messages, which would point straight to Provine. He is the person who gave each of these girls a toggle to interact with them online."

Mind reeling, Kane gaped at him. "Yeah, but without the boyfriends having a toggle, could he hack into their accounts as well? I remember in Chad's statement he mentioned Kate sent him a message to change the time of their date through the games hub."

"If the killer is capable of remotely manipulating a single player's game interaction, hell yeah." Wolfe's expression was bleak. "He is *good*, damn good. I am surprised he hasn't tried to breach my firewalls on our cellphones or the department's mainframe, but right now, it is as safe as the Pentagon's security system. If he had as much as tried to tamper with anything we would be lighting up with alerts."

"Where is Lionel Provine? Have you been keeping tabs on him?" Jenna's eyes flashed with anger. "The weasel. Did Emily connect her laptop to his damn circle of friends or whatever?"

"Yeah, she did, but only so I could monitor everything he was doing. I'll check the logs again the moment I get home, just in case he opened a connection last night, but so far, Provine seems to be quiet. As far as I know he didn't trigger the alarm I set on her firewall and he hasn't moved from his apartment either, unless he found the tracker." Wolfe's brow wrinkled as he pressed buttons on his cellphone. "Nope, according to the app, his car is still in the same place. If either of our suspects had driven anywhere, the trackers would have alerted me, which means Provine could have an alternative means of transport and Rogers could have walked here." He cleared his throat."

Pulling out his cellphone, Kane scrolled down his list of contacts and found Provine's number. He shrugged. "I'll call him. You never know, some of these ass—Ah, Mr. Provine, this is Deputy Dave Kane. I am just looking over our budget for the rest of the year. I wondered if you could arrange a discount for the sheriff's department if we buy in bulk?" He winked at Jenna. "You can, that's great. I'll speak to Deputy Wolfe and we'll drop by next week. No, thank *you*." He disconnected. "Well, he is in the store. I can hear games in the background and voices."

"Smartass." Wolfe removed his hat and used wipes from his bag to clean his sweat- and mud-streaked face. "He thinks he is invincible and untraceable. If he is involved in these murders, he has to make an error either online or at the scene. I found hairs and fibers this time. He didn't wash the body and is getting careless in his rush for a fix."

"We'll need to keep him under surveillance." Jenna pushed a strand of black hair behind one ear. "I wonder if he is going to be at the dance at the fairgrounds tonight."

"If he isn't, we'll have to arrange surveillance." Kane rubbed the back of his neck. "I think he'll take the opportunity to kill again while everyone is at the dance. It wouldn't be too difficult to lure a girl away in a crowd, and the fairgrounds are filled with places to hide."

"Count me out." Wolfe's eyes narrowed. "I'm taking Emily and I don't break promises to kids. After working since before six this morning, setting up tests on the evidence, and doing two PMs, I'm owed the time."

"We planned to go too but watching Provine is more important." Jenna bit into her bottom lip. "I do understand you are working two jobs and I don't expect you to pull extra shifts. You had better get going. We'll finish up here. How long before we have any DNA results?"

"On the evidence we found on Aimee, three days. The other victims' samples should be ready this afternoon." Wolfe's mouth twitched into an uncharacteristic smile. "I'm hoping I have enough to convict the killer. I did find cells on Kate's hands, most likely sweat dripped from the murderer."

"Brilliant!" Kane bent to gather all the used equipment and pushed everything into a bag. "Can you call me after you inform the sheriff?"

"Yeah, not a problem." Wolfe's nostrils flared as he stared at the large bag of stinking discarded coveralls, gloves, and booties. "I need to make a new rule as M.E. I want all contaminated materials from a crime scene placed into an incinerator, not into the garbage. I'll take it with me. There is one at the funeral home but I'll ask the mayor to have one installed at the sheriff's department. The contaminated trash can you have there is an environmental joke." He grabbed the bag Kane held out for him and headed toward his SUV. "I'll catch you later."

Kane took the crime scene tape from his bag, tossed one end to Jenna, and walked into the forest, looping the tape around trees until he had made a full circle. He emerged to see her tying her end securely around a pine tree on the edge of the trail. He twined the tape around the opposite tree then pulled it across the trail entrance and fastened it beside Jenna's tape. "That will keep everyone out but we've done a thorough search of the scene." He smiled at her, glad to see her rigid stance relax a little. "What next, ma'am?"

"I think we should pay Lionel Provine a visit. I wouldn't mind seeing what his demeanor is like and we have an excuse to drop by now." Jenna's dark gaze searched his face. "I'll ask him if he is going to the dance tonight. If he is going, we'll park outside Aunt Betty's Café and wait for him to leave then follow him to the fairgrounds."

"We'll be able to keep a close eye on him." He gathered up his bag and headed for his SUV. "How did you like driving my ride?"

"I'm not sure what you did to the engine but it takes off so fast it should be illegal." Jenna dangled his keys between her long fingers. "Handles well. I'm jealous."

He gave her a sideways look, glad she had coped with the murder scene better than the last time. "I can make your vehicle faster and beef up the suspension, if you like? I'll look at it the next time we get some downtime." He threw his bag into the back of his SUV then climbed behind the wheel. His body ached with weariness and he had to attend a dance. *Tonight is going to be a long night.*

# CHAPTER FORTY-EIGHT

Standing in front of a full-length mirror, Jenna stared at her reflection, wondering if the fringed sequined shirt she purchased was a bit over the top. Since arriving in Black Rock Falls, she had spent the rodeo carnival weekends on duty and in her uniform. She pirouetted in her soft leather cowboy boots, checking how her butt looked in the tight blue jeans. The hat had cost her a fortune; black and made from beaver, it fit her head perfectly. She looked the part and hoped the "Learn the Texas two-step" DVD she purchased online would at least make her moves on the dance floor acceptable.

With Rogers still on the run and Lionel Provine attending the dance, she had everything under control. Kane had monitored Provine's store all afternoon and Rowley had taken turns with Walters to keep him under surveillance until he showed up at the dance. With all eyes watching Provine, he would have to be a fool to attempt anything tonight.

A horn beeped outside and she headed for the door, making sure to engage the alarm system on the way. She picked up a tiny purse, stuffed her keys and cellphone in her pockets. Closing the door, she turned to see Kane leaning casually on his black SUV, dressed all in black with a leather vest over a shirt embroidered with six-shooters. He resembled a gunslinger from the Old West. She slid inside and noticed his Glock sitting in the console.

"Do you think you'll need a weapon at the dance?"

"Uh-huh, never leave home without it." Kane's mouth twitched. "I have a holster in the small of my back but it digs in a bit when I'm driving."

"I couldn't fit my Sig in my purse." Jenna shrugged. "It would have looked a bit obvious if I'd worn a shoulder holster with this outfit considering we are supposed to be undercover."

"Don't worry; I have a backup strapped to my ankle. If you need a weapon."

Jenna smiled. "I somehow knew you would."

"You look spectacular tonight, ma'am." His long lashes dropped over his eyes. "Am I allowed to say that or is it stepping out of the bounds of our professional relationship?"

"You may." Jenna's cheeks grew hot at his frank appraisal but deep inside it felt good to have a compliment. "You look like you just walked out of an old western movie."

"Oh, *shit*. The shirt is new." His mortified expression made her giggle like a teenager.

"No, no… you look great." She grinned at him. "You'll be fighting off the women tonight."

"Nah." He started the engine and headed down the driveway. He flashed her a perfect white smile. "Tonight, I'm undercover. Oh, by the way, in the glove compartment you'll find our earbuds and wireless transmitters. The microphone attaches to your shirt and the reception is amazing. We'll be able to keep in touch with Wolfe and Rowley just in case anything happens but with the four extra deputies and Walters on duty at the fairgrounds, we should have a quiet evening."

She reached into the glove compartment and pulled out two plastic bags. "This is different to what I'm used to. How do I turn off the microphone? I don't want all my deputies listening to everything I say."

"Press it—it's like an on and off button."

She turned the device over in her hands. "So how do I speak to each one individually?"

"Once you turn it on, you'll be speaking to everyone, so use names. Just remember to turn it off when you've finished." Kane's full lips turned up at the corners. "I remember one time we had this guy on the team who'd forgotten to turn off his mic and went into the bathroom. Let's say his time in there was explosive to say the least, and he sounded like a pig in labor." He chuckled. "I was standing next to another agent each side of the president of the United States in front of a press gallery, and it took every bit of my willpower not to burst out laughing. That guy never lived it down."

"Oh my God. That's the funniest thing I've ever heard." She could not believe he had met the president. "I didn't know you worked that close to POTUS."

"Yeah, after my last mission, HQ was worried I'd been compromised so I was moved to the White House." He slanted her a blue gaze. "It should have been safer but it seems there are no safe places anymore."

Her cellphone belted out a ringtone and she glanced at Kane. "That's Wolfe. I wonder what couldn't wait until the dance."

She pressed the phone to her ear. "Alton."

*"If you're with Kane, don't put me on speaker."*

Flicking a glance at Kane, she shrugged. "Sure."

*"The DNA trace I found on Kate Bright is a match for Dave. As she was in the water, this has to be a secondary transfer. The problem is, he was covered from head to foot like me when we found her, and I had bagged the hands before I asked him to help me lift her into a body bag."* Wolfe cleared his throat. *"I don't believe for a second Dave killed anyone, and the only explanation is the killer rubbed the body with something belonging to him, like a sweaty T-shirt or even a sock."*

She heard Wolfe's sharp intake of breath. *"Do you know where he was at the time of death?"*

She stared out the window as the trees flashed by and swallowed the lump in her throat. "No but I'll find out. If this is a set-up like I believe, then you'll find the same result on Aimee's body."

*"I agree because the other strange thing I found consistent to both murders is the fibers. They are identical to the crime scene coveralls we use. I tested the fibers for DNA as well and both swabs came back a match for Dave Kane."* Wolfe's voice had become hard and serious. *"Were the ones he used for Felicity's murder thrown in the trash outside the sheriff's department?"*

Jenna winced. "Yeah, I'm afraid so. I didn't think to have them incinerated."

*"This will be considered indisputable evidence in court. You'll have to ask him to prove his whereabouts, but in my opinion, someone is setting him up for the killings. I'll talk to you later, Emily is anxious to leave."*

"Okay, we're heading for the fairgrounds now." She disconnected, turned in her seat, and met Kane's curious gaze. "Where were you when Kate was murdered?"

"Don't *you* remember?" Kane raised one black eyebrow and the nerve in his cheek twitched. "I was with you."

At no time did she doubt him, not for a second, but the week had been a complete blur. "I wouldn't ask if I *knew*, would I?" She glared at him. "For Christ's sake, Dave, your DNA was found on Kate Bright's body."

"What do *you* think?" Kane's blue gaze narrowed as he stared at the road. "I may be a cold-blooded killer but do *you* believe I'm capable of raping and murdering girls?"

*"No*, of course not, but Wolfe said he can't suppress evidence in a murder case." She touched his arm, feeling the bunched muscles under his shirt. "This week has been one long day to me, and with this evidence you'll need a rock-solid alibi."

"Well then, it's just as well I was with *you* most of the time. Let me see, I was at the office until six, at Aunt Betty's Café having dinner with you until about seven thirty then we drove home, had coffee at your place, and I walked back to my cottage around eight. You called me at eight thirty and told me Chad had found Kate's body. I'd have to have superpowers to commit a murder somewhere in between." He turned the SUV into the parking lot at the fairgrounds and headed for the area allotted for the sheriff's department vehicles. "I'm glad you told Wolfe someone was setting me up. I need to know you trust me and I'll appreciate someone on my side if this evidence hits the courts."

"There will be plenty of people who remember seeing us at Aunt Betty's."

"I'm sure, especially Susie Hartwig. She must have mentioned going to the dance ten times. I wonder when she'll give up the chase." He gave her an eye-roll then rubbed his chin. "Okay, what else did Wolfe say?"

Relief flooded over her and she swallowed the lump in her throat. "He found your DNA on Kate's palms and on fibers consistent with the comparison samples taken from our crime scene coveralls. He believes the killer took them from the garbage and rubbed them on Kate's hands." She looked into his closed expression. He had become the detached professional again. "Likely he'll find the same result on Aimee's body."

"The murdering son of a bitch is trying to set me up. Dammit, I dumped ours in the trashcan outside the station. I mean, who the hell takes the risk to touch contaminated material?" Kane snorted in disgust. "Well, I'm sure *you* remember where I was *last* night."

She cleared her throat. "I remember. Come on." She pushed open the door. "Earbuds in, mics attached. Let's get this guy."

"Yes, ma'am."

# CHAPTER FORTY-NINE

The spicy smell of barbecued ribs, fried onions, and beer smacked Jenna in the face the moment she stepped from the SUV. People flowed into the fairgrounds from every direction wearing brightly colored clothes and cowboy hats, but the way they dressed did not disguise the air of unease rippling through the crowd. The threat of a killer in their midst hung over the carnival like a wet blanket. Parents kept their children close to their sides and she could not help noticing the way people bunched together, their worried expressions darting in all directions. Every stranger was a potential threat.

The uneasy chatter rose and fell over the loud country and western music blaring out of the huge hall. Flashing fairy lights lined the pathway leading to the entrance and they joined the line to the hall. Apprehension of allowing the dance to proceed flowed through her but the mayor had insisted the event take place as usual. His idea to flush out the killer might cost another girl her life. With the threat of a serial killer on the loose, she intended to keep everyone on high alert for the evening.

The Blackwater deputies moved around the entrance and she had spotted a couple near the parking lot; no doubt, Duke Walters would be inside. She decided to use her new communication toy and went through the names of all the deputies, asking each one to check in. Glad to find Deputy Rowley had Provine in his sight, and in fact had been speaking to him earlier, she relaxed a little. "This communication device is fantastic." Turning off her mic, she grinned at Kane. "I'm surprised with all this noise I could still hear everyone reasonably well."

"Yeah, Wolfe knows his gadgets." Kane gave her an appreciative glance. "I know you don't dance but will you have a go around the floor with me? It would be a good excuse to scope the room and see who is here."

"Yeah but don't make it too obvious, we are meant to be enjoying ourselves."

"I think the people here would expect us to be watching out for their safety." He sighed. "Come on, Jenna, taking the first step is the hardest."

Suddenly concerned she would make a complete fool of herself, she glanced at him. "I'll give it a try but don't expect too much."

"You'll learn the moves in no time." Kane's wide back turned toward her for a second as he handed in their tickets, then he smiled at her. "You pick up new moves in hand-to-hand combat fast. Dancing will be a breeze."

Hoping her self-taught skills would pass muster, she nodded. "Okay."

As they walked inside the brightly lit hall, she eyed the twirling couples on the dance floor. She caught sight of Jake Rowley dressed to the nines leaning casually against the bar, his gaze moving around the room. Since Kane's arrival more than six months previously, he had worked with Rowley to improve his skills, and in fact, Rowley's input in investigations had been invaluable. He seemed to notice the small important things people overlooked. She trusted him to watch Lionel Provine, and if he made one move toward a girl, she would know. Her gaze drifted over the dancers and she noticed Lucky Briggs and Storm Crawley spinning around the floor with a couple of women, all smiles and laughter as if oblivious to the lingering threat. Although they had given her a scare, she discounted both men as possible killers from the evidence, and their alibis for Kate's murder checked out.

She stood in the jostling crowd at the edge of the dance floor, nodding greetings at the townsfolk. In her periphery, she noticed Susie Hartwig making a beeline for Kane. "Told you the women would be falling all over you." She laughed as she continued scanning the room.

"Save me." Kane held out one large hand and his blue eyes sparkled. "Come on, show me your moves, we can watch everything from the dance floor."

Jenna stepped into his arms and they moved together with ease. Although Kane's eyes never left the crowd, he kept up an easy conversation with her. After the third song, she discovered the Texas two-step might well be her favorite dance. She smiled up at him. "I'm beat and I'm not attempting the boot-scooting. I need to take a look around."

"Sure." Kane closed his long fingers around her hand and led her toward the tables set around the hall. "There's Wolfe. I'll go get some drinks and see who is at the bar."

She took a seat at the table and smiled at Wolfe. "Everything okay? Where's Emily?"

"On the dance floor." Wolfe gave her a look of despair. "You have no idea how difficult it is raising three daughters without their mother."

"You are doing a great job."

"Nah, I mess up more times than you imagine." Wolfe huffed out a miserable sigh. "For instance, Emily asks my opinion on what she is wearing. She wants a man's opinion. Now, I see her as my little girl, so I put my foot down on allowing her to wear short shorts and have a bare midriff." He shook his head slowly. "She is growing up way too fast." His attention had not left the dance floor.

Jenna followed his gaze to see Emily dancing with a young man. All smiles but respectfully dressed in blue jeans and a western shirt with sparkles. "She looks great, what are you worrying about?"

"She is impulsive and I'm sure she lacks the fear gene." His mouth flattened to a thin line. "I'm frankly scared to buy her a car, although she has her license. She is too much like me. The other girls take after their mother."

Feeling sorry for Emily, she patted him on the arm. "Lighten up, she's been through a hard time, she needs a night to have some fun."

"I'm trying."

Not long after Kane came back with a pitcher of cola and glasses, Emily came to the table with Julia, one of Aimee's friends. Jenna smiled at her. "Having fun?"

"Well not really but I'm glad Emily dragged me out, I couldn't stop crying. My parents are here as well for extra safety. Have you noticed the ring of men standing around the dance floor? It looks like the townsfolk are on full alert waiting for someone to make the wrong move."

"It's safe, there are deputies everywhere." Emily tossed her long blonde hair over one shoulder and turned to her father. "I'm going to the bathroom with Julia and then getting a hot dog. We'll be back soon."

"I'll walk over with you." Wolfe's cheek twitched.

"Dad, *please*. I'm *seventeen* not seven." Emily's eyes flashed with anger. "I'll be fine. I'll be a few feet away and make sure I'm in a crowd. Okay? Watch my things. I'll be back in five." She pulled a bill out of her wallet then dropped it with her cellphone on the table.

"Don't you think you should take your phone?"

"I'm hardly going to be making calls while I'm peeing and I have my brooch as a backup if anything happens. Stop worrying." Emily flounced off with her friend and disappeared into the throng of noisy people.

They sat in awkward silence for some time and Jenna noticed the way Wolfe checked his watch then his cellphone every few minutes.

She cleared her throat. "Why don't you ask Rowley if he can see her? He is at the bar to watch Provine. He should be able to see the refreshments stand from there."

She waited, listening to the conversation in her earbud. Apparently, Rowley had not seen Emily buying hot dogs at all but there was a long line. Her attention fixed on Wolfe, who was drumming his fingers on the table in agitation. "Can't you locate her via her tracker?"

"Yeah." Wolfe's brow furrowed as he held up his cellphone to display the screen. "It gives her location as the fairgrounds. As this area isn't in the maps, it comes up as a single location. It doesn't tell me exactly where she is in the area at this moment."

"Would you like me to check the ladies' room? No doubt there will be quite a wait there as well."

"Yeah, thanks. I wish she had taken her phone with her." Wolfe offered her a weak smile. "I *know* I'm overprotective but after what's happened this week, I have cause."

"Not a problem." Jenna strolled toward the door.

# CHAPTER FIFTY

He mingled with the crowd, enjoying a hot dog and commiserating with everyone's complaints and worries about the murders of the young girls, but deep inside he reveled in their distress. The constant chatter and suspicious glances from everyone brought the reward of the last images of his dead girls. They would never see the pale skin and staring eyes of his girls or watch the life slip away like the snuffing of a candle. Those memories belonged only to him.

After joining a group of parents huddled protectively around their children, he scanned the area. Of course, most young girls had adults protecting them but not all the girls listened to the warnings of their parents. His attention moved to Deputy Wolfe's daughter, Emily, and her new friend Julia as they made their way, unescorted, from the hall. Arousal hit him in a rush. He wanted Julia. He smiled inwardly, how trusting she was; in fact, he could have plucked her from the street a number of times during the week and not a soul would have known, but the idea of an easy kill had not interested him. Here under the noses of everyone would mean his crimes would be infamous and he would live forever.

He eased his way through the crowd and out the door, nodding congenially at everyone he passed then caught sight of the girls making for the ladies' room. Thrills ran through him at the idea of killing both of them but doing so would be difficult with so many people strolling the fairgrounds and with more deputies on duty than ever before. *One girl will have to do for now.*

To avoid anyone seeing him near Julia, he turned away and headed for a suitable hiding place. A cool breeze had dried the slick of sweat on his brow by the time he reached the dark entrance to a hay barn. From his position, he could view the people coming in and out of the dance. He touched the knife at his waist, the leather sheath well concealed by his long shirt. Time would be of the essence; he could not linger to enjoy cutting his girl. He grinned. Although the one in the forest had whet his appetite for more quick kills. The startled look in her eyes and the way she trembled as the life flowed from her would remain with him for a long time.

He stared at the ladies' room door then checked his pockets to make sure he had everything he needed. His cellphone slipped into his hand and he wet his lips. Excitement curled in his belly. In his dark hiding place, she would not see him. He chuckled and watched the deputies patrolling the other end of the fairgrounds.

None of them could outsmart him.

He would have two more girls before leaving Black Rock Falls. He craved to hold Emily Wolfe's life in his hands despite her father being a deputy, and then to kill the sheriff slowly—although not the age he preferred, she would fight well and be worth the effort. Cloaked in shadows, he leaned casually against the doorframe, his gaze resting on the wide walkway sloping down toward the promenade.

"I'm waiting for you, Julia."

# CHAPTER FIFTY-ONE

Moving through the mass of hot bodies and inhaling a variety of odors, Jenna made it out the exit and followed the brightly lit pathway to the restrooms. The line of women waiting went halfway back to the hall. She walked to the end of the line, pushed inside the bathroom, and called out Emily's name. No one answered. Noticing Susie Hartwig on her way out of the building, she caught up and walked beside her. "You haven't seen Shane Wolfe's daughter, Emily, have you?"

"Yeah, she was waiting some ways back with Julia. I guess they went to the restrooms over by the main arena. They're under the stands and I heard a few women saying they were heading over there. We all warned them not to go because the lighting isn't good but they wouldn't listen and went off in a group. They thought if they stuck together they'd be okay."

Worried the two girls might be wandering through the fairgrounds alone, she needed to cover all bases. "Are there any other restrooms close by they might use?"

"Oh yeah, there is another one down by the promenade. Do you know where the souvenir and food stalls are set up during the day?"

Jenna nodded. "Yeah, I know the place. Thanks."

She hit her mic button and contacted Wolfe. "She is not at the restrooms outside the hall but people have seen her and Julia. I'm heading to the main arena restrooms now. If she is not there, I will look at the ones by the promenade. Go and check the food and soda lines in case she has returned."

*"Roger that. Wolfe out."*

She hit her mic again. "This is Sheriff Alton, is anyone in the vicinity of the main arena or the promenade?"

One of the Blackwater deputies responded, *"Yes, ma'am. I'm at the far end of the promenade near the entrance."*

"Keep your eye out for Deputy Wolfe's daughter and her friend. Call me if you see them."

*"Yes, ma'am"*

Breaking into a jog, she headed toward the main arena. People clumped in small groups, chatting or wandering around, likely cooling off after dancing, but at the main arena, the place looked deserted. The lights were out but the summer sun still offered a bright twilight. A rush of fear hit her in the pit of the stomach the moment she entered the dark walkway under the grandstand. Would two girls be stupid enough to go here alone, especially as Emily knew the current danger? Gathering her wits, she listened intently in the hope of hearing voices over the thumping music belting from the dance hall. Going into a dark corridor with a serial killer on the loose was unnerving, hand-to-hand combat training notwithstanding. Taking out her cellphone, she accessed the flashlight and moved swiftly along the dark corridor toward the sign above the ladies' restroom. The moment she arrived, the muffled voices coming from inside calmed her nerves. She pushed open the door to find a small line of women waiting to use the facilities. "Emily Wolfe, are you in here?"

When no reply came, she looked at the line of women. "Has anyone seen a girl with long blonde hair recently?"

The women wore terrified expressions and shook their heads in the negative. "Keep together, don't leave anyone behind when you return to the hall."

She turned and ran out the door and back to the main arena. She hit her mic. "Wolfe, no luck at the main arena, heading toward the promenade now. All deputies with the exception of Rowley be on the lookout for Emily Wolfe. Alton out."

Fear cramped her gut but she took off at a run toward the promenade area. Dancing advertising signs illuminated the entrance to the fairgrounds and banners with various events flapped in the breeze. She noticed a fall of blonde hair and jogged toward a group of teenagers chatting by a refreshment stand, her gaze doing a visual scan of everyone in the area. The blonde-haired girl in the group turned around and gave her a wide-eyed stare. She smiled then bit back despair at not finding the girls and changed course.

After contacting Rowley to make sure he had eyes on Provine, she headed back to the hall. Emily was mature and levelheaded. Causing her father so much worry seemed out of character. When she placed herself in danger at the computer shop, she made sure her father had her back. *She must be okay or she would have activated her tracker.*

As she reached the hall, Kane, Wolfe, and Rowley walked outside. "What's happening? Who is watching Provine?"

"Walters is chatting with him now." Kane's gaze moved over her face and he handed her a bottle of water. "We've done a recon of the hall and Emily isn't there."

Jenna drank greedily from the bottle. "I want everyone else searching for her. Break the fairgrounds into sections and get the deputies to check in once they're cleared."

"Yes, ma'am." Kane's gaze moved over the fairgrounds. "Where do we start?"

Panic welled in her belly. Everything was moving too slow. She couldn't just stand there, she had to do something. "Get them organized, Kane. I'm not waiting. I'm heading to the backlot—that's where I'd go if I wanted to murder someone."

When Kane started issuing orders into his mic, she looked at Wolfe's drawn face and started to jog toward the back of the fairgrounds with the deputies on her heels. "She hasn't activated her tracker yet?"

"Nope." Wolfe's pale gaze moved across the mass of buildings spread out in all directions. "I hope she is just cooling off somewhere and chatting with friends. She's met quite a few since we moved here." His cellphone let out a piercing ringtone. "That's her tracker brooch signal. We'll be able to hear her but it's not a two-way. I'll put my phone on speaker, move away from the noise."

*"Daddy? I know the name of the killer."*

# CHAPTER FIFTY-TWO

Emily Wolfe wished she had alerted her dad earlier. After what had happened to Aimee, she had promised to tell her father when someone was in danger. In fact, she should have told him the moment she walked out of the restroom and discovered Julia had taken off to follow a stupid character. She had seen players nearly run over trying to catch a character. They seemed to fixate on the game and forget their surroundings. Her father's stern warning not to trust a soul had filled her mind, but in fear of her friend's safety, she bolted in the direction Julia had headed. She doubted a killer would try to kill two girls walking together. She had seen Julia in the distance, her head illuminated by the screen of her cellphone.

After leaving the lighted areas far behind and moving into the backlot, she feared for her safety and was about to call out to her friend to stop when a man stepped out of a dark building as if he had been waiting for her to arrive. It seemed creepy strange as if he just happened to be in the deserted area of the fairgrounds. A tingle of fearful anticipation ran down her spine and she melted into the shadows, but the sight of Julia speaking with someone she knew convinced her something was terribly wrong. *Dad thinks the killer knows the victims.* When the man bent to look at the cellphone, she recognized him. He'd been right in front of them all along, yet nobody had suspected him.

From the body language, he had offered to escort her to find the character, and they headed toward a long, dark building. She had seen Julia's grateful smile and immediately hit her tracker button.

Her short message to her father lacked the vital information he required, and he would be fuming not knowing her exact location. As she pressed her back against the cool brick wall of the stables and turkey-peeked around the corner, terror like nothing she had experienced before gripped her.

In the dimly lit interior, Julia strolled beside him, her head focused on the cellphone in her hand, chatting like there was no tomorrow. Her friend had failed to notice the man beside her was swinging a black sock filled with something heavy. She had no doubt that in the next few moments she would witness Julia's murder.

She wanted to scream out a warning and rush to her friend's aid, but even the defense moves her father had taught her would not stop a psychopathic lunatic. Legs heavy, she moved back a few steps, hoping the slight crunch of the gravel under her boots would not give her away. Sweat trickled down her back and she swallowed hard, wishing the shadows would conceal her. She had to get help but the moment she opened her mouth, the killer would hear her.

Heart pounding, she lifted her shirt to bring the glittery guitar brooch containing one of the trackers to her mouth and kept her voice to a whisper. "Dad, I'm at the other end of the fairgrounds, the last stable block, on the right. Come quickly. It's Reverend Jones. He's going to kill Julia."

Palms sweaty and heart thumping against her ribs, she crept forward. Hearing a thump then the sound of something hitting the ground, she trembled uncontrollably. She had to know what was happening to her friend and took a quick peek around the corner then froze. Julia lay sprawled on the ground, her arms and legs twitching, but Reverend Jones was nowhere in sight.

The need to run bunched her muscles and she darted out of her hiding place. As the crunch of footsteps came close behind her, she opened her mouth to scream but the sound came out in a whimper. Gasping for air, she chanced a look over one shoulder. He was less than five feet from her and gaining fast.

The leather soles of her new cowboy boots slipped on the gravel but she had a head start and could run fast. She headed for the blacktop in the middle of the grounds and took off at full speed. Behind her, his footsteps pounded on the road and she could hear his heavy breathing getting closer. *I have to escape.*

She lifted her knees and sprinted toward the lights. Her dad would be coming and she just had to reach him. If she could make it around the last building, she would be in the open and he would see her. The heavy footsteps thundered behind her. A strong hand grasped her hair and pain shot up her neck as Jones wrenched her to a halt. She twisted and stared into the face of evil.

Clawing at his face and eyes, and trying to knee him, Emily fought using every move her father had taught her. "Daddy, *help* me."

Gasping, she lifted her knee sharply and hit pay dirt. Jones made a long moaning sound and let go of her hair but seemed to recover in a split second. Pain shot through her face from his punch and she staggered then broke away and ran. Her vision blurred, tears streamed down her face but she made it around the last building and could see people heading toward her. "Daddeeeeeee."

"He can't help you now." The reverend's voice had changed to a sinister growl.

The sharp tug on her scalp pulled her to a standstill once more and she fell to the ground with the weight of him on top of her. Winded, she gasped in a painful breath. The stink of him filled her nostrils and his sweat dripped onto her face. She had clawed his cheeks and blood oozed from the corner of one eye.

She caught the glint of a knife and screamed, "Daddy, help me!"

"I'm so going to enjoy killing you." Jones's blood-streaked lips curled into a smile.

The promenade lights blinked in the sharp blade as it rose high in the air. Unable to fend him off, she waited to die. The next moment, Sheriff Alton crashed into them and locked both hands around the reverend's wrist. Her head came down on his nose in a sickening crunch and one foot locked around his waist.

"Drop the knife, you're surrounded." The sheriff rolled to one side and slammed his hand into the ground. "Drop the damn knife."

"Bitch." Jones swung a fist at her face. "I'll cut you so bad your mother won't recognize you."

The sheriff ducked the punch then rolled the reverend away from her. Terrified, Emily dragged her leaden body away. The reverend reared up but the sheriff had his arm in a death grip, her legs locked around his waist, and she was squeezing so tight Jones's face was turning blue. Footsteps came running and in the blink of an eye, Deputy Kane had ripped the knife from the reverend's fingers. The deputy had Jones by the throat, lifting him high in the air.

"Put me down." Reverend Jones's eyes bulged as he fought to breathe through his bloody nose. He moved his gaze to Sheriff Alton. "I had a special time planned for *you*. No game, no rules, just you and me and a knife."

"Shut your mouth." Deputy Kane's eyes flashed with anger. "One more word and I'll tear your head off."

"Stand down, Kane." Sheriff Alton's worried face came into view. "I want this animal alive, but get him away from Emily."

"Great tackle, by the way." Kane's lips twitched as he shoved Jones toward the gathering deputies.

"Oh Jesus." Her dad, white-faced and angry as hell, kneeled beside her and gathered her into his arms. "You are so grounded for life." He checked her injuries, muttering curses under his breath.

Head spinning, she sat up slowly. "Julia is in the stable. The last one, way back there. He hit her over the head." She pointed in the direction. "She was moving, so she might be okay."

"I'm on it." Sheriff Alton turned her concerned gaze toward Deputy Kane. "With me. Rowley, take care of the prisoner and call the paramedics."

Emily looked up at her father. "I remembered everything you taught me. Look at the damage I did to him, and if he'd killed me, I would have his DNA under my fingernails."

"We'll talk about this later." His daunting expression gave no hope for a reprieve. "Can you stand?"

Biting her bottom lip, she nodded. "My head is sore. He punched me in the face too."

"So I see."

Flashing lights came into view as the paramedics drove toward them, sirens blaring. She looked at her father. "I don't need to go to the hospital. If you think I'll need an X-ray on my head, you can do that, can't you?"

"I think an ice pack will suffice." His pale gray gaze moved over her face. "You did good, kid. You survived because we planned for all contingencies, but if you ever put yourself in danger like this again, so help me, I'll lock you in your room until you turn twenty-five."

Emily smiled at him. "You have the killer. Do I get points for that?"

"Nope."

Two deputies arrived to escort Reverend Jones to the lockup. Emily sat in the back of the ambulance and allowed the paramedics to tend her injuries without complaint. Her dad had walked away and was speaking on the phone, no doubt to the Department of Homeland

Security. He had mentioned the killer was probably responsible for identical murders across the state. With a dangerous man in custody, the Black Rock Falls Sheriff's Department would likely need assistance.

A wave of relief flooded over her at the sight of the sheriff and Deputy Kane carrying Julia in his arms. Her friend had one arm wrapped around the handsome deputy's neck, and as they came closer, she could hear her talking. When he deposited Julia into the ambulance, she smiled up at him.

"I'm fine now. You didn't have to carry me, but thank you."

"You should thank Emily, she saved your life." Deputy Kane's full lips curled into a smile, he touched his hat and walked away.

Seeing the dreamy look in her friend's eyes, Emily snorted. "Don't waste your time." She glared at her friend. "By the way, I nearly got murdered because of you. The reverend was going to stab me so I tore his face apart with my nails." She pressed ice to her face. "I'd be dead if the sheriff hadn't flown through the air and tackled him then held him until Deputy Kane arrived. You should have seen her, she was amazing."

"You look a mess." Julia stared at her. "I guess you'll be going to the hospital with me."

"No, but I'm glad you're going to the hospital. You need your head examined after running off like that alone."

"I *know* that now." Julia pulled a face. "I'm going to be grounded. I promised my parents I wouldn't leave the hall. They are going to be so mad." She frowned. "Oh shit, here they come now."

Emily took one look at the sour expression on her father's face and sighed. "Yes, they will, but not half as mad as my dad is with me right now."

# CHAPTER FIFTY-THREE

Five days later, Kane strolled into Jenna's office and waited for her to look up at him. "They've picked up Steve Rogers just outside Blackwater. The deputies are bringing him in now but when they interviewed him, he gave them a signed confession to killing his wife. They'll be here before twelve."

"That's great." Jenna leaned back in her chair and gave him a long, considering stare. "If he pleads guilty, it will make our job a lot easier." Her mouth turned up at the corners. "The mayor called me and, would you believe, the new road he had planned to his property has been axed and the funding is coming here. This means we get two new deputies, the computer system that Wolfe wanted, and money to spare."

Kane dropped into a chair and grinned. "Lockers for our personal items would be something to consider. There are a few rooms sitting empty, we could turn one into a locker room and have a keypad to get in and out so it's secure."

"I'll add it to my list."

He rubbed his chin. "Wolfe has finished his reports; he'll be here soon to give us the evidence he found at Jones's house and update us on what he discovered on his computer."

"I know you wanted to be involved in the search of Jones's residence but with your DNA on two of the victims and me as your only alibi for Kate's murder, it was best I ordered him to handle it with Rowley." Jenna gave him an apologetic look. "Waiting for one of Helena's forensic team to go in with them was the correct thing to do."

He nodded. Her quick thinking had removed any conflict-of-interest accusations. "I appreciate your consideration, ma'am."

"While we're waiting for Wolfe, bring me up to date with the Rogers investigation."

As a familiar headache threatened, he rubbed the scar on his head. "I've collated the evidence against Rogers; even if he hadn't admitted guilt, the case against him would have been solid. I'll print it up and have it on your desk within the hour."

"Good work." Jenna gave him a bright smile. "When Rogers arrives, I'll send it along to the DA with his confession. I'd say the county jail will be taking him off our hands."

A knock on the door heralded Wolfe's arrival.

"Come in." Jenna's interested gaze flicked over his face. "Shut the door. I take it you have finished your reports on the Jones case?"

"Yes, ma'am." Wolfe deposited two folders on her desk then eased his large frame into a chair. "He made a mistake and one that usually brings down serial killers. In one word: trophies. We found sixteen different locks of hair taken from his victims and all are under DNA analysis. We hope to link him to similar killings throughout the state. He worked as a preacher all over and arrived here some months ago. According to the GPS on his car, he often traveled to other counties during his time here. I have matches for all of our victims; it's enough evidence on its own but I have proof he used the Golden Wizard game, the one where the kids collect the virtual reality characters, to lure his victims."

Kane leaned forward in his chair. "So, Lionel Provine is in the clear? Surely, we can get him on something. He was luring young women to join his private group."

"I agree." Jenna looked expectantly at Wolfe. "What he is doing is creepy to say the least. Yet he comes up clean on priors. How did your interview go with him?"

"I think he was a pawn in Reverend Jones's game but we'll need to keep an eye on him." Wolfe stretched out his long legs. "Jones is a Black Hat hacker and used his ability to rewrite the codes on games. Jones told Provine he worked as a programmer in a major games company before God called him into service. He actually convinced him for a twenty percent share of his profit, for the church of course, he would make him rich. The idea was to invite teenage girls to join an exclusive group of gamers. Jones agreed to supply the toggles to gain remote access to the kids' computers and bonus codes to give out as enticements."

"How did Provine make money giving out bonus cards?" Jenna frowned. "It seems a bit lame."

"The money part of the deal came from the same agreement I heard Provine use with Emily. He told the 'exclusive members' of his club he would supply them with bonus cards if they convinced their parents to buy merchandise from his store." Wolfe shrugged. "Kids who play games would do just about anything to get the bonuses, and Provine didn't believe the idea was exploitation. When I questioned him, he did wonder why Jones insisted he only enlist teenage girls into the club but he did give the boys who came into his shop the cards as well."

"So, Reverend Jones kept a low profile and put Provine in the line of fire?" Kane frowned. "You thought he was manipulating the game but how did he hack the girls' cellphones?"

"Yes, I'd like to know that too." Jenna's mouth turned down. "I had no idea carrying a cellphone made a person vulnerable."

"He didn't hack the cellphones, he used the game interface. The toggles gave Reverend Jones remote access to their computers. He spied on them using their webcams to track their movements. When he wanted to lure a victim to his pre-chosen spot, he programmed the next sequence of the game. The girls played on their cellphones and, using the camera interface, collected the virtual characters in real time. The characters popped up close to them."

Kane nodded. "Yeah, I saw Aimee playing that game in Aunt Betty's Café—it was like the character was in the store. Freaky."

"Ah yes, I've seen them heads down staring at their cellphones and running around like crazy." Jenna shook her head. "They collect the characters as part of the game, is that right?"

"Exactly, and Jones tweaked the game so he could literally use the characters like a trail of breadcrumbs leading straight to him."

Kane frowned. "How did he send the message to Chad to change the time of his date with Kate?"

"I have evidence he hacked the online games room to send messages using the kids' usernames. I found the messages he sent changing the time of Kate's date and the one sent to Aimee from Julia. They originated from Jones's computer." Wolfe's pale gaze narrowed. "He made an error and didn't delete the files. I think he believed he was invincible."

"I'm impressed." Jenna flashed him a white smile. "The DA will be fascinated with the details and I'd bet due to your conclusions The Department of Homeland Security will be extending the case throughout the state."

"Yes, as you requested I have kept them up to date with my findings." Wolfe scratched the blond stubble on his chin. "I take it Jones will stand trial here? Will he be remaining in the county jail?"

"Yes, I would say from these results, our initial charge of attempted murder of Emily will be upgraded to murder in the first for Felicity, Joanne, Kate, and Aimee." Jenna's look was troubled. "We still don't have a motive. What pushed Jones to kill?"

Kane tapped a folder on the desk. "The DHS sent over a file. He has been on a watch list for some time so I'm not sure why they didn't arrest him on suspicion earlier. His cruelty to animals goes back years.

When he attended high school, the local police implicated him in the drowning of a girl but he wasn't charged. He graduated top of his class and won a scholarship to study computer science." He met her gaze. "His mother, as we assumed, was a prostitute and took her johns home. They lived in a tiny apartment, and from Jones's garbled statement, his mother made him watch, and at times, the men used him as well. His mother performed abortions for the local hookers and ordered him to assist her. The DHS included photographs of his mother and she wore bright red lipstick."

"Do they mention why he left the flowers?"

Kane winced. "Yeah, when his mom got mad with him he picked her wildflowers and she forgave him. He actually said, 'They all wanted me to bring them flowers.'"

"So why did he kill young women?"

Kane sighed. "He isn't saying, but who can figure out the mind of a psychopath?"

"I would have never picked him as a killer in a million years. He seemed like such a nice, caring man. I can't believe I called him in to help with grief counseling." Jenna pushed both hands into her dark hair and stared at him. "Was he a reverend?"

"Yeah, and I would imagine he became a preacher to get close to girls. When you think about it, it is a good cover. Who would suspect a reverend?" He winced. "He slipped through our net."

"I saw pure evil in him when he was attacking Emily." Jenna moved her gaze to Wolfe. "How is she doing?"

"She is still very upset for not telling me about Aimee but after preventing Julia's murder she is a bit better." Wolfe's smile was genuine. "She feels instrumental in finding the killer of her friends."

"That is good to hear, I'm looking forward to her continuing her internship." Jenna flashed a white smile at them. "I'm very proud of my team. We were the only sheriff's department in the state to stop

Jones's killing spree and we've taken two murderers out of circulation. You have both excelled, as did Rowley and Walters." She cleared her throat and eyed them from under her lashes. "But don't get too comfortable, I'm still going to be cracking the whip."

Kane leaned back in his chair and glanced at her. He had to admit Jenna led them to perfection. He had respect and deep affection for her. "So, case closed, ma'am?"

"Yeah." Jenna's warm smile made her eyes sparkle. "Case closed."

He returned her smile with a grin. "Now we'll have time to work on those dance moves of yours. I'll have you boot-scooting by the fall dance."

"That's what I like to see in my deputies." Jenna chuckled. "Ambition."

# A LETTER FROM D.K. HOOD

Dear Reader,

I am delighted you chose my novel and joined me in the thrilling world of Alton and Kane in *Bring Me Flowers*.

If you'd like to keep up-to-date with all my latest releases, just sign up at the website link below.

www.bookouture.com/dk-hood

I really loved writing about Jenna Alton and David Kane, and it was fun introducing Shane Wolfe into the team. I think I am going to have fun exploring his expertise in the future. I love forensic science and researching every aspect of the crime scenes.

If you enjoyed my story, I would be very grateful if you could leave a review and recommend my book to your friends and family. I really like to hear from readers because when I write, it's as if you are here with me, following the characters' story.

I would love to hear from you, so please get in touch on my Facebook page or Twitter or through my website.

Thank you so much for your support.
D.K. Hood

DKHood_Author

dkhoodauthor/

www.dkhood.com/

# ACKNOWLEDGEMENTS

To my fantastic editor, Helen Jenner, and all the amazing Bookouture team who have worked with me to make this story possible. Also, thanks to Kim Nash and Noelle Holten—the best promotion team ever.